WAR OF OUR ERA

WAR OF OUR ERA

THE BREAKAWAY CHILDREN

GERARD DORI

gatekeeper press
Tampa, Florida

This book is a work of fiction. The names, characters and events in this book are the products of the author's imagination or are used fictitiously. Any similarity to real persons living or dead is coincidental and not intended by the author.

The content associated with this book is the sole work and responsibility of the author. Gatekeeper Press had no involvement in the generation of this content.

War of Our Era: The Breakaway Children

Published by Gatekeeper Press
7853 Gunn Hwy., Suite 209
Tampa, FL 33626
www.GatekeeperPress.com

Copyright © 2024 by Gerard Dori
All rights reserved. Neither this book, nor any parts within it may be sold or reproduced in any form or by any electronic or mechanical means, including information storage and retrieval systems, without permission in writing from the author. The only exception is by a reviewer, who may quote short excerpts in a review.

The cover design, interior formatting, typesetting, and editorial work for this book are entirely the product of the author. Gatekeeper Press did not participate in and is not responsible for any aspect of these elements.

Library of Congress Control Number: 2024945982

ISBN (hardcover): 9781662956249
ISBN (paperback): 9781662956256
eISBN: 9781662956263

Acknowledgments

For Cpl. Micheal Blake Wafford.
For LCpl. Ryan Eugene Deady.
Always faithful, my brothers.

Table of Contents

Prologue	1
Chapter 1: In Our Galaxy, in Our Future	5
Chapter 2: There Are Those Who Know Our War	25
Chapter 3: Our Reality	37
Chapter 4: Our Opposite	51
Chapter 5: Our Fate	79
Chapter 6: Ours Is Always Theirs	93
Chapter 7: Our Beginning	107
Chapter 8: Our Awakening	137
Chapter 9: Our Battle	153
Chapter 10: Our Low	173
Chapter 11: Our Change	191
Chapter 12: Just Our Kind of Crack	213
Chapter 13: Our Escape	241
Chapter 14: Our Love	257
Chapter 15: Our War	281
Chapter 16: Our Era	297
Epilogue	313

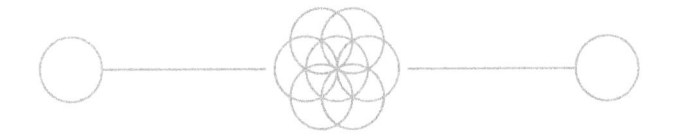

Prologue

The people of Earth, and especially the leaders of the newly formed UNE, were more than willing to approve the transfer of tens of thousands of people to Mars. Overpopulation was becoming a real issue even after birthing restrictions were enacted centuries ago.

It had not been easy for the original pioneers of Mars. Terraforming had been ongoing for decades, but the planet was still not 100 percent habitable. Massive amounts of supplies had to be collected and then transferred millions of miles to the newly founded city of Jazeera. Even then, the suffering was extreme, and people died due to disease, starvation, or while terraforming. Hubs had to be constructed, water had to be found and collected, and the food situation had to be solved.

Every year there was to be a massive shipment of food, medical supplies, and construction material to help expand and make Mars at least habitable. Eventually, the shipments stopped, and the planet relied solely on what the newly arrived refugees brought with them.

Through determination and a lot of luck, Mars slowly turned into the paradise it was today. More and more people arrived. More wealth, more goods, more will to succeed was pumped into the planet, which led to the forming of the Council of Peers.

From across the planet, people and representatives argued over the best course of action as far as forming a government. They squabbled over the fine points of it, but ultimately, they settled on a definitive overall picture of what they wanted the government to be.

There would be little to no government. It was an almost completely free planet. Local law was elected yearly, and the people of Mars, having left the tight grip of government on Earth, desired nothing more than their individual liberties. Do whatever you want as long as it does not affect others.

The planet thrived. People being left to their own desires was the catalyst for growth, and more people flocked to the once-red planet. The UNE kept watch over what they thought was just a colony, laughing at the people who would endure such a hard life when everything they needed for a happy life was on Earth.

Over the years, more reports kept trickling into Mars, informing the First Panel of the Earth of the successes of the planet. The air was breathable, crops and livestock were feeding the people, and commerce was flowing, even to and from Earth. The UNE had to get their hands more directly into the honeypot. They restarted the shipment of building materials and sent advisers and educators.

After a while, they eventually set up a UNE base for the transport of goods and a central hub where the people of Mars could come for aid. The UNE then began to attempt to suck the planet dry like the leeches they were.

The people on Mars became increasingly agitated toward their former overlords and boycotted any goods received from Earth. They pulled back the critical food production that Earth needed for survival. Tensions rose, and the boycott of traded goods hurt the people of Mars just as much as they presumed it was hurting Earth.

An uneasy, unspoken truce was established for the sake of commerce, but there were a few who still resisted the UNE and everything they stood for. If the boycott would not work and the people still had a need, then the opposers were forced to form a new strategy, and that was how piracy was born.

Why should the UNE make profits from Martian sweat? It would just be beneficial to seize said goods and then sell them to the people at an extreme discount, and the people were overjoyed at the thought. The pirates became extremely wealthy, and the free people of Mars got the goods that they needed. The pirates even stuck it in further by buying the latest technology from Earth and installing it in their vessels. Armored guards had been brought in to help protect the cargo from the marauding pirates, and of course, the armored suits were taken and immediately implemented into the pirates' bag of tricks.

The pirates became heroes, and that was just too much for the adventurous Samuel Cleber to resist. Politics was just too boring. He needed adventure, and he signed up—using a false name—and began his illustrious career. Both sides were irritated by the other, and the UNE saw the pirates as a direct threat to the prosperity of Earth. Action had to be taken.

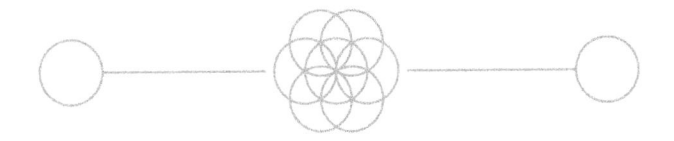

Chapter 1

In Our Galaxy, in Our Future

The *Validus* was still as it floated in the vast, dark, and silent space of the galaxy. Many found it uneasy and were unsettled at the thought of the openness, but not the captain of the ship, Samuel Cleber. It had taken Sam years and much sweat to make the *Val* what it was today. It was sleek in design for maximum stealth and was powerful enough to outrun anything in the known world. It lacked any grace in atmosphere, but space was the *Val*'s natural habitat.

Thirty minutes to intercept, so he got on his all-hands coms and announced it to the crew. Most of them were veterans of multiple jobs and had been with Sam from the start. They had just never left his side, and that was the way he liked it. He swung around to the side of his suit, detached the main power cable keeping its start-up power unit charged, crouched down, and then entered his suit from the back.

Entering the suit was like crawling up its ass, and it was common to use the expression "brown hole" when describing that part of the suit. He had to go arms first and stand up into the one-thousand-pound full-armored battle suit. Once inside, he stepped his legs in, closed the entrance, and initiated the start-up procedure.

The power unit that kept it in sleep mode was replaced by its power cells, and Sam's armored suit came to life. The gel expanded, conforming to fit his body up to his neck and securing his head in place. At the same time, his heads-up display came to life. Finding his bearings, he ran a full system check.

The onboard system, or simply OB, followed Sam's every move and, as always, was learning. The more Sam used his armor, the more familiar the OB became with its operator. He wasn't sure how the advanced processor worked exactly. All he knew was that the OB was monitoring the frequency of his brain, so it knew what he wanted and instantly gave him whatever information or readings he was after.

If he thought it, so would the OB. It was a slower process than being directly connected to the suit, but Sam was strongly against direct connection with any OB or AI. With a direct connection, an interlink was surgically placed in the brain. To many, once a link was established with an AI, the human wasn't the same afterward.

At the same time, the OB was taking readings from millions of sensors embedded throughout the suit's gel and relayed all the info back to it for processing. The OB processed the information and instantly gave instructions to the suit's motors to move the specific parts it needed. The sensors were so sensitive that Sam could gently crack an egg to cook this breakfast and at the same time could also literally bend steel. The onboard system was state-of-the-art and pretty much the standard on all vessels, both manned and unmanned.

He pressure-sealed his suit, made sure there weren't any alarms, and was satisfied that he was ready to go. This allowed him to focus on his ship's command room and then his board team. The remaining crew—which was just Ameera, the ship's pilot, and Helena, the ship's navigator and copilot—was already locked in the command room and had sealed themselves in.

"You guys ready?"

"Yeah, Sam. Good to go," replied the girls. "Sam, fifteen till intercept, so power down in five."

"Copy that."

The ship's scanner had a pretty far-reaching scan, and it was always common practice to shut everything down so they didn't get detected by anyone waiting or on approach. He was sure Ameera could run down any ship, but he always liked to lure his prey in close before springing his trap.

Sam then turned his attention to the board team and saw all five were ready to go.

"Is board ready?"

"Fucking right, boss. I'm even commando in my armor right now."

"Gods, Akari. And to think when we found you, you were such a sweet girl."

"Easy access," Tucker chimed in.

"Is Big Bertha charged?"

"Yes, Sam. Big ole girl is charged and ready."

"Okay, copy that."

Sam could switch comms over to talk to just the board team, just Ameera, or any individual on the ship. But in general, he kept an all-hands comms so everyone on the ship knew what was going on. He quickly turned on his individual to the member designated number 6 though.

"You good?"

"Yeah."

"It's all right to be nervous. On my first job, I had no idea what was going on. Just stay back, keep your eyes open, and don't fuck up."

"I can do more than just stay back."

"You've been briefed. You know you're definitely not going through the hole. Not on your first job. Just watch, help where you can, and like I said, don't fuck up, or I'll kill you, and then I'll send your mother flowers."

"Well, that's nice. At least you'll send Mom flowers. She probably won't be surprised 'cause she figured one of us would kill the other at some point."

"Don't make it today. Now shut the fuck up, I'm switching to all comms."

"All hands, prepare for vacuum and anti. Ameera, give us a count."

"All hands vacuum and anti in five . . . four . . . three . . . two . . . one. VA!"

The middle section of the ship went to zero gravity and vacuum, and all six one-thousand-pound armored battle suits immediately adjusted to the new environment. Little spurts of stabilizers fired up, keeping all the squad in place.

"We have VA. Ameera, let's pop the hatches."

"Copy that. All hands, I'm popping her in five . . . four . . . three . . . two . . . one."

The ceiling and walls of the ship gave way to the vast open space, and all six of the crew couldn't help but get that little shudder as they looked out at the emptiness. The massive EMP Mark XI cannon, gloriously nicknamed Big Bertha, unfolded. And with it, Sergio's long-range scope began searching for its target.

"All right, Ameera, set us up for success."

"It's done, boss. You have a perfect angle for a shot. It's on Helena and Serg now."

"You know I don't miss," said Sergio. "I ain't gonna miss later tonight when we're back home neither."

"You definitely missed the other night," Ameera sassed back.

"Ameera, are we ready for shutdown?" Sam interrupted.

"We're ready, Sam."

"Helena, going dark, confirm position."

"I confirm, Sam. We're in perfect intercept position. No maneuvering necessary, we're good to power down."

"Copy that. Ameera, it's on you."

"Shut down in five . . . four . . . three . . . two . . . one . . . Kill power."

The ship went dark.

"Powered down," Ameera said from command in a softer tone.

With the ship practically 100 percent shut off, it got very quiet, and the crew matched the quiet tone of space.

"Ten mikes, people. Everyone ready?" Sam asked the crew.

"Yeah, Sam, let's fucking rage!"

The crew all let out a nervous chuckle.

"Copy that," Sam said, chuckling to himself. "Call signs from here on, people."

"Roger, One."

The next nine minutes passed ever so slowly. Comms traffic was always limited to emergency only. Sam never knew if they could pick up on it or not, but since he could detect comms traffic, he assumed they could as well. Sam's interceptor was, however, the best money could buy and rigged with state-of-the-art equipment, but why chance it.

They sat and hovered, just waiting in the emptiness. Some of the crew moved constantly about, looking at weapons, checking their suits over and over, even though they'd checked it a dozen times. Some stayed motionless, like Sam, with who knows what was going through their minds.

With that stillness came his favorite part. He wondered to himself, just sitting there floating, if he was sick in his head. Sam was immersed in his favorite part of the job. He craved this more than any other part—more than the planning, more than the actual performance of the job, and even more than uncovering the rewards. Sam lived for this. Everything else in his life, he could probably give up—or at least learn to live without—but he could never give this up.

It was the anticipation of the action, the massive buildup of adrenaline and the shaking that came with it. He could never tell if anyone noticed his shaking. Sam was always afraid they would think he was scared, but he couldn't control himself because of it. It was the same after a job. As soon as he knew the "action" was over, his shakes returned as he calmed down, and he had to control himself. The crew all knew it, but they didn't care. They knew Sam was the best.

His heart was racing, and he was primed for the explosion of action. It was almost like an addiction, and the only way to satisfy his craving was the job. He saw Two, aka Serg, look down and take control of the ship's magnified scope to "paint" the target. Helena likewise was readying the massive EMP cannon mounted on the deck, which was linked to Serg's scope. It was too much for one person to shoot that far and calculate the insane speed the vessel was traveling in. They both needed their OBs to check each other's data for maximum accuracy. The slightest movement could change every calculation, and they only had one shot. If they missed, their target would scream by at danger close. Everything depended on the two operating Big Bertha.

"Target in scope," Serg relayed, using the sensors in his gel to control the scope of Bertha. "Looks like you're right again, One. This one tried to take the easy route. They never learn." Serg made the slightest adjustment to the scope, moving Big

Bertha, and said, "Target is not adjusting course, and she . . . is . . . now . . . locked."

"Confirmed, target acquired. Stand by, Two." Helena was equally focused at her station, zeroing on the incoming ship. She double-checked Serg's figures and hovered her index finger over the display, ready to fire. "Okay, we are green, Two," she said as green display indicators came to life. "All hands, going hot."

There was no sound from the EMP cannon, which shot out its concentrated wave at the speed of light. All that came from the weapon was a hiss as it discharged into space. The crew looked on as the EMP wave flew straight toward the cargo ship and impacted the command room perfectly. The only members of the crew that saw the impact were Serg and Helena with their scopes, who confirmed the hit to the crew.

"Direct hit! She's slowing down!"

"Good shot, guys! Ready on my command."

The ship's fail-safes, which operated in the event of power down, fired, and the ship rapidly began slowing. The Gs on the ship were intense as its drive shut down and fired its atmospheric thrusters almost at full. Sam was searching for the ship with his longer-than-normal scopes outfitted on his armor, then he saw the light in the distance that had to be the cargo ship approaching. He gave a short-range notification light to all hands and immediately started tracking it on his heads-up display.

Seeing the vessel on approach made Sam's heart and adrenaline begin to pick up even more. His heart was pounding so hard in his suit he wondered if the crew could hear it through his comms. The OB calculated the cargo's path and speed in a flash and picked up that there was very little comms traffic coming from the ship—only small bits of data sending position back to its owner or operator. He was pleased to see his contact info was spot-on as always.

Time to intercept—thirty seconds. With his heart racing and his breathing increased, Sam steadied himself, took a deep breath, and braced himself for the blast toward the cargo ship.

Ten seconds. The crew could see the ship now firing its reversing thrusters. It came closer and closer until, finally, the thrusters went silent.

"She's dead, One!"

"ON ME!" Sam barked out to all channels.

At that moment, all six armored battle suits fired their suits' thrusters at full and rocketed toward the disabled ship in formation with Sam in the lead. They were screaming toward the ship.

Sam called out, "Almost to her, people. You know your jobs. Four, let's get to the hole."

The honor of the hole was strictly volunteer among the crew members—with the idea that the first person in the breached ship got his or her pick of the loot. The crew generally knew what loot they were after, and having first pick was a big drama when they got back home. The downside to all this was, of course, the first one on the ship was always in the most danger of being injured or killed by either human personnel or the ship's automated defense. It was hard getting people to commit to battle, and this was Sam's little way of motivating people to do the necessary, because if no one volunteered to go in the hole, it would always be left to him.

The hard part was over. The EMP had done its job, temporarily shutting down the cargo's OB, and all the emergency systems had worked and stopped the ship. Early on in interplanetary travel, people learned quickly what happened to an object that was traveling at an insane speed and didn't have the ability to stop. After a couple ships turned into flaming balls of mass headed to the planet surface and smashed down like meteors, the elders quickly determined a fail-safe had to be implemented.

Emergency stops were installed on all ships and fitted so no one could remove it without completely destroying their ship. When the onboard lost the ability to control, the emergency stop fired and stopped the ship dead in space. It was a safety measure that Sam had been using for years to halt the ships he wanted. The only flaw in his technique was that due to the rampant piracy across the stars, designers were constantly upgrading shielding for the OB. It would reboot in the event of an EMP impact, and if Sam couldn't permanently disable the ship, it would restart and blast off regardless of where Sam and his crew were. Because of this ever-upgrading shielding, the OB didn't take long to restart all systems, so the key to pirating a vessel was speed. The crew had to know their jobs to the letter for speed.

Sam fired his thruster in reverse to slow them down, but they still smashed into the ship. The time for subtleties was over, and there was no need for a gentle touchdown. The armor could more than handle the impact, and it absorbed enough that the crew barely felt the impact. The first job was the permanent disabling of the ship, and Sam left that to Two—and normally to Four, but since Akari had the hole honors, Sergio was teamed up with Five for this job.

"Two and Five, how's it lookin'?" Sam asked.

"Not bad, One. She's an older model, so I bet she won't even reboot, but I'm isolating the thrusters, we aren't going anywhere," Tucker relayed to Sam. "You can start to board, you're good to go."

"Copy that," acknowledged Sam. "Myself, Three, and Four are almost ready. Getting the last charge in place as we speak. Six, are you in position?"

"I'm in place," replied John.

"Keep your eyes open, and watch our backs."

Akari and Sam worked quickly to place the premade charges in what they thought would blow a hole directly to the cargo bay of the now permanently disabled ship.

Entering through the cargo hold had its drawbacks, and Sam was constantly at a back and forth with himself as to the best boarding practice. Entering this way had the benefit of shortest path to the loot and less chance of encountering any resistance in the form of crew or automated defenses. So far, cargo captains and crews had not been manning cargo bays, and most of the time during travel, it was at zero gravity and using minimal power, so it made it an ideal place to enter. The flip side was, when a ship was at vacuum and was carrying live cargo or organic matter, it was instantly destroyed when Sam and his crew entered the ship.

That was why many captains entered through traditional airlocks, but that took time, sometimes a lot of time, and it gave the enemy crew precious time to form a defense if they chose. Sam and his crew generally didn't like fair, straight-up fights, and going for a frontal assault was not in the playbook. There were wild crews like that, but not the *Validus*. Sam wanted the least amount of risk and exposure for his crew.

* * *

Every second counted from disabling the ship and to breaching her. Disabling it was important, for obvious reasons, but the hole was just as important. Delaying could give the ship's personnel time to organize and get weapons and get suited up in their armor, if they had any, so the team worked quickly. They got the last one in place, thrust away slightly, and Sam on his all-hands comms gave his order.

"EXECUTE."

"FIRE IN THE HOLE!" Akari yelled out.

The controlled blast worked perfectly. It created the desired hole size, and an instant after the concussion faded and the room equalized, Akari was thrusting in the hole with weapons up. Since she was first in, her weapon of choice was dual auto shotguns on each arm. In case the room was heavily defended, she could lay down massive amounts of thermite projectiles down in a short time. Although there had been new and impressive weapons developed over the centuries, some old weapon designs were still used, minus gunpower. The modern energy clip had more ass behind it, and there was still nothing like a good auto shotgun for room clearing.

Immediately after Akari entered, Sam was right behind her, also packing an auto shotgun, but he preferred his mini on his strong hand. Like the shotgun, his mini could bring a lot of firepower in a short time, firing armor piercing rounds at an extremely rapid rate. Luckily, though, both Akari and Sam didn't need to use their weapons this time.

Akari entered the room, checked her fatal front, then immediately swung right to clear that section of the room, firing her thrusters to continue to search. Sam entered swinging left to clear that section. Three was last in. Dre's job as third in was to back up the first two if they needed help, and if no help was needed, it was his job to set up an overwatch and watch his crew's back.

Dre's job once in was security while the other two dealt with cargo. He thrust to a good position and started to continuously scan the area, watching for any potential danger. Sam and the rest of the crew all breathed a little easier now that they had entered the ship and knew that there would be no resistance this time.

"All clear, people. We are checking cargo. Two, do you have comms yet?"

"Yes, One. The channel is ready whenever you are. Three is moving to opposite side of the ship to complete his sweep, and I will fully disable the transmitter."

Sam saw that Serg had, in fact, gotten into the ship's comms and had overridden the all-hands channel. Sam switched over to it and addressed the boarded ship's crew.

"All hands, this is the captain of the vessel boarding your ship. Your ship has been disabled, and we are commandeering all cargo. We will be gone in moments. No one will be harmed unless we have to. Stay where you are, and it will all be over soon."

Sam kept it short and to the point and divulged as little info as possible. He was aware that other captains gave out their names and the name of the ship they captained, but to Sam, this was a massive error and had all to do with vanity. He didn't want anyone knowing who he was for the obvious reason of remaining anonymous to authorities.

"Sam! I need you!" screamed Akari.

"What's up?" Sam asked, thrusting quickly to her.

"Look," said Akari as she pointed to the cargo.

Sam thought the cargo was supposed to be machine parts, but instead, he was looking right at military-grade weapons.

"Fuck me," was all he could say as he and Akari stood over the crates, hovering with their thrusters.

"This can't be . . ." said Sam, "What the fuck? It's a weapons transport. Why is there even weapons, and why would a weapons transport go unguarded?"

Then Sam answered this own question and quickly shouted orders.

"All hands, eyes up! I don't like this, we're out of here!" Sam's info was always first-rate. His gut told him something was wrong, and he had learned to trust it.

It was at that very moment that the UNE forces on board sprang their trap. Out of compartments in the cargo bay, fully armored UNE marines came charging out, immediately firing on the intruders on their ship. Akari was hit before she even had a moment to process what was going on or react to Sam's orders. She was nearest to the marines and didn't even have a chance to return fire. She was hit so many times Sam was almost sure she was instantly dead.

The second he saw the marines, he fired his thrusters at maximum, and it was this quick reaction that saved this life. He flew across the cargo bay, slamming into the ship's bulkhead, letting out a loud thud, and landing almost side by side with Dre. He was lucky as well. He had his back to the springing trap but was in good cover behind the fastened crates and not at all exposed to the firing marines. Dre had fired his thrusters like Sam, but he did so in a more controlled manner. He started returning fire as he bobbed and weaved in zero gravity as best as he could using the secured cargo as cover.

"CONTACT, CONTACT!" both Sam and Dre were yelling into the comms.

The marines were still firing on Sam, and he had to thrust behind cover again.

"Dre . . . hold there! Watch right!" Sam ordered while bringing his mini up and firing at the charging marines.

In the heat of the moment, Sam didn't even realize that he had used Dre's name. The chaos of battle had started, and in the first few moments, Sam had countless thoughts racing through his head. He was still in shock that he had walked right into an ambush and was questioning who got it wrong or who betrayed him. He was not exactly aiming at any of the marines charging but was more or less what they called spraying and praying. He just fired at the marines' general direction instead of taking well-aimed shots or using controlled bursts.

This was the madness that happened at the onset of every firefight, and with the massive amount of projectiles Sam was throwing toward his enemy, anyone else in the galaxy would have looked for cover or at least hesitated in their charge. Unfortunately for Sam and Dre, they were up against marines, and no amount of fire could hinder their charge or deter them from killing everyone they saw.

The first moments of chaos and confusion happened to everyone; it was just the way battle was. But the great warriors and leaders, which Sam was, always composed themselves after that initial shock, and Sam did exactly that. All battles or firefights, even though they only lasted minutes, seemed to last forever to those involved. It all happened so fast.

After a second to gather his wits, Sam counted four marines rushing at him at multiple angles. Four marines against two pirates were not good odds, and Sam knew he was in trouble. He snapped out of his haze.

"Sam! We're coming!" Serg yelled into the comms.

"Fuck, Dre, we're fucked! Hold them till Serg comes!"

"Sam!"

Dre was still darting from cover to cover, firing at the marines with his lay rifle with deadly accuracy. His laser rifle was the newest and greatest model of Xi rifles. It had the fastest recharge rate of any lay rifle and longest capacity on the market. On the other hand, he sported an auto just like the rest of the board team. His Xi, however, had nowhere close to the old mini rate of fire, but it had serious knockdown power.

Dre, unlike Sam, could not just hold down the trigger and let his rifle eat. He had to take well-aimed and controlled shots, and this was exactly what he did, hitting one marine square as it moved from cover toward the breach. Sam was confident that that marine was out of the fight and began focusing on the next target. Unfortunately for Dre, the remaining marines realized the threat Dre posed with his powerful rifle and focused all their firepower on him.

The UNE marines were a sight to behold. These individuals were recruited as children and trained in the art of war their entire lives. All were the unwanted children of Earth—meaning that their mothers gave them up at birth for a very small onetime payment. All they ever knew from their first memory was the military, and it was their family.

They had been trained and instructed to absolutely obey every order without moral question. Once given an order, they would carry it out and complete it or die. In their minds and belief system, it was almost sought after and a massive desire for each combat marine to die in combat. It was a religion to them. To reach their afterlife or whatever they believed to be their version of a supreme afterlife, it was paramount that a UNE marine died under fire.

They were fanatics, if not zealots, in their pursuit of mastering their trade of warfare as if war were a religion. There was no negotiating with them, and they never showed mercy to anyone or anything. They were all given body mods to enhance physical capabilities, and they also had interlinks installed for direct access to their OBs. This gave them not only enhanced physical abilities but also elite problem-solving and communication capabilities. They moved and fought as one in their signature battle armor, and a marine squad was one of the—if not *the*—deadliest groups in the known universe.

Sam watched out of the corner of his eye as they focused on Dre and he received multiple hits across his armor. He fought off the first two hits, but the third caused Dre to slump over, knocking him out of the fight.

"Dre is down!" Sam screamed into his comms.

In a flash of a second, Sam was alone against three remaining marines and helpless to go to the aid of his two friends, both now floating motionless in the bay with madness surrounding them. Sam didn't have much time to process before they again focused their attention back on him.

Instead of returning fire, Sam crouched behind the cover he had found and surveyed what little options he had. The marines would be on him so fast it was pointless to wait for his other teammates. They wouldn't get there in time, and he didn't want anyone else to get hurt. His first option was to stand and fight, and that option, he thought to himself, would probably end in him getting his head blown off. The second was to make a break for the breach and try to get to out of this confined space he was in. The benefit was that once outside, his teammates could help him in the fight, and they might prevail. The problem with that option was that he would almost certainly never even make it full thrust before the marines tore him to pieces, and even if he did get out, the marines would still probably cut him to pieces along with the rest of his team.

They were closing in on him, increasing their thrust, and he had only a couple precious moments. So Sam decided on his first option.

Better to go down fighting than running, he thought.

"We're fucked, guys! Fall back, and get outta here! Ameera, Serg, get them out!"

Sam closed his eyes and made a small prayer to the gods, thanking them for his time in this universe, and in the same moment, he felt sorrow that he could not say goodbye to his loved ones. With his mind made up and at peace with his decision that these were his last seconds to live, Sam stood up, releasing the fiercest battle cry he could, and faced the charging enemy.

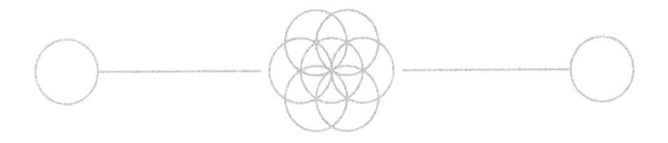

Chapter 2

There Are Those Who Know Our War

It's easy to look back at an engagement after it was all over and dissect what went wrong and what someone could do differently to change the fight's outcome. But while the fighting was actually going on, there was absolutely zero time to think. In a strategic sense, commanders had all the time in the universe to formulate and execute a battle plan, but when it came to the most tactical decisions, quick and decisive choices needed to be made and executed. The luxury of time was not a factor, and a bad decision most of the time was better than no decision. Sam's decision wasn't necessarily a bad one, but luckily for him, someone else decided to act—and act very quickly.

John, being the newest member of the crew, was in his position of guardian angel. It was perfect for new and inexperienced crew members because during a heist. They had very little responsibility other than being a lookout, and how often was a lookout needed in space? The likelihood of another ship approaching during a job was slim to none, and even if one was approaching, the ship's pilot or navigator would pick it up. Basically, it was a way of getting new pups like John in the action without them getting in the way.

John was perched up at the top of the ship when he heard Sam's contact announcement and very clearly heard the weapons fire beneath him. Whether it was hearing his brother in trouble, bravery, or complete lack of understanding of what he was doing, John fired up his suit without hesitation and maneuvered his way to the cargo bay breach that Sam and Akari had made.

"*Dre is down!*" he heard while he had his thrusters firing wildly as he came to the breach. When he entered the cargo bay, to his amazement, he saw the three remaining marines firing at someone tucked in cover, but again, to his amazement, all three were mere meters away.

"*I'm fucked, guys! Fall back, and get outta here! Ameera, Serg, get them out!*"

Dre had dispatched the marine moving to cover the entry/exit, and John practically ran into the backs of the marines when he entered. He was so close that his default move was to point and blast, and because he was so close, it was nearly impossible to miss. He raised his two lay rifles and fired directly into the marines' backs. One marine was blasted across the cargo bay, running into the other as its armor gave a red glow where the rounds had made an impact. The marines, after seeing another member go down, roared in rage, and one of them turned to face the new threat.

John fired again with both weapons at the marine turning to him, and both rounds found their marks. His lay rifles burned holes through the marine and his armor, smoldering as the marine flew back as well. The remaining marine then turned to face John, but doing so exposed his back to Sam.

Sam was rising to fire just as John was entering the cargo bay. It was a complete act of luck or possibly even fate that timed the two brothers' attack exactly at the same moment, and luck was definitely on their side for this engagement. The marine was caught in a perfect cross fire.

Sam fired his thermal shotgun and mini sabots into the remaining marine, but he refused to go down. Sam's weapons, in particular the mini, didn't have the knockdown power of the lay rifle, and the last marine stood for what seemed forever and received round after round, refusing to drop. He tried to raise his weapon at John, who was firing at the marine as well, but Sam took his time and released the thermal slug at the marine. He blew his arm off at the shoulder, and finally, the marine went limp, floating in the cargo bay. The engagement was over.

Sergio and Tucker entered the bay immediately afterward with weapons raised. They stood frozen as they surveyed the carnage and floating armor. For the longest time, no one said anything or even moved. It was Ameera who finally spoke.

"Sam! Are you there? Anybody?"

Hearing Ameera's voice, Sam snapped out of his frozen state.

"Yes . . . Yes, we're good, *Val*. All hands, all clear. We have two down! Six, you take Four. I'll take Three! Two, I want you and Five to clear the rest of the ship. Everything, Two. Breach what you need. If there are any bodies on board, I want them, but I expect this thing is all auto."

"Copy, let's bounce, Five."

"I'm with you!" Tucker yelled as the two fired away.

Both Sam and John fired over to their downed teammates and were at first happy to see that the suits had, at least to their eyes, sealed the impact of the rounds so Akari and Dre would not be in vacuum. Both had to move quick because although there were minimal first aid capabilities in the armored suits, it took a long time to move them back to the *Validus*. It took even longer to get them out of the suits, especially if they were unconscious or if the suit had lost power or so damaged that they had to open it manually.

Sam reached Dre and hardwired directly to Dre's suit, pulling the reinforced cable from his own and connecting to Dre. Sam and his team set up for direct access to any other member of the team, and it allowed the OBs to work together instead of against each other. He brought up Dre's medical status and saw first that Dre was alive. His suit had sealed all the impacts, and the gel had even sealed the wounds on Dre's body. Sam had to confirm once back on the *Val*, but a quick glance showed that the armor had taken much of the rounds and Dre wasn't in critical shape.

"Ah, fuck, man," Dre said, coming back to his senses. "That knocked the fuck outta me. How bad is it? Fucking burns."

"It's not that bad, my friend. I think your armor took most of it. Your shoulder looks good, but I don't like the one in your side, it probably took too long to seal. We need to get you back. Can you move? You need to get to vacuum asap."

"Yeah, man, gimme a hand, my thrust is gone, and my suit has alarm all over the fucking place."

"One!"

"Go, Six."

"Four is dead."

Sam paused. Akari had been with him for almost a year. Internally, he cursed himself, but he needed to focus first. He and his team weren't done and clear yet. There would be time for mourning, reflection, and anger later. Sam first had to get his shit and his people together.

"Copy that. We'll get her back after. Three needs the attention now. Get him on board," he said somberly. "*Validus*, stand by to move to transfer position, but wait till I clear the rest of the ship. Six is inbound. We need to move, people," Sam's voice was rising into his comms. "I don't want any more fucking surprises. All hands, acknowledge!"

Sam heard his order acknowledged from each member and moved over to John and put on his private channel to him.

"Thank you," he said while giving John a light head butt. "I owe you. We'll talk about everything later. We need to focus now."

"Okay, I'll take care of Three."

"Get him back, then head back ASAP to help. We're going to need it."

Sam thrust over to Akari. He couldn't see her through her armor, but he rechecked that she was indeed gone. It wasn't the first casualty Sam had seen, but it was the first under his command. He felt terrible, but he had more pressing matters to get to. He began his sweep of all the weapon crates. Each weapon probably had a tracking ID embedded into it, and before anything on a highjacked vessel was touched, it was first thoroughly scanned to identify if there was an ID so it could be removed. It was not hard to do, but it was time-consuming. Normally, each crate had an ID attached to it, but since these were weapons, each individual piece was tagged.

As Sam went through more and more containers, it became more and more apparent that this was going to be among the—if not *the*—largest score anyone had made. Most pirate captains were happy to get some consumer goods or organic products that were being shipped, because those could be sold easily on the market back home. The real prizes were machine parts or any equipment because they were in high demand back home. But military-grade weapons would most likely make a small fortune. It was money enough to even consider retiring from pirating altogether. But there was still a lot of work and deals to be made before anyone saw any profit for this job.

All together, there were fifty crates of weapons, all with ten lay rifles inside varying from armor models to standard nonarmor models. Sam moved as fast as he could to scan every weapon and remove the IDs from each. John had returned from taking Dre over to med bay and reported to Sam that the ship's automated doc was taking care of him. John joined Sam in scanning weapons as fast as they could, and the two had all five hundred completed by the time Serg reported in.

"Ship's all clear, Sam," he said over the all-hands comms. "Sorry, but took a while getting through the OB's security. As you guessed, the ship is auto."

"If that's the case, we are gonna blow this thing when we leave, so I need charges placed as well. If you need anything, call it in. Any questions?"

"You wanna blow the ship? Are you sure? We never go that far," asked Serg in a doubting tone.

"Yes. In this case, I don't want to leave anything behind. Someone is obviously on to us, or we got fucked, or we just got unlucky and ran into a random ambush, and I'm not giving anyone anything. No trace. It's possible we've been IDed already and that the marines definitely recorded and sent away everything, which brings that up. *Validus*, Nav, did you pick up or track anything other than standard transmissions while everything was going on?"

"Nothing, obvious. We jammed what we saw, but we'll look into it."

"If there was anything sent, it's too late now, but we need to know."

"We'll let you know."

"Okay, copy that. We've completed the scan and sweep of the ship. We're all clear. Repeat, all clear. *Val*, move to transfer position. Five and Six, you can move the cargo. Myself and Two will look at the marines and take care of Four."

Sam fired his beast to life and made one large leap to the first marine, which was the last to go down. He came down hard on the cargo floor and began examining the floating marine. As he expected, the wound was too large, and the marine died almost instantly after having its arm blown off. He directly connected to the marine and began his hack of the marine's OB. He didn't have difficultly retrieving the data that he needed. The OB had fail-safes and firewalls to block intruder access. But the marine was dead, and the OB was linked to its marine's brain. The brain was dead, so the OB was dead. All that didn't matter anyway, because all data was purged the moment the marine lost his cognitive functions. He stored what data he could grab from the marine to be analyzed at a later time then moved to the next marine. It was the same, and then he fired to the next one, and finally to the last one—the one Dre brought down.

Sam again thudded next to the marine jacked into the beast and was surprised to find that the marine's antihacking was still operational.

Sergio fired in, "Charges placed, Sam. Where you need me?"

Sam switched to his private channel with Serg. "This one's alive, it looks like his OB is still up."

"Can't be. Where was he hit?" he asked, thrusting over to Sam and the marine.

"Shit. Dre's shot hit the power. The suit went dead. So inside is an alive and maybe conscious marine."

Sam had never even heard or dreamed of capturing a marine, let alone seeing one. But in this particular instance, the marine's battle suit had failed when it was hit. The marine lay there unable to move, trapped in the half-ton suit, and Sam could only imagine the raging animal inside.

"I see," Serg said, pausing for a moment to gather his thoughts, floating in the bay. "Man, I don't have to tell you the risk of bringing that thing on board, but it's your call, boss. I've never spoken or let alone seen a marine out of its armor."

"What's your opinion?"

"I know it's fucked up, but let him be. There's no risk leaving him, and there's no telling what he will do on board."

"I'm not a murderer."

"Gods, Sam. Be real."

"We could use the intel. Hacking won't get shit on directs, you know that. We can find out why they are here, what they know."

"And you think that thing knows anything?"

"Maybe, maybe not, but I can't just leave him here. It's not right."

Sergio just shook his head in his armor.

"Give me a minute to think it over. In the meantime, let's get Akari back on board."

"All right, Sam."

Serg grabbed Akari, threw the lifeless armor over his shoulder, and fired back over to the *Validus*.

Ameera had the bays open still, and the remaining crew were loading the crates on board. Sam had remained, just floating in thought. He had stood over Akari earlier, saddened by his fallen comrade. Again, his emotions and thoughts began to rise, and Sam pondered internally at the possibility being him the one lying there in the cargo bay instead of Akari. One different move and everything could've changed, but he shook those thoughts out for the time being and brought his mind back to the present.

He stood there for a couple of minutes, questioning what his move was going to be. He stood so long and motionless that by the time he made up his mind, the rest of the crew were done and were all standing, stabilizers firing, just staring at Sam, wondering what was going through his head.

Sam switched to his all-hands comms. "Okay, where are we? Is transfer done?"

"Yes, transfer complete. We're ready to bounce out on your order," confirmed Serg.

Sam again paused for a moment, running a mental check that he completed everything that needed to be done.

"Serg, I know we have one issue left, but is there anything else you see that we need to do?"

"No, Sam, I think we're good."

"Very well then. Okay, guys, we have a live marine on board, and we're going to take him. After we close up, since we don't have a brig, I need the most secure place in the ship to stick him in, and I'm thinking of the arms locker. But since it's packed, I need it cleared. Serg, can you get him back to the *Val*? Tuck, take John and get it ready, will you? If you can find some kind of restraints to put him in, we'll need that as well. Okay, let's get to it, then we'll get the fuck out of here."

The whole team confirmed, and Sam and Serg fired over to the marine.

"Come on, fucker," Serg said as he grabbed the armor with one hand. "You're lucky, I would have left you to be blown to shit," he continued. "Listen, Sam, if this fucking animal puts us in jeopardy, intel or no intel, I'm gonna take care of it, understand? Now, we all follow your orders underway, but if I feel for a second that it's him or me, you can bet I'm gonna look after me 100 percent of the time. All I ask is that you don't put me in a position where I have to make that choice, okay?"

"I hear ya."

"I don't fucking like this."

"I know, my friend. It'll be okay."

Sam and Serg both fired their thrusters, with the marine being pulled by Serg. They crossed the short distance, and the whole crew readied for recovery.

"All right, Ameera, all hands and cargo are on board. Go ahead and close the hatch."

"Copy, Sam, closing."

The bay closed, enclosing the crew and massive EMP cannon. Vacuum was achieved throughout the hold.

"*Validus* sealed, Sam. I have green across the board."

"Confirmed vacuum here as well, all green. Go ahead and equalize the ship, and then let's get some distance. I want a visual when we blow her, so not too far."

"You got it, Sam."

She equalized the ship and at the same time engaged the *Val*'s thrusters. The blue flames produced by the core came to life. She piloted the craft to a safe distance and reported to Sam.

"Sam, we're clear and equalized," she said as she cut thrusters and spun the *Val* around, perfectly executing the maneuver. "You ready for some grav?"

"Let's have it."

"Coming online now."

The grav came online, and the crew had to increase their thrusters to land their armor in their "lockers." They touched down, and the whole crew went about their post job routine, only this time there was no celebration. Everyone was quiet.

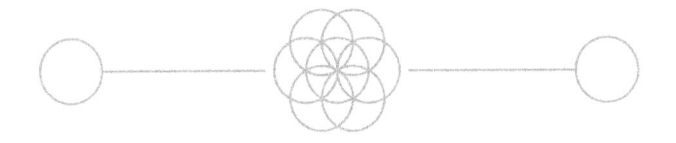

Chapter 3

Our Reality

Sam opened his armor and began the sleep procedures then slid out of it the opposite way he entered. He reattached its charger and put the safeties on all the weapons. On the return trip, he would have plenty of time to do all the maintenance on his suit. After all, it was his favorite. He then ordered John and Tucker to take the marine to the armory before leaving their suits and asked them to find any restraints they could. He headed to the command deck of his ship, which was down the crew quarters up and on the second level. Sam ran up the stairs and saw that Ameera had the command deck doors open already and was waiting for Sam.

"I want that ship destroyed before we do anything else."

"I heard you, Sam. Chill, boss."

"I promise I will chill when I see that ball of light and I'm headed home."

"If you say so," Ameera acknowledged without looking up from her station.

"Doors coming open, guys." Helena reached over from her copilot station and swiped the screen open.

"Ah, never gets old."

"Can't argue with that," Helena said, gazing into the stars.

"Serg, go ahead and blow your charges."

"Copy. Fire in three, two, one."

They saw from the command deck a brilliant flash of light that had once been the highjacked ship. Watching it explode, Sam took a couple of deep breaths and started to calm himself like his mother had taught him. He was still jacked up from all the strain that had been on him for the last hour. He needed to relax, but first he had to make sure things got cleaned up first.

He got on his comms, which was throughout the *Val*, and announced to the crew, "All right, give me thirty mikes to unwind, and clean up before we settle in for the ride home. We need to tend to Dre and then our prisoner. Tucker, after you take a minute for yourself, see if the auto doc needs any help with Dre. Me, Serg, and John will deal with the marine. Tuck, Helena can give you a hand if need be. I'm silencing my direct comms."

He exhaled and closed his eyes for a brief moment then continued, "I don't know what to say, my friends. We lost one of our own, and it was only by pure luck that we made it out alive. We'll get through this together like we always have, as a crew. I'll see you all at dinner. Sam out."

Sam silenced his comms and headed to the arms locker to have his first encounter with a UNE marine. As he was making his way toward the locker, he said out loud to himself, "What the fuck was I thinking?"

He entered the weapons locker and was happy to see that John and Serg were there and already working on the marine's suit. Sam had cursed himself, walking through the *Val*, that he hadn't fully disabled the marine's armor. He did, indeed, do a quick diagnostic on the suit before the transfer was over, but he had forgotten to pull the damaged power unit completely. If he had pulled the power then, there was absolutely no way the suit could come back to life. All of Sam's team were now out of their armor, so the marine could have easily torn through the ship if it got powered back up.

"Good thinking. I flat-out missed it," Sam confessed.

"It's all right," said John. "We all missed it, but disaster averted. So how you wanna do this? I suggest just removing the helmet if we can. That way the armor will still be holding him down, and we can see who and what we are dealing with."

"Yeah, that'll work. How much air does he have left?"

"Plenty," replied Serg, not even looking up from his work. He had already begun the drawn-out process of manually removing the helmet. "Just give me a minute, and I'll have it off."

"You need a hand?" Sam asked.

"Nah, I'm good. Just be a sec."

Sam went over to John, who had just finished pulling the power completely from the marine's suit.

"Thank you, John. I was surely fucked, but you saved my ass. I owe you."

"You would have done the same, but honestly, I didn't really think. As weird as it sounds, I just went in."

"It's not weird at all. I'm just glad you did, but now, after replaying everything, I know we got extremely lucky. It could have turned out drastically different, and Mom and Dad could have lost us both. Next time—and pray to the gods there is never a next time—don't put yourself in danger for me ever again."

"We'll see."

"I'm serious, John. Our parents don't even know what we are doing out here. Actually, they don't even know we are out here. Imagine what they would think if something went wrong and they lost two sons." Sam sighed as he was trying to explain his thoughts. "Listen, thank you, you were incredibly brave, and your quick thinking or instincts saved my life. Just in the future, be careful."

"You got it, Sam."

The two clasped hands and embraced each other. Sam released him and placed a hand on his shoulder, nodding and smirking, proud of his younger brother.

"You two done?" Serg was sitting behind the marine just watching the exchange. "That was fucking weak, but this thing is ready to come off, plus I can't watch this anymore."

"Yeah, Serg, off with the thing," Sam gestured, indicating to go ahead.

He slid a chair in front of the downed marine, turned the chair around facing backward, and took his seat. They had put the marine in its battle armor in the sitting position, so Sam was face-to-face with the thing. John positioned himself standing at Sam's side and readied himself, looking at Serg to finish his task.

Serg released the armor's pressure seals, and the customary hiss sounded throughout the locker. Serg gave the helmet a swift jerk and slowly lifted, grunting mightily due to the gravity and the weight of the armor.

It was not what any of them expected in the slightest. Sam had the impression that he would see a deformed, raging man animal. Instead, what he saw wasn't a man at all. Beneath the thousand-pound armor was a woman.

All three were taken aback because they expected some hard-looking creature, but the marine woman actually had a certain beauty to her. She had blond hair, which was currently cut very short, very fair skin glistening with sweat, and few but not elaborate scars on her face. All the men, after looking the marine over, immediately focused on her eyes.

They were fierce but were a beautiful brown color that, at the moment, were focused dead straight at Sam. She sat there with one of the fiercest gazes any of the three had ever seen, and it was immediately clear to the three men that this person was a serious individual. Sam was mesmerized with the marine, and the look he returned to her was one of awe, fear, and disbelief.

It was John who finally broke the silence.

"What's your name?"

The marine blinked once and slowly shifted her gaze toward John. Unfazed by the marine's icy glare, John only asked her the same thing again.

"What's your name? Can you understand what I'm saying?"

Her only reply was her continued icy stare.

"Do you have a name?" asked Sam, repeating what his brother asked.

The marine again shifted her focus back to Sam and said nothing.

"Well, if you understand what I'm saying, then I'll tell you that you are now my prisoner. You will not be harmed unless you intend on violence yourself. These men will be removing the rest of your armor and seeing you are restrained. They will bring you some food, water, and anything else you need. I am in command of this ship, and if you want to talk at some point, you can ask for me."

"I know who you are, Samuel Cleber. Pirate, thief, murderer, and son of Mars. The only thing I have to say to you is, your planet, your people, and your family have defied us for long enough. Pray to whatever false gods you pray to, but even they can't save you from what's coming."

"And what is that?" asked Sam, unable to feint his fear any longer especially after hearing his name.

The marine didn't answer, just gave a sinister smirk and then turned her focus on something else in the room, removing eye contact from the group.

Sam, John, and Serg gave a quick glance to each other, and John motioned them to exit the weapons locker. All three walked out of the hatch, and Sam sealed the heavy armored door behind them.

Serg, in a very questioning and drawn-out tone, said, "Okay ... what the fuck was that?"

"Not exactly what I was expecting," said John, standing with arms crossed and scratching his chin.

"Yeah, no shit," Serg mimicked John's pose. "How did she know who you were? And most importantly, if a grunt marine knows who you are, I'm sure the panel knows who you are. Not good, Sam. I say we get our asses back home. You have to let your parents and the council know about this."

"I agree, but this is not going to go well," Sam confessed, clearly a little rattled by the marine's response. "They have always preached a nonviolent solution to the problem, and now their son is about to tell them that he's doing exactly what they have been speaking against for years. I'm not sure if I'm more afraid of the UNE or our parents' wrath."

There was a pause in the conversation as all three in the hallway contemplated what had just happened.

Sam then turned his attention to John and spoke to him directly, "Anyway, we have a little time to decide our move on our return trip, but I want you to think about not involving yourself in this. This being your first run, I'm sure no one knows you're here. You're a grown man, just giving you my opinion."

"I pushed to be here. Not right for me to go running for cover."

"Just think on it, but for now, can you two finish up with our guest? And I'll let Ameera know it's time to go home."

"All right, boss," Serg said as he turned away.

John didn't say anything but followed Serg's lead and went back to the weapons locker. Sam turned down the hallway, turned on his comms link, and hailed Ameera.

"Ameera, status?"

"All quiet, Sam. Orders?"

"Let's go home, and make it quick."

"Copy, Sam. On to Mars."

* * *

"How's Dre?" Sam asked, taking a seat in the crew quarters.

"He's been better. His wounds are bad, but he'll be okay by the time we get home." Tucker let out a slight chuckle. "He'll have some good scars that he can impress the women with at the bar, and he seems like himself. He's already bitching that he should've downed one more marine for you, and he's back to being our Mongo. I pumped him full of meds and gave him a sedative, so he'll be out for a while."

"Thanks, Tuck. And how 'bout the rest of you? Everyone as good as can be?"

"All good, but if it's all the same, I'm gonna get gassed up tonight," Serg said as he poured himself a stiff drink. "We got time on the return trip to recover, and I ain't gonna fucking sleep unless I pass out, so here we go." He upended the bottle he was holding on to.

"I'm with you on that. Pour me one, Serg," Tucker chimed in.

"While you're at it, I'll have one," Sam said, sliding a glass to Serg.

Ameera walked in right behind Helena and said, "Might as well pour a round for everyone, honey."

"Where's John?" asked Helena as she took a seat at the crew table.

"He's finishing dinner, then gonna take some food to our new prisoner."

"So about that, Sam," Ameera said as she swirled her drink around. "Listen, this is your ship, and while we're underway, we follow your orders, but what the fuck, Sam? You brought that thing on our ship. What can you possibly gain from that thing? It's not like you and me. For all we know, he's been trained to fuck with you, give you false information, and it's certain he's trying to escape and kill us all. You should have left him on the ship."

"First, 'he' is a 'she,' and to be honest, I don't know what we'll gain, if anything, from her." Sam paused to let the sincerity of his words soak in. "But I promise, if I even think for a minute that she will hurt one of you or this ship, I will send her out the airlock without hesitation. They obviously know about us. I haven't told you yet, but she knew my name. If I can learn anything at all about what they are planning, I'm gonna try."

"Wow, hold on, they know your name?" Tucker said, leaning in on the table.

"Yes, she called me by my name in the armory. Honestly, a little unnerving, but again, now more than ever, we need intel. This changes things. Guys, we all hate the UNE, and the council has been tiptoeing around this for a long time, but they are gunning for something, or at least trying to bring us in line. I don't know shit, and I need to know what they're up to. If a fight is coming, I want to know about it. Info is power, so I'm told."

"Sam, that thing doesn't know shit. Throw it out the fucking airlock. They killed Akari," Ameera interjected again.

"And we killed three of them. I know we're all emotional right now. You guys are family to me, and I love and respect each and every one of you. Let me talk to this marine. Word is, they aren't supposed to be taken alive, so hopefully, we have her at a disadvantage. She might never have been trained in how to handle being captured. Let's give her a minute to calm down and see if she talks. It might be worth more than just data collection."

"I got dinner, people," John yelled, bursting into the room, then throwing the large pot down on the table. He was totally unprepared for the current mood of the room. He continued, but at a more relaxed manner, "It's just a stew, but I'm not a cook like Tucker there. Worst case, we have week-old bread to choke it down," and gave a nervous chuckle.

Sam slid a glass over to John as he took a seat and then raised his. "Thanks for cooking, John, but first, I'd like to raise our glasses to Akari. She was new to the crew compared to all of us, but she became part of us very quickly. I'm gonna miss her enthusiastic personality and that she always told it how it was. To Akari."

"To Akari," the crew said, all downing their drinks.

"I, ah, was going to give her share of the loot to her family, plus a hefty bonus, if everyone is okay with that."

Everyone nodded in agreement.

"Does anyone have anything they want to get off their chest?"

The crew looked around the table at each other, shaking their heads.

"What a fucking day," Sam said as he set his glass next to Serg and the bottle, indicating a refill.

Serg refilled his and everyone else's in the room.

There was silence for a long while as the crew of the *Validus* dished out John's stew and ate their meal. All except Serg, who preferred to drink his dinner tonight. All that could be heard was the clinking of dishes against the metal spoons as the crew ate and the occasional thud of a glass being put down after a drink on the wooden table, which Sam specifically ordered for the ship. What could they say at that moment? The loot that they just captured from the transport would make them all very wealthy, but there was not a smile on any face or a sound of laughter at that dinner. Such was the atmosphere when a friend was lost.

It was Sam who finally broke the silence when dinner was almost done.

"I need a watch set up for the marine. I don't want her unguarded. Twenty-four seven, is that understood? We'll all take a watch, and I want everyone armed just in case." Sam paused again to gather his words.

"I'm going to go to my parents and tell them everything. The council needs to know and form a plan. I want all cargo unloaded and stored before I go to them, and I'd plan to lay low for some time. I have no idea how they'll react, but I'd assume we won't do any runs anytime soon. I'm not going to tell them about the cargo we have and definitely not going to tell them anything about you. I think my parents would be more upset with me if they found out I'm running with you pirates than the fact that I'm pirating."

All the crew chuckled at that.

Serg, feeling the alcohol kick in, said, "Sam, you can tell them all about me if you want. It's not like I don't have a colorful reputation. Ha!"

"You're just too famous, Serg!"

"Sam, you sure about this?" Tucker said, turning the conversation back. "I know you'll be fine, but you don't need to fall on the sword."

"No, I need to take responsibility. I've been lying to them for years now. They knew I didn't give a shit about politics, or whatever the fuck they do in the council, but they are speaking out against pirating. I want them to know from me and not a rumor what I'm involved in, so this is what needs to be done. If it comes to it, Serg and Ameera can take the *Val* up to get some loot while I stay grounded." Sam paused for dramatic effect, grinning from ear to ear. "As long as I get my cut."

At that, the crew burst into laughter, and everyone started sliding their glasses back to Serg, who had produced another bottle.

"Why the fuck not."

And Sam slid his glass to Serg again. He needed to drink enough to pass out. Drink the day away.

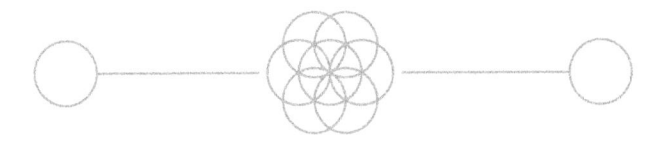

Chapter 4

Our Opposite

Millions of miles away from the crew's position, at the capital of the UNE, located in the First District, the panel of administrators overseeing UNE operations on Mars got their first reports from the marine squad they were all monitoring. Even with all the advances in technology, most of UNE's panels required meetings to be conducted only in person.

Security was one of the—if not *the*—highest concerns in the UNE, so from the earliest forming of the United Nations of Earth, it was mandated that meetings be held in person to avoid anyone listening in on any conversations. Low-level briefings and information were still passed over links, but no devices of any kind were allowed in a high-level meeting. Each panel member was scanned thoroughly before being granted access and entrance to a series of the most secure rooms in existence. There were multiple meeting rooms, each of them with their own security measures. It provided an extra layer of security not only from outsiders but also from other panels looking for some inside information.

Due to the strict in-person-meeting-only policy, each panel member of every panel in the UNE had to live in the district grounds so they could be called upon in a moment's notice. This also made it easy for the UNE to keep a constant eye on their own. All members in one location.

"So Gerard's little shit came out on top."

"I told you, we were way too light on this one. We should have had three times the marines lying in wait. What makes it even worse is that some idiot tried to send weapons on the same transport, and now they are in those degenerates' hands. Our forces on the planet need those weapons, this is just unacceptable."

"So those peasants acquired some new toys, who cares? And we agreed that they'd potentially not take the bait if they scanned more than one ship. It had to look as normal as possible, but some fool tried to earn some credits, and due to his actions, we currently have him arrested, and he and his family are on their way to the camps. And how did they neutralize one marine squad? I thought the marines were among the best in the UNE force."

"They were, but as you can see, there was an unaccounted-for member, who we know now is the other son." The panel member looked down, trying to recall the son's name from memory. "John. Still, it's no excuse. The marines had surprise on their side and still were defeated. They paid the price, and apparently, so will we. We must report this immediately," he said, closing his report. "Our little game of kidnap the son failed totally, and now they are aware something is going on."

"They had to know there was going to be a reaction. Piracy has been a problem for decades now. We have been increasing garrison numbers, and we started choking more and more supplies from Mars, which made them turn to piracy even more. I mean, for fuck's sake, the pirates are becoming fucking national heroes. We created the problem and thought we could force them into submission by kidnapping one of the royal family and forcing them to terms. Now I'm afraid we just added to the fire."

"Perhaps it's time to stop playing around and go for complete control. Total occupation and immediate overthrow of their little play government. Their 'free' planet is making things difficult here on Earth. It will be costly, but in the long scope of things, UNE control is what we are all after. One quick, decisive action."

"I'm inclined to agree," one panel member spoke up. "We'll end up spending more resources slowly assimilating the people into our way, and who is to say that will ever happen? As our colleague mentioned, it's been decades that we have been going with this hearts-and-minds campaign, and I'm afraid the situation has been progressively getting worse. Our garrison, if we can even call them that, is undermanned, completely lacking in training and equipment, and most of the personnel are native to Mars and could care little about the UNE, I'm sure, other than the credits they receive. If our goal is total control, then we need to stop dicking around and go for total control."

After the entire panel sat quite for a couple minutes, the panel chairman spoke up.

"I want full reports on potential plans, total cost, chance of success, the whole works. I am not going to approach the First Panel without being 100 percent confident of success and every detail worked out. If they decide to approach the president, that will be their decision. I know no one on this panel decided on the current strategy, but I want to create the winning one. Does anyone have anything further to add?"

"I do, sir," one junior member spoke up.

There was a hesitation in the member's facial expression, clearly displaying instant regret at speaking up. After calculating his options, he decided to go ahead with his original thought but with a less direct statement than originally intended.

"I am in no way saying that this option would be the best course of action, and we haven't even considered or mentioned this yet, but consider going a different direction and completely leaving Mars." He paused for a minute to let the idea sink in for the rest of the panel. "We would have to negotiate the trade of goods, but no garrison equals less cost, and we could definitely use the manpower and resources elsewhere. It would solve the pirate problem because that could be a condition for us to leave Mars. Mars would have to police their own and make Mars responsible for the grain transport. Lastly, it would provide time to build up our forces and quell domestic issues we are having. Mars and its people have been the outcast and unwanted of Earth, and they have been a problem for us since it was first colonized centuries ago. They have been slowly draining us and will continue to do so until we put an end to it."

"Are you suggesting independence?"

"Isn't that basically what they have now? Their leading family has no real power but heavily influences their committee of peers, and they basically govern themselves, meaning there is little government at all. We all know why they left, I say let them have it. I believe they will come crawling back after the only semblance of order leaves and the mob takes over. At that point, they'll welcome us back with open arms. Again, I'm suggesting this as an alternate option, I'm by no means saying this is the way forward."

"Interesting idea, young man. However, you failed to mention one key possibility where the mob takes over and decides not to send Martian food our way. Then, my boy, we are truly fucked. Earth would starve, and we'd have to mount an expedition anyway."

"That is a possibility, sir, but either option has its risks involved. For example, what if our total occupation fails? That is a certainty too that food will stop and that Earth will starve."

"Now, that's absurd. Are you suggesting UNE forces couldn't overtake Mars? Fuck, man, they have no army, space force, or even a militia, for fuck's sake. The only authority present—if you'd call it that—is their, what do they call them, executive officer and officer of the law offices that here on Earth have been phased out for almost a century."

"Historically, sir, people have overcome greater odds. Back in the days of nations, there were many cases where common people toppled their nation's government forces."

"And that is why the UNE got rid of the primitive nations. We are the United Nations only in name. I should not have to educate you why we had no choice but to assume planetwide control. I find it extremely unlikely that those farmers and peasants could do a thing to us. The only problem I see is logistics, keeping our forces supplied and fed, which is the problem I want this panel to figure out. Do not consider abandoning Mars to these rats. UNE must and will prevail!"

"Sir," another member spoke up.

"Yes, what is it?'

"One positive out of this situation is that it is very possible our contact was not compromised, so they could be of further use to us in the future if need be."

"Yes, yes, I very much forgot about our little pirate asset. Let us figure something useful for our informant in our planning. It might be beneficial for the asset to simply supply us information, or perhaps we could use them for another potential trap. Either way, I want a full report completed on the asset as well and expect it along with potential occupation operations. Now, if there is anything else . . . No? This panel is dismissed. You have one week."

* * *

Sam couldn't face his parents right away. He had plenty of time on the return to Mars and had for the most part figured out what he was going to say but hadn't thought out how to start.

Hey, Mom, Dad. Remember when you told me pirating could do no good? Well, surprise, I'm a leading member, and by the way, Earth knows who I am, so get ready, I guess.

He would just wing it; it always seemed to work in his favor more times than not.

"Attention, passengers, coming off thrusters and calculating for entry. Our angle is actually looking nice, so hopefully, it won't be too bad, but I'd still strap in."

Upon hearing Ameera, Sam and the crew headed to the command deck to assume their spoken-for seating and strapped themselves in.

"Is Dre good back there?"

"Yeah, he's good. Still bitching that he wants out, but the regen is still doing its work. He had way too much exposure. I juiced him up for the landing, so he's enjoying the ride."

"Definitely taking longer than I thought. When we land, get the big ox somewhere comfortable, and get him some good drink and smoke."

The port, as it was simply called, was the main and almost sole official landing site for the capital of Jazeera. Since it was such a busy station, there were almost constant flights coming and going, keeping the steady stream of cargo coming to and from the mother planet, Earth. This, of course, was perfect for Sam because it made it easier to come and go as he pleased.

"On final approach, people," Ameera said over the *Val*'s comms. "Looks like we're in store for a pleasant entry, we're lining up almost perfectly."

"Rarely happens," Serg added. "I'll take it. Our luck is still running, looks like."

"Hopefully keeps up," Helena chimed in. "Entering atmosphere in three . . . two . . . one. All right, we're in."

Ameera and Helena, in the pilots' seats of *Validus*, opened the shielding that protected the view port and gave them a bird's-eye view of their approach to the landing site. They could just as easily make the landing with the shield closed, but the crew very much enjoyed looking at the beautiful planet they called home.

Mars was a beautiful green, lush with vegetation, and every so often, the *Val* glided over crystal clear lakes and rivers. The centuries of terraforming, although not 100 percent complete, had been doing its job.

Ameera took manual control for actual landing, and although the ship's OB could more than handle a landing, Ameera preferred to remain sharp and perform manual maneuvers from time to time. The ship's landing gear came out, and Ameera softly touched the *Validus* down in its normal landing spot and started to power down the engines.

"Touchdown, people. Welcome home. I'll shut down the ship, and then I'm signing off." Ameera looked over to Helena. "Good job as always. I'll see you around. Get ahold of me after things settle down. We'll go get fucked up one night, I'll get Sergio to watch the kids."

"Sounds like a great plan. I myself am going to get good and smashed tonight, probably partake in some booze and high-quality herbage and perhaps find something to drag back home," Helena said with a little sass.

"We all know you and Tucker been having at each other. I don't know why you two hide it."

"We know you all know, but it's fun right now to keep it like it's a secret, plus we all know the policy. When it's business, it's business, and we try to keep to ourselves when we are on a job. Maybe one day we'll shack together, but not now, it's still too new, ya know."

"Well, enjoy it, honey, 'cause when you get to my position, you're gonna have that man baby with you constantly. Serg and I basically are with each other all the time, which is the way we like it, but it has its issues." She paused for a moment. "But what am I saying? Enjoy yourself, and like I said, if you wanna get fucked up with or without Tucker, let's do it."

"Okay, I'll be in touch."

The two exited the command deck and walked through the ship, seeing everyone moving about, eager to get off the ship they had been contained in.

Ameera walked into the cargo bay and was immediately hit with that beautiful clean Martian air, which was spreading throughout the bay because the doors had been opened. She stopped for a moment, took some deep breaths, looked around the landing zone, and sought out the person she was looking for.

"Hey, Cap!" she yelled from the doors of the cargo bay across the landing zone.

"Any problems this time?" Cap, the crew mechanic, asked. "You didn't hurt my ship, did you?"

Cap had been the mechanic for the *Validus* for some time now. Sam and the crew just couldn't do all the maintenance themselves, so they brought Cap in. No one knew, including Cap, how she got her name. It was all she knew, and that was what everyone called her. She wiped her hands on a dirty rag as she approached the ship.

"I don't see anything too bad."

"Nope, you got it easy, just standard fuel and maintenance."

"All right, you guys do any good?"

"Yeah, not bad," Ameera said, clearly trying to contain information from Cap.

"Oh, that good, huh. Hopefully, I'll get a nice fat cut of whatever you got. Hey, Sam!" Cap yelled out, seeing Sam walk down the bay. "When can I expect some money? Something tells me you gotta nice score."

"What makes you say that?" Sam asked back.

"You always get a nice score!"

"You get your cut when you get your cut, Cap, and if you bust my balls like you always do, I might look for another mechanic. I'm in no mood to fuck with you," Sam said as he walked past the two.

"What's up his ass?" Cap asked, watching Sam walk away.

"Don't blame him, he has a lot on his mind," Ameera told Cap as they watched Sam walk away. "We'll explain later."

"Okay, whatever. I'll see to the ship. You keeping it here in port or moving?"

"We'll move it later, but first, come with me. You're gonna want to see this shit."

"After you." She gestured toward the *Validus*.

The two walked back into the hold of the ship.

"Oh boy . . . Okay then," Cap just kept repeating as she stood with her arms crossed, looking at the weapons. "Is Selena taking this shit? By tomorrow, everyone in the city will know what we have."

"No, they won't! Sam want everyone quiet on this one."

Cap picked up a pebble off the ship's deck and tossed it up in her hand. "Gonna be hard to keep this contained once we start moving it."

"We are moving them to one of the caverns after dark. One of the boys will be by later, so until then, keep it quiet, Cap," Ameera said as she gave Cap a pat on the shoulder and walked out.

"Yeah, sure thing. I'll just do what I'm told like always. One of these days, I'm going to get pissed and walk. I don't like being a member of the crew and kept out of the loop."

"That's Sam's call, and you know it." Ameera was getting frustrated. "Can you just once not complain and just do it?"

"Yeah, yeah, I'll do it." And she grumbled something to herself as she walked away.

She had a frown on her face, realizing once again she had to be kept in the dark. She hated it, and it made her feel like she was not part of them. She took a deep breath and smiled as she looked at "her" *Val*. It always calmed her working on it. She shook off the last conversation and went back to work.

* * *

As Sam walked away from the crew, John was in the armory with the newly acquired prisoner. He had demanded that she be kept under watch at all times with the crew rotating duty until they decided what was to become of her. John volunteered for first watch. Being the newest recruit, his responsibilities were limited, and if he wasn't on guard duty, he wasn't exactly sure what to do. Sitting by himself with the marine and always at a distance, John digested what had happened and now all the consequences of the choices Sam made.

Not knowing what to do, John started thinking to himself about what he would do and how he would prioritize things. Dre was stable but definitely needed some attention. He was by far the number one priority. After that, he had to let someone know about Akari and also had to decide what to do with the captured marine. As he was thinking that exact thought, he turned to the marine and noticed she was staring at him. It wasn't the extreme glare he received before like she wanted to carve his heart out, but still fierce nonetheless.

"You have something to say? You haven't said shit the whole way back."

She didn't respond, only blinked.

"What the fuck do you want, crazy?" John asked again as the marine continued to stare. "Okay, I'm not a mind reader, spit it out."

There was a long moment when the two didn't speak but just looked at each other.

"Okay, crazy, since I have time to burn watching your ass, I'll play. Now, what do you want?" John questioned as he stood and started to stroll around the armory. "It's obvious you would like to kill me, so that's easy. I won't guess that. And you obviously think I'm a handsome man."

At that statement, John noticed a slight cringe in the marine's face, and John smiled, knowing he succeeded in fucking with the marine a bit.

"Made you cringe, that stone-faced stare is melting away. Okay, seriously, though, let me think here." And after a short pause, he said, "I got it! You're hungry?"

No response.

"You're thirsty?"

No response.

"Oh, fuck, you have to go the bathroom?"

At that, the marine just stood in her restraints, but there was the ever-slightest smirk across her face when she rose. This was the first time John truly got a good look at the ship's prisoner. Before she had been in her beast suit and not stood before on his watch, but now he got his first good look at her, and he couldn't help but admire her absolutely perfect physique.

She was as tall as he was, and he could easily see that she had to be one of the fittest human beings he had ever laid eyes on. He couldn't help but think to himself that she was beautiful, which was probably showing across his face. The marine seemed not to care.

"Here's the deal. If you try anything or make any quick moves, I'm going to fucking kill you. Even though it would be a shame to kill a beautiful creature as yourself, I am not fucking around. Before I move one fucking inch," John stated as he started to raise his voice, "you are going to make some sort of gesture that you agree and understand me. Now, do you agree?"

The marine known as Commander put her chuffed hands out and gave John a very slight nod.

"See, that wasn't so hard, was it? Before we decide what to do with you, I'm going to get you talking to me. I'm going to make it my personal mission in life because, unfortunately, at the moment, I have nothing better to do. Okay, I'm leaving your arm and leg cuffs on, but I'll take off the restraints from the bulkhead. If you're good, I'll get you some water and something to eat. Let's go, marine lady."

* * *

Before leaving the *Validus*, Sam had stopped by to see Dre and make sure he was all right. Since he was stable and in good spirits, he asked Dre if he could wait until nightfall before moving him and seeing to a med spec. Dre agreed with no issues and told Sam he was all right, just needed to sleep at the moment. Sam asked him to check on John every so often. Upon leaving, he also told Serg to wait until nighttime to move the cargo and the marine because now the *Val* had way too many eyes on it and too many nosy people snooping in trying to see what was going on.

He asked Serg to also let Tucker know he was next watch in eight hours so he needed to get cleaned up and get something to eat. Sam would eventually take a shift, but he had much to do before that happened, and the next task was one he was dreading the entire trip home.

He was going to see Akari's parents. He was pretty sure she had a love interest, but he wasn't sure who it was. Anyway, her parents deserved to hear first. Sam had never lost a companion before and had no idea what he was going to say, but he knew he had to go there directly before gossip in the port eventually went around.

Walking away from the landing zone, he ran into Ameera and Cap and almost instantly regretted his reaction to Cap. Cap was a good person but fucking annoying, always on about with money. Sam paid his people well, and Cap was no different, but she never seemed to have any, which Sam knew was due to gambling. He would deal with paying his crew later, including Cap, and although she had her problems, she deserved absolutely zero special treatment.

Sam's interaction with Akari's parents went as he expected. He received the blame and even was struck by Akari's mother, but Sam weathered it all, and in the end, he was holding both her parents in an embrace. He told them that although it would never make up for her death, Akari would get her share and that if they needed anything, Sam would do anything in his power to help them out.

With that done, Sam was mentally and physically exhausted, and he knew it was time to retire for the day.

* * *

There was only one place in the galaxy that Sam wanted to be at the moment. He had gone pretty deep into the city, preferring to walk instead of taking the auto transport. This allowed him to gather his thoughts in the upcoming encounter with Akari's parents, but now he wanted to get to the bar with all possible haste.

He jumped in one and told the auto nav to take him to Selena's. It was nearly dark, and Sam knew the bar would be packed with customers, but he didn't care. He needed to see the one person around whom he could fully let himself go. Selena and Sam were never formally married due to Sam being a "public figure" and Selena being a bar owner / black market dealer.

There was also the issue that Selena was what the people called "pure blood," meaning that she was a descendant of an Indian bloodline. She could trace her lineage all the way back to Earth during the time of nations before people became almost unrecognizable in regard to their lineage. The people of Mars had over the centuries mostly blended, but not all people, and Selena was indeed a rarity for Mars. Her family was dead set against Selena interacting with anyone outside her "own" people, so to not upset anyone's feelings, they kept their love hidden from the world. They never displayed it in front of anyone. Only a select few knew of the two, and they were going to keep it that way, but behind closed doors, the two acted as any man and wife and madly in love with each other.

He entered the bar, and Selena, tending to the packed crowd, saw Sam enter and immediately saw something was wrong. He walked to his usual table situated in the corner overlooking everything and was pleased to see Serg and Tucker there having dinner and drinks.

He walked over and slid in, asking, "Mind if I join you, degenerates?"

"Sam!" the two echoed, sliding over to even out the space, making room for Sam.

Selena had made her way over and asked if they needed anything, setting down Sam's typical drink, homemade Martian brew. As she did, so the two made eye contact, and in that second, both told each other they were happy to see the other.

"As you can see, fellas, crazy busy tonight, but if you need something, just holler, okay? Me or one of the girls will get ya what you need."

"What's on the menu tonight?" Sam asked Tucker as he lightly brushed Selena's leg as she walked away.

He didn't care. It was hard enough to keep his hands to himself, and he wanted her even more on this particular night. On top of being pure blood, Selena was exotic and a world-class beauty. She had perfect olive skin, long, thick dark hair, glorious green eyes that looked like emeralds, and a body that all men couldn't help but notice. She was immediately noticed everywhere she went, and she knew it. She took pride in her appearance and loved that as she walked away from the table, all three men were watching her as she went back to the bar.

"You're one lucky bastard, you know that, Cleber? I'm sure many men would gladly trade one of their balls just to have a shot with her."

"Right, Tuck, you know we're just friends," he said, giving Tucker a wink. "What you guys eating, and are the girls joining us?"

"I don't know. I know Ameera wants to be with the kids tonight, so I don't think she'll make it this way, and I'm gonna take care of moving Dre, the cargo, and our guest later. Couldn't tell ya 'bout Helena."

"She'll be up later," Tucker confirmed. "We're gonna spend a little time together before my watch, and I think I'm going for Selena's special, the fa . . . fa . . . ji . . . tas, I think they are called. Am I saying that right?"

"Fajitas, yeah, bull's-eye. You can't go wrong with those. I think I'm going for the stew and some rolls. I want a good base before I drink too much. You guys order any vape?"

"Yeah, here. I felt like vanilla tonight."

"One of my favorites." And with that, Sam took a long inhale and almost immediately felt its effects, relaxing his mind and his body. Then he said as he was exhaling, "Oh my gods, I needed that."

"That'll set you right, my friend."

The three sat in silence for a moment while Sam took another long draw and leaned back in the booth.

"Listen," Serg said, leaning in looking right at Sam, "I don't know how and when to bring it up, so I'll just ask. How'd it go at Akari's?"

"Like you think it would, Serg, and not right now please." Sam continued to lean back, not engaging with Serg. "I'll tell you all about it, but just not now, okay?"

"Yeah, yeah, no problem, just you need to talk to people too, and me and Tuck and Dre are always around. I know you got Selena, but just saying."

"I know, but let's just eat, have some drinks, little vape, and just try to enjoy the evening. We'll talk about everything tomorrow after I meet with my parents, and we plan what we can do, all right?"

"Okay, Sam."

The three went on staying somber with an occasional laugh here and again. Helena showed up before too long, and Sam and Serg left for the evening to give the two privacy. Serg went back home to Ameera before he returned to the *Val*, and Sam went up to the bar and had one more drink, preferring to sit by himself for a moment.

Selena went over to Sam once the crowd started to go home for the evening and asked, "Mine or yours? Doesn't matter."

"How 'bout yours? Mine is trashed at the moment."

"Mine too, but who cares. Why don't you head there now and get cleaned up, and I'll be along shortly. I'll have one of the girls close up."

"Okay, hurry please. I've been gone for almost two weeks, and it's taking every ounce of my will power to not grab you here right now."

"Calm down, you pirate. I'll take care of you when I get home. Now, get the hell out of here before I let you grab me and have you here on the bar in front of everyone."

"By the gods, I love you."

"Get going, you pirate."

"See you in a little bit."

* * *

Sam didn't have to go far to get to Selena's place. When she built the bar, Selena had multiple dwellings built as a multistory building, and Selena took the top floor for herself. She spared no expenses, and her bar as well as the dwellings above were considered by many to be the central hub of the port. Many other businesses sprang up around her bar, and over time, it ended up being a very nice area.

Selena not only ran her bar but was one of the main middlemen in the ever-thriving market on Mars. She could get her hands on almost anything, and if she couldn't, she knew people who could. She was a busy girl. Sam noticed she almost never sat still and was always looking into something, on the comms conducting business or getting alerts about new information. It didn't bother Sam at all. He kind of enjoyed being with a woman who was so connected and influential. He got his intel from various sources, but Selena was by far his most-trusted and go-to girl. He never went anywhere else to sell his cargo—Selena had a monopoly on that.

He got himself cleaned up, grabbed some of his clothes that he had left, sat himself down, and let his mind wander, specifically about how to approach his parents the following morning. He still had no idea what he was going to say.

In the end, he was probably just going to tell the truth, and whatever happened after was going to happen. He didn't see too many possible outcomes. He never gambled, but he would bet a considerable amount that the UNE knew about him and that soon there was going to be a reaction from them.

How much of a reaction, he was still unsure of, but he was guessing, first thing was, they would have to watch the garrison closely and see if there was anything unusual going on. He made a mental note to contact one of his people in UNE to see if they knew anything. Most of the garrison were native Martians just needing the funds to survive, so hopefully, someone would have something for him. All in good time, he would find out everything. This was not the time to be sloppy.

Selena unlocked the door, walked in, and shut and locked the door behind her.

"Cleber, get over here."

"Yes, ma'am," Sam said, jumping from the chair and walking over to her, getting nose-to-nose with her.

Selena, keeping her eyes locked on Sam, slid her hand down his pants and grabbed Sam's manhood, which was standing at attention now.

"This way, my dear." She guided Sam into their room, where the two unleashed all the built-up love that had been brewing for weeks.

"Before we go to sleep, I have to know."

The pair was lying in the bed recovering. Selena was still naked, and Sam was running his hand over her body while they talked.

"You don't have to get into details, but you can if you want. What happened?"

"Fucking mess. Long story short, the ship didn't have machine parts as you said. It was full of weapons. They were no doubt headed to the garrison, but that wasn't even the biggest surprise. The ship also was carrying a marine squad, which ambushed us as we entered the cargo bay. Akari didn't make it. Dre got hit, but he's okay for now. And I was almost gone if it hadn't been for John."

"My gods. I'm sorry, Sam. Poor Akari, she was a good one." Selena nodded her head for a moment and said goodbye to Akari. Then suddenly, she turned back to Sam. "Wait, what? A marine squad, what the fuck?"

"Yeah, I don't know anything yet, but one of the marines survived, and we took her on board, and she knew who I was. It was a no doubt trap specifically aimed at killing me, so someone gave us up. I'd look into where the info came from. I'm going to look into my people. There's no telling who it was. I don't know how else they could have set this up, it had to be someone selling info to them."

"Wow, you have a marine?" She paused a moment to think things over. "You think she could tell us something?"

"I doubt it. I'm going to try, but I wouldn't count on it."

"Well, what's your next move? You know the UNE knows about you, so no sense in hiding anymore. I'm sorry, my love, but you might have to go to your parents for protection."

"I'm going to them tomorrow, but I don't want to involve them if I don't have to. I've been going back and forth on what the right move is, and to tell you the truth, I have no idea what to do. I know sometimes the best thing to do is nothing, but that feels wrong to me. I just feel like there's no secret anymore, so the UNE is going to make a move. They have to."

"Huh, I think you're probably right there. You better find a place to lay low for a while if you don't want your parents involved. I'd also move your cargo as soon as possible. If UNE finds that, then who knows. You want me to help with it?"

"Of course. The crew is moving it to our normal spot, but just be careful with this one. Bring people you can trust."

"I will. You want me to sell it off? We'll be rich if I do that. On the other hand, if I start moving this shit, it won't be long until everyone on Mars knows what I have."

"No, you have a place to hold on to it until it calms down. There are too many unknowns that I have to find out about before I make a move. I don't like being blind like this. It's just too fucking much."

"Okay," Selena said as she was lightly rubbing Sam's freshly cut head.

He was getting worked up again, and she wanted him to calm down.

"I like your hair short like this."

"Less maintenance, my dear."

"Relax, my prince, it's late, and you need some sleep, but before you do, do you have another one in you?"

"I'll do my best, my Latina goddess."

* * *

Sam woke to the sound and smell of breakfast being made in the kitchen. Whatever she was making smelled delicious, and Sam rolled himself out of bed, making a loud groan as he stood up, and stretched his achy muscles. He walked in the kitchen wearing only a pair of shorts to see his Selena still in her sleep clothes, which was next to nothing, frying something in a skillet. He just smiled at her, walked over, and gave her a healthy kiss good morning.

Looking at the clock, he said, "Gods, it's that late. I slept most of the morning away."

"You needed it. Plus, we were up late," she said, winking to him.

"Yeah, fuck it, there's no rush. I wanna get a good workout before I go to my parents." Sam stretched mightily. "Being trapped on that ship for a couple weeks made me miss running in the fresh air."

"First, breakfast. Here's some coffee and orange juice, and I've made eggs chorizo and tortillas for us. I had one of the girls go to the market, so there's some fresh fruit for you."

"Chocolate!" Sam almost shrieked at seeing the delicious sweet treat Selena set next to his plate. "How'd you come across that?"

"Was headed for UNE headquarters. I figured they didn't need it. It'd be a shame to waste some Earth chocolate on them."

Sam smiled at that. He loved that Selena was just as much of a pirate as he was.

"Mind if I turn on the screens to see what's goin' on?"

"Not at all." Selena commanded, "Display on. News,"

A standard news broadcast came up on the display.

"Authorities are on the lookout for an outlaw crew that just this past week viscously attacked an unarmed supply ship headed for UNE headquarters here on Mars. According to reports, the outlaws boarded the ship unprovoked and brutally murdered all crew members on board then destroyed the ship with explosives. Four were lost in this latest attack on private vessels just trying to bring supplies to the people of Mars.

"Following the attack, the UNE has issued a statement, and I quote: 'The UNE is utterly committed to the protection of its people, both citizen and noncitizen. Efforts are currently underway to avenge this latest in a long history of unprovoked and brutal attacks against honest merchants and law-abiding UNE personnel. Rest assured, every effort is being made to bring these criminals to swift justice,' end quote.

"We will have more on this story as it develops. So that brings me to my first question as I bring my cohost into the discussion. Have these outlaws, who at first were thought of as saviors robbing from the UNE and giving to the people of Mars, gone too far? I mean, they aren't giving anything away. From what sources on the street inform this network, these outlaws are making huge profits for themselves. They choke off the normal supply line and charge insane rates for goods and are now using extreme violence to obtain these goods."

"I'll say, personally, this has gone too far for me," the co-anchor confirmed the question. "The UNE is trying to ship goods and keep lanes open, and these outlaws are keeping the UNE from supplying the people of Mars with what they need. I think, in short, it's time to deal with these outlaws strongly. Unfortunately, that means the UNE will have to get heavily involved here on Mars. Not only will they have to greatly increase their presence here, but they will also have to commit to patrolling the lanes to and from Earth. They'd have to sacrifice much to ensure the Martian people are taken care of, so I think it's time for Mars and its people to do their part as well."

"But many here on Mars don't want UNE here. Many are upset with the garrison that's here already, and a lot of people feel the UNE muscled its way into Mars after all the hard work was done making this place the paradise it is today."

"Sure, the UNE should have done more during the first days of colonization, but that was generations ago. Mars has become more than just a group of colonies struggling to get by. There needs to be a government in place to oversee all resources. Earth needs Mars, and Mars needs Earth. It makes sense to have a unified government to oversee the best interests of both planets."

"It sure would help solve these violent attacks on shipping and bring much-needed supplies to the people of Mars. Perhaps welcoming the UNE to Mars would be the best solution for all."

"Screen off," Sam barked. "Same old shit, but if we lose public opinion, we're fucked, and you can kiss our free planet goodbye, and I'm too old to go start a colony on a different planet."

"Your only thirty-six, Sam. What do you mean 'too old'?"

"Shit, you know how rough it is on Titan, and I know you know the stories about this place. Children dirty and dying of starvation, every day is a fight for survival. No, thank you, I'm quite comfortable here as a rich pirate with a Latina goddess."

Sam ate his breakfast with all the grace of a barbarian. When he was done shoveling the meal in, he finally came up for air. Selena sat down to eat her breakfast, and Sam winked at her.

"I know you won't leave," Selena continued their previous conversation. "Go on your run, clear your head, go talk to your parents, and get back here. I'm setting up a dinner with the crew. We're gonna celebrate and have some fun tonight."

"I got work to do with the prisoner and cargo."

"I'll take care of the cargo, and as far as the prisoner, take her to your place, and you stay here. Have John watch her. He practically lives there anyway."

"Yeah, both of us don't care much for the bullshit in the government center. Vivianna seems suited for that, so she can carry on the family tradition for all I care."

"How is your sister? I haven't seen here in a long time."

"She's good. Always caught up in the family business, but she's smart, and she knows what she is doing. She was smart enough to see you for who you are," Sam said as he pulled Selena close to him. "How 'bout I go for a run, and when I get back, we'll take a shower together?"

"I can do that. But get going, I got shit to do, and you have to make lunch with your parents. Your sister set that up for you, so don't be late."

"Yes, yes, I'll get there on time, plus you just helped me finish my run faster."

"Huh?"

"I know that you and a shower are waiting for me at the finish line."

Selena smiled widely, in love with the man next to her. "I love that evil grin of yours, Samuel."

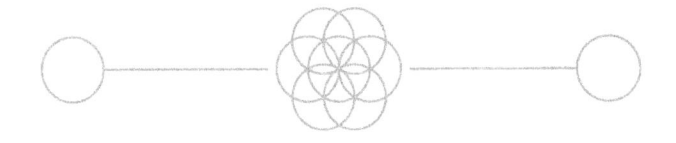

Chapter 5

Our Fate

Sam needed his runs through the streets of Jazeera. The city had grown exponentially since he was a child. Every year, more and more arrived from the crowded, dirty streets of Earth seeking opportunity and, above all else, freedom.

On Earth, you were monitored every second of your life. Being registered at birth, the UNE watched your every move. Violations were a way of life, and too many could land you in a penal city where forced labor was the punishment or way to atone for your violations. As soon as you ended up in a labor camp, you never left.

But here on Mars, people were free to pursue their own agendas. If you wanted to drink smoke and fuck? Have at it. You wanted to open a business and try to make money? Have at it. Nobody or no government was going to stand in your way. It was worth everything to Sam not to let the UNE get their disgusting hands on this beautiful planet.

Earth was dark, pollution-filled, overpopulated, and void of any pure nature anymore. That's the beauty of Mars. The founders and their descendants kept Mars clean. That's why, even after years on Mars, the air was still clean and the water crystal clear and free of contamination.

The streets were alive this late morning. Shops and restaurants were open, and people were enjoying another beautiful Martian day. The city was perfect to Sam. It was crowded enough that one could get lost there, but not too overcrowded to where walking—or in Sam's case, running—was a chore. Most newcomers went far out of the city to grab a piece of land and make a living. There were hundreds of small communities stretched across the planet all living off the land, raising and growing their own food with no one in the universe to bother them. In short, they were at peace.

Sam knew as he was finishing his run that they would have to fight for that peace, and that was what he was going to suggest to his parents and the council. Free and independent Mars. UNE must leave, or they would be made to leave. Sam thought of how the situation had become so jacked up as he ran faster and faster, trying to run out the anger, the shit he stored in his head, the building hate that was brewing for the UNE. How did it come to this?

* * *

He walked through the district after his run and headed to the house of the first citizen, which was adjacent to the chamber of peers. Back to the place of his upbringing. The District of Peers, as it was referred to, was the center of what one would call government on Mars.

The Martian people would never accept the rule of a government. But they did embrace Gerard Cleber and his wife as spiritual and thought leaders. It was a strictly an administrative title, but Sam's parents did hold seats on the Council of Peers, which was made up of ninety nine leading members of Mars, with Gerard voted in as first citizen.

Their voices were extremely influential but ultimately held no real power more than any other member on the council. They held the ceremony seats as head of the council, but their vote was equal to every other member. The first family, established during the colonization of Mars, had long been residing in the first citizens' residence, and it was Sam's mother and father's time to continue their duties.

It was always funny to Sam that Mars had a first citizen. He had learned through the histories that the Council of Peers, when they originally formed, didn't know what to name the administrator of the council, so first citizen it was. Next in line would be Vivianna and her husband, if the council deemed them worthy. They would continue the traditions of the first citizens, and Sam and his brother would possibly get seats on the council if worthy, but on the current course, that outcome seemed highly unlikely, at least for Sam.

He wanted nothing to do with the show that was the first family. Always proper, never impolite, always duty-bound to serve Mars and its people. Sam was all about helping his fellow man, but not at the cost of sacrificing his own happiness. No, he was perfectly fine with losing his status as first citizens' son and passing that on to his nephew.

As he continued his climb onto his childhood home, he passed countless law offices, temples, historic buildings dating back hundreds of years, community centers, theaters, and lastly, the famous Gardens of Mars.

The gardens were the envy of the dark and polluted Earth. One hundred acres of the most beautiful and well-manicured flowers, trees, and bushes known in the universe. It surrounded the crown jewel of the Martian civilization—the Library of Jazeera.

Sam stopped and had to smile as he remembered himself and his siblings, along with their group of friends, running and playing throughout the gardens. When he got older, they established a spot where they were out of eyesight and could sneak in drinks, have a little smoke, and maybe get lucky with a girl. Vivianna found out about it, and although she would never rat on her brothers, she scolded them both, reminding them that their reputations were written in ink and very hard to erase or correct once inscribed in memory.

Sam weaved through the gardens, finally making his way to his old home, and although he knew he never wanted to be involved in the politics of Mars, this was still his home. He found comfort as he walked through the gates of the residence and around the massive fountain. The all-imported marble fountain was another historic landmark. Sam was told since he was a child that it dated back over a thousand years ago and that it was from the palace of a king of Earth known as the Sun King. Since Sam and his ancestors came from the same place on Earth, his ancestors decided to purchase and import the fountain rather than see it destroyed during the UNE purge.

He entered his childhood home and was happy to see Vivianna obviously waiting to greet him.

Sam gave his big sister a healthy hug and said, "I've missed you. Thanks for setting this up. How have you been?"

"You know me, I'm good. Gustavo is getting big and terrorizing the place. He reminds me so much of you and John. Francisco constantly wonders if there is any of him in the boy whatsoever."

Both smiled and chuckled. "You know us Clebers, we have some strong genes," Sam said as he took Vivianna by the arm.

"How's Franky boy? He still the eager one to prove to our parents that he deserves you?"

Vivianna chuckled. "He's great. He loves me and Gustavo, so that's all I care about. He's a good father and husband. He's not as rough as my brothers, but I'm happy."

"Will he be joining us?"

"No, he said that we need our family time. He gets it."

"He's family, he can join if he wants."

"I'll fill him in later. Besides, he has meetings today to keep him occupied. Since Father recommended him and he got an appointment to the council, he's been busier than ever. He's already so busy with the family businesses and now, ha."

"Ah, he'll be fine. Besides, he's got the super boss to keep him in line."

"That's right, and don't you forget it," Vivianna demanded as she and Sam continued their lazy pace to the dining area.

"Sam? What's this meeting about? Why did you ask to speak to Mom and Dad like it's some official business or whatnot? Are you in trouble with your pirating bullshit?"

"That's an understatement. I fucked up bad, and I'm coming to Mom and Dad for advice."

"Sam." Vivianna stopped and looked him square in the eyes. "Fill me in. I want the big picture, skip details. Now go."

Sam told her the recent events that had happened, leaving the details out, especially the part that it was John who saved him. Growing up, Sam and Vivianna were always close, and it was John who was not always included in Sam and his sister's inner circle, but that had all changed as they grew into adults. The three were a crew. Inseparable. And each one of them would go to great lengths to protect the other. Sam not giving details about John was his way of shielding him from all that was going to happen, even though he would love nothing more than to have John at his side.

"I see," Vivianna said as she and Sam continued their walk. "This is going to impact everything. Wow. This is big. I need some time to think on it, but what are you going to say to Mom and Dad?"

"Well, I want to go to the council, and I'm going to suggest independence, but I want their input and blessing, I guess."

"Sam, we are basically independent."

"Not really. There is a UNE garrison here on our home that at any minute can start terrorizing the population and start enforcing harsh UNE policies on us. It's only a matter of time before they make a strong play at totally controlling us, and here's the brutal truth—we can't do anything to stop it."

"Serious times here. Well, as you said, the UNE knows about you, and they will, at a minimum, call for your arrest."

"Yes, on which the council has two choices. Give me up or tell them to go fuck themselves. Everyone hates the UNE, but they came to Mars to get away from the violence. I don't know if the council and the people of Mars are ready for a fight, but if we can spread the word that they are coming for our way of life, then maybe we have a chance."

"First, you have to survive Mom and Dad, then we'll see about waging an interplanetary war with Earth. What have I always said, Sam? 'One battle at a time.'"

They entered the main living area, and Sam was pleased to see his parents sitting down together, enjoying the start of their lunch in the outdoor area. It was a beautiful day out, and the first couple had the fountains on. The flowers and plants scattered throughout also gave a vibrant color to the area.

"Sam, my dear, join us, and you as well, Vivianna. It's been too long since we all sat and had a meal together."

They gave their parents both an embrace and took their seats around the table.

"How are things?" Gerard Cleber, the first citizen of Mars, asked his son.

Sam always thought in the back of his mind that his parents knew, but he was most definitely not going to lay it all out this early in the conversation. He was pausing too long when Vivianna noticed and interjected to stall for time.

"Feels weird. We're missing John," she said, eyeballing her brother.

"No, we're not," John said as he very bullishly entered the room, oddly enough at the perfect time.

He took a seat at the table, stopping to hug his parents and sister. As he sat, he made eye contact with Sam and then Vivianna, the three exchanging a "What the hell is going on?" look.

"I thought since you were coming that we'd all have lunch together," the family matriarch said, barely holding back her excitement. "We haven't been together in a couple of months, and well, I'm just simply not a fan of that."

"She's been excited all morning since Vivi told her," their father confirmed to the group. "Been pestering me all morning, asking about what we should serve for lunch, so I hope you're hungry because she cleared out the markets for this one."

"I'm starving," said John.

"So, Sam," his father said, looking over his way, "what's all this that you want to talk about?"

Sam looked at his siblings and then back at his parents and said, "Why don't we eat first. Mom's right, we haven't had a meal together in a long time."

"Great!" his mom said as she clapped her hands. "I'll go tell the kitchen staff that we are all here. I hope they are as good as they cost."

* * *

"Man, I kinda miss the service, not gonna lie," Sam proclaimed as he took a piece of finely cooked Martian steak, which was served á la carte. There was enough food to feed twenty people, and Sam intended to try to finish it to the very last bite.

Weeks of living on the *Val* and eating stew and stir-fry took its toll on Sam, and he was craving a proper meal. Selena's breakfast was delicious as always, but he needed this badly. He called the server over and asked for a glass of Martian red. Everyone followed suit. The family finished eating and found themselves laughing and telling jokes as they drank their wine. None of them noticed that they kept refilling their glasses, and before they knew it, midafternoon was fast approaching.

Sam's father was the first to notice and said, "Good gods! It's been three and a half hours. I have meetings."

"Wait, Dad," Sam said in a frantic tone. "I need to talk to you. I need to talk to you all, and it won't be easy, but I just need to get it out. I feel like I should warn you, it is not pleasant news, and although I've had a great time this afternoon, I'm sorry to say, I'm going to ruin your day."

"Sam, my boy, what is it? You've known since you all were children that you can come to your mother and me about anything."

"We'll see how you feel when I'm done. Here it goes."

* * *

His parents took it better than Sam expected, but dealing with situations was one thing the first family excelled at.

"That is not what I was expecting, but okay, we have to deal with this immediately. I'll call an emergency meeting of the council. We will decide the best way forward and how to address this mess. I can't help but feel disappointed, Samuel. We asked you not to get involved, but then again, you are your own man. We will do everything to help, but you must face the consequences of your actions. Whatever they may be."

"For the gods' sake!"

All eyes shifted to the matriarch of the family.

"What was he supposed to do? Sit idly and watch? We raised our children to do what is right. The UNE are not messing around this time. We have been dancing with them since we were children, Gerard, and now it is time for all the history to come to a head. I'm sorry, my beloved family, but it's time to break away from the UNE for good. I for one will not sit by while my child faces the consequences!"

"Independence is what we all desire, but at what cost? Do you honestly think the UNE will just let us go? I guarantee that they are making serious moves this very minute. People's lives will forever be affected by your actions, Sam. I'm sorry, but it's the truth. If the UNE comes in force, we will be powerless to do anything about it. I'd love independence, but it will be hard fought, and people will die. Perhaps our loved ones. I cannot support something where I know we will cause pain. We negotiate and give them what they want minus our son, but that is for the council to decide. As for now, everyone, lay low. We will meet again tomorrow morning as a family. Sam, is there anything else you need to say, or does anyone have anything to say?"

The room went quiet, and the brothers exchanged looks.

Then John spoke up. "It's not all Sam. I was there."

"Dear gods, boys!" Gerard roared, standing up tall from the table as he did so. Although considered an elder, he was still a powerful figure, and the boys were still in awe of their father.

"You said yourself, you raised us to do what is right, and I thought helping my brother was the right move." John paused as he held his head high. "I'm proud that I will always have my brother's and sister's backs no matter what. I'm good with my actions, I'd do it again."

"That's not all," Sam interjected. "John saved me. If not for him, I wouldn't be sitting here. I owe him, and we'll just leave it at that. Also, in the spirit of coming clean . . ." Sam paused, letting out a long breath. "We captured a marine. They know our names. They have been watching. There is a major response coming, I know it."

"You have one of them?" Vivianna asked.

"Yes, under guard. She hasn't said much."

"She? Interesting," Vivianna asked with her normal grace.

"Is that all?" their father asked as he placed both knuckles on the table, peering into his children's eyes. "Yes? Then we have work to do." The elder pushed off the table with his fists and left the table and the room, walking briskly and immediately, starting to call for his staff.

"You know your father, children," she said, rising from the table while the rest of the family followed suit. "Passionate, fierce, and an absolutely unstoppable force when he puts his mind to something. You all are so much like him, I laugh myself silly sometimes."

"We're also a lot like you, Mother," Vivianna included.

The ever-elegant matriarch and council member eyed her daughter and gave her a loving smile.

"I'm going to help your father. He needs my calming presence for his mind to work right."

She gave each child a kiss on the forehead, then brought her boys down to her so she could reach them.

"Take care of each other. No matter what happens, promise me, you will all never abandon each other."

They all promised their mother, and her eyes watered as she left the room. Sam sat back down in his chair, and instead of sitting properly as he did at lunch, this time he lazily slouched. He started rubbing his temples and stretching his neck, giving out moans as he did so.

"Sam?"

"Yes, Vivi?" said Sam, still rubbing his temples.

"Sam, I would like to see this marine of yours if you don't mind."

"If that's what you want." Still rubbing his head, he said, "Wait, why?" as he became alert, dropping his hands and sitting up in the chair.

"I want to learn all I can about this marine, the UNE, and what we might face," she said, rejoining Sam at the table.

"I guess," Sam said, eyeing his brother for approval.

"She'll be fine. The marine lady isn't all monster."

"Don't assume anything, John. She is playing all of us—of that, I am sure. She wants to size us up, no doubt."

"I'll be all right, boys. Now, when can I go?"

"I'll take you there now if you wish. I was going to check in on Dre and then our guest, but we can see her first."

"Sam, do you have any pull with the rest of the pirate crews? I strongly suggest we ease up on the raids at the moment, and I can't believe I'm going to say this, but I think you should go into hiding for a while. We can't give up what we can't find."

"I'll say something to the crews, but they are their own minds, and as far as hiding, I was thinking of laying low, but maybe I should drop off the radar for the time being." He gave out a long exhale. "I'm so sorry to put you in this position. I can't just sit and do nothing. I tried to keep you out of it, but like you said, things are coming to a tipping point. I thought I was doing good, now it's all fucked up."

"Sam, we are with you on this," John said, sitting at the table. "I'm choosing to do this. You did not drag me into it."

There was a moment of silence between them. "We all have our jobs to do."

"Wait, what am I supposed to do?" John asked.

"How about you set up operations at our normal spot outside the city. Start gathering what you can as a staging point. At least from there, we can use the tunnels, and for the most part, stay out of sight. I'd say it's a good spot to lay low. We can observe the city and get in and out if need be."

"All right."

"I'll let the others know soon enough, but for now, let's keep this as quiet as we can."

"Okay, Captain Obvious."

The three chuckled.

"Okay, Vivi, let's go. I'm going to talk to Selena real quick if you don't mind."

"Not at all. I was going to do the same with Fransico."

"Let me know if you need anything," Sam said, eyeing John.

"I'll be good. I'll leave you be, and I'll ask one of the crew if I need anything."

John hugged his sister, gave his brother a punch on the arm, and headed out.

Sam and Vivi both followed suit, both of them linking to their respective loved ones. Sam told Selena what had transpired. He told them that he was officially going into hiding effective first thing tomorrow.

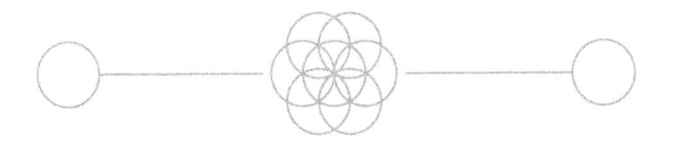

Chapter 6

Ours Is Always Theirs

She had arrived on Mars many months ago. She knew it would be a long assignment, but missions like this were no mystery to her, and it didn't matter because she loved missions like this. It was intoxicating to her to assume a new identity and make a new life. She could become someone completely different from who she really was, and when it was over, that new person would be erased from existence, and then on to the next assignment and the next person she would become. This mission was almost at its end, and she was having this feeling that she hadn't had in a long time that some part of her wasn't ready to give this one up.

Her mission was simple. They wanted intel. Get close, set the trap, and get out. A master at her craft, she knew she would have to be embedded deep before she could produce anything of value, so she got straight to work when she arrived at the planet.

Her story was the same as almost everyone else on Mars. She was fleeing the UNE, wanted for some minor crime, but it was bad enough it would ruin her life if she stayed. She was starting anew and had no attachments and no possessions. She landed in Jazeera and immediately decided to concentrate her efforts in this city exclusively. There were other established towns and cities across Mars, but the capital, Jazeera, was by far the most developed and had the greatest potential of developing an asset. The other civilized centers were still in their beginning stages, and she definitely wasn't crawling her ass in the underground cities where the first colonists settled—dark and dirty. She was just fine staying topside.

Investigating her new city, it didn't take her long to figure out that a certain bar was the center of Martian gossip, so she looked for a dwelling close by and settled in. She stayed in a public house where she had her own tiny room, a shared bathroom, and most importantly, a short distance from the bar. To properly set up her identity, she needed to find work—and quickly. Although she had a small fortune on her, she needed to set her story as a runaway with nothing and desperate for any work or living. She was extremely attractive, which gave her a massive edge, and she knew it and used it.

Her first instinct was to go directly to the bar and ask for a job, but she wanted to be offered a job, so until then, she got work as a part-time worker in a clothing shop. The clothing was disgusting, poorly made, and smelled of the chemicals used to dye and wash the material, but fashion wasn't a major concern for her. What was appealing about this particular store was that it gave a great vantage point to observe the entire community around the bar.

It didn't take her long to figure things out on Mars. There was virtually zero concern for spies, and these peasants probably couldn't pronounce *espionage*, so she wasn't expecting too much trouble. But she had to be cautious nonetheless. If she had to stay here for a long time, she was sure she was going to set up the best backstory she possibly could.

She found out that a certain Selena ran the bar and that she was always coming and going. Always on the move. She also quickly noticed that many of the pirates that were flagged in her official brief frequently visited Selena's establishment, including the famous Sam Cleber. She wondered why he would come to this shithole of a bar, but then she saw Sam and Selena together one evening, and she chuckled to herself.

He's in love with her.

That was her in. She knew what she had to do. She had to get in that bar. Selena wasn't going to hire a rough street girl. She needed to stand out a little and needed Selena to come to her. She needed a date, and who better to target than a pirate? It took her a couple of days to find him.

From the looks of him, she had taken it that he was a serious individual, but then she saw him stumble out of the bar one evening, and she concluded he was a "work hard, play hard" type. She even saw him joking with the famous Sam himself. It would be fun for her. She was allowed to have a little fun while on assignment. Set up and ready to begin her work, she looked at herself in the mirror and became the Martian runaway.

She saw him and a handful of pirates walking to the bar. She threw on some Martian rags, but she knew she looked good in them. The clothing was more revealing than she normally wore, so her slender, toned physique stood out among the Martian peasants. She waited for her prey to come to the bar, and then she pounced.

"Where did you come from?" he said as she walked by.

"I live here. This is my territory."

"Is it now? Well, since you're so familiar, why don't you show me around."

Giving a slight giggle, she said, "Well, I'm fairly new here, so not that familiar. I was trying to get the courage to go in the bar. It looks like the place to be."

"You've never been? Well, it just so happens we're heading there now. Mind if I escort you, or are you meeting someone?"

"No, I don't know too many people here. I got here a couple months ago and been laying low, ya know."

"Where you from originally?"

"Some shithole on Earth, but I had to leave."

"Got ya. Well, how 'bout we don't worry 'bout where you been. How 'bout we just try to have a little fun tonight."

"I need a little fun. Let's do it."

"I'm Dre."

"Mia."

"Nice to meet you, Mia. Come on, dinner and drinks on me, and you can meet some of the guys."

She smiled widely both at the idea of her new plaything and that she was inching closer to her real target.

These people are too naive, she thought to herself as she smiled at Dre. *They have been living soft, as far as espionage goes. They have no idea.*

* * *

Over time, Mia had become very comfortable among the pirates of Mars. They sure knew how to celebrate a score. It was nothing like she had ever seen before. These pirates had a code, an unwritten code that if you broke, you were almost dead to the rest of them, and her target, Dre, was one of the worst of them.

She at first welcomed her new plaything and thought of him as merely that—nothing but a discardable item—but her "curiosity" kept her right where she was. She became Mia through and through. So much so that she scared herself on a couple of occasions, forgetting why she was there, falling deep into the world of the pirates.

They lived for the moment. Every moment was enjoyed to the fullest. When they worked, they put everything into what they were doing, and when it was time to enjoy life, they certainly did that to the fullest as well. Dre was again the most extreme, which she loved. Dre worked, partied, and loved Mia in this fashion. He wasn't going to do something stupid like propose marriage, but when he was there and she was there, they only had eyes for each other.

She had gotten the job offer from Selena that she was looking for. At first she declined the offer, saying she was happy where she was at, but when she was offered again, she pounced at the opportunity. She said she would happily start anywhere, and she was informed that when she worked at the bar, she would be required to do any job that Selena asked. She was highly intelligent, so more and more, Selena gave her more important tasks, and she followed through to the letter.

Selena noticed and gave her more responsibility, eventually becoming the day-to-day bartender while Selena did whatever else she did. All Mia had to do was keep working, and sooner or later, Selena would have a need.

"Mia, I'm short a body. Do you want to earn a little extra money? You don't have to do anything but stand next to me."

"I can always use extra. When and where do you need me?"

"Tonight, right after we close, I have a meeting. Do you know how to use a weapon?"

Mia just nodded but was truly surprised when Selena asked about a weapon.

"Okay, tonight then."

They showed up, just the two of them, in some remote, backcountry outpost far away from the city. The two had to take an all-terrain vehicle for many Martian miles to get to the meeting point. Right from the start, Mia knew this was a dangerous situation. There were four people they met, all dirty and broken down. You could tell that life on Mars was different for them than the rest of the planet.

"You got what we need?" one of them asked Selena.

"I got it if you have my payment."

"We have that."

"All right then, give me my payment, and you can unload all this shit."

"Just you two out here?" one asked, looking around at the horizon.

"I wouldn't do that if I were you." Selena was standing her ground. "Even if we don't kill all of you, you will never buy any of our wares again, and I'll see to it that all of my counterparts don't do any business with you either. Since you obviously live in a fucking hole, I'll just tell you that I am not someone you should fuck with."

"Now, calm down, little lady, I was just asking, that's all. Here's your payment. Guys, unload the lovely ladies' ride so they can get out of here."

"Thank you, Ali. That wasn't so hard now, was it?"

"I didn't mean anything, Selena. It's just two beautiful women out here alone is strange, that's all."

"I'm sure you didn't mean anything at all, Ali. Just like I didn't mean anything when I said I'll kill all of you," Selena explained as she was verifying receipt of payment on her portable OB.

"Would you ladies like something to drink while you wait?"

"That's very kind of you, but no, thank you, we are supplied and do not wish to take anything from you."

"Offer stands. We will have you unloaded in a minute."

"Wasn't sure what to expect from these guys," Selena said, turning to Mia. "I normally do runs solo or with someone else as backup, but he's gone at the moment."

"You mean Sam?"

Selena turned quickly and gazed at Mia, reading her from top down. The sun was rising in the sky, and she turned and looked at the beautiful sunrise, taking her time to reply. She weighed her options and eventually replied to Mia, who had joined her looking into the sunrise.

"Yes, Sam and I . . ." she paused, not able to find the word. "Sam and I . . "

"I understand," was all Mia had to say.

Selena turned back to Mia. "And that's the last time I hear anything like that out of your mouth. Understood?"

"Yes."

"In case you haven't noticed, I don't give a fuck who you are or what you do outside work. That's your business, and if you wish to continue to work with me, you'll remember I am an extremely private person. Not many know about what you just mentioned, and we both wish to keep it that way. Keep your mouth shut and eyes open, and I'll make you rich. If you can do that, we have an understanding."

"I can agree to that."

"Very well then." Selena paused and kicked some Martian rocks with her almost-knee-high boots. "How did you know?"

"Well, I didn't 100 percent until just now, but I see you two. You guys cannot keep your eyes off each other. I can see that from Earth. That wasn't surprising. What is surprising is us way out here selling what I assume is pirated goods. I figured you to be a savvy businesswoman, but pirate fencing is one I wouldn't have guessed."

"Mia, my dear, you have no idea."

"I can help if you want me to, with whatever you need."

"Why is that?"

"Credits is number 1. I left Earth and the UNE because I had nothing and was going nowhere. Poor and struggling is not the life I have in mind."

"And number 2?"

"I fucking hate the UNE."

"Maybe we can find a use for you, but it'll take time. Keep your head down, do your work, and prove you can be trusted."

"I can do that. I've been practically running the bar for you."

"The bar is just what's visible to the public and just the tip of the iceberg. If you want to see what we really do here, like I said, every day is a test. If you get good grades, you graduate to the next level. You did good tonight. Most of the girls wouldn't be able to handle a simple deal like this, but you were calm and under control. Next time it might not end so nicely. Practice with a weapon so you can defend yourself and, most importantly, defend me. Ask Dre to show you. I have eyes as well, my dear."

Mia blushed uncontrollably. "Yeah, Dre is too much fun."

"He's also one of our best fighters. He's one you want with you when shit gets real, so pay attention to what he says, he will teach you right."

They both looked around at the beautiful Martian sky as the sun rose higher and higher.

"We are all done, Selena," Ali said, walking toward the pair.

"Thank you, Ali. If I come across any more machinery for your little cave drilling, I'll get ahold of you. Anything else you need me to keep an eye on?"

"Meds, Selena. Always meds. Our old and little ones are struggling this year, and we are at dangerously low levels."

"I'll find some for you, and maybe I'll have Mia here run it to you. That is, of course, if you promise to behave yourselves."

"Of course, ma'am."

"Take care, Ali. Mia, let's go."

The ride back was long, and both women sat in silence, just looking out at the beautiful arid Mars, which was turning into lush green vegetation as they got closer to Jazeera. The transport was fast, and more importantly, it was undetectable.

The long trips from settlement to settlement never really bothered Selena at all. She rather enjoyed a quiet moment to just think and sit. Normally, Sam went with her, and most of the time, he sat in silence with her. The other times, the two had at each other while the transport raced across Mars. She was happy that Mia could sense she didn't want to talk, and she looked out at the landscape, letting her mind wander. Mia followed suit but eventually broke the silence.

"I've never been outside the city. I haven't seen this much openness ever. It's kind of unsettling."

"And I've never seen Earth. How about you tell me about it, like where you're from."

She didn't have to lie about this part. "Like everyone, I was born in the birthing district and assigned to partner group.

Unfortunately, both are departed. One was cancer—the other, drink and drugs. I was alone at nine. Joined some kid groups from other kids who were alone, and that's that. I stole what I could, ate what I could find, and killed when I had to. It was no place for weakness. I grew up moving from place to place, avoiding the UNE whenever I could. Eventually, I was almost caught and had too many authorities looking for me. I was lucky and gave everything I had to get here on a cargo ship. The rest, you know from there."

"Sounds rough, but the good thing is, here you can have a fresh start like so many. And no one will be looking for you here."

"I've grown quite fond of this place."

"And that's why we have to keep it the way it is. If the UNE get their hands on this place, then it's only a matter of time until our way of things is gone."

The two sat in silence again for a while, returning to their gaze out at Mars.

Selena, deep in thought, suddenly turned to Mia. "You know about the pirates here, right? You're not stupid—of course, you do. How about this . . ." she said, letting it build for a moment. "Tell me what you think about the pirates."

Mia, very puzzled, looked at the floor of the transport. "You want me to say it?"

"Yes."

Mia looked at Selena. "You are the pirates."

"I knew you knew, best out with it. We have many moving parts, and I need good, smart people. You won't be privy to everything, but you'll be in. If you dip your toe in the water and don't like it, you can stay at the bar, no worries, but if you're interested, I have work."

"I am, and yes, I knew. I think most of Jazeera knows."

"Ha. They don't know shit. Only that we leave and come back and then sell them shit."

Both the women laughed.

"We're having a party tonight. You coming?"

"I'll be there."

"We are very guarded. It's weird for some people, but we have to hide who we are. Some other crews don't care, but we do."

"So are you part of Sam's crew?"

"Gods, no! I facilitate many things for many crews. Like I said, a lot of moving parts. I just have a soft spot for Sam's crew." She grinned as she thought of her pirate. "You won't know why, just that you have a job to do. Do your job, and more will come. Eventually, you'll be in so deep you couldn't even imagine living another life. I warn you, it's like a drug. As soon as you get a taste, you'll want more."

"I like it. I'm happy here." She paused. "And with Dre."

The two giggled like girls and continued their ride. Mia looked away from Selena, worried that she was losing herself. Did she really mean that? It felt natural. She didn't have to act. It was a scary thought. It sank back deep within her. She had what she wanted—she was in. Now she could ask around and find a weakness.

She moved slowly, to not cause too much attention. She watched, waited, and probed where she could, again to not cause suspicion. The pirates left, came back, and sold their shit just as Selena had said. Their schedule was irregular. Sometimes gone for days, then gone for months. They always returned with much loot. Mia concluded Selena must have one heck of an informant in the UNE garrison—or possibly, but not probably, an informer on Earth. She had made a mental note to follow up on that if she could, but to never jeopardize her primary mission in the process.

This went on for months—Mia running cargo for Selena, receiving and delivering messages from crew to crew, and whatever else Selena needed from her. Her responsibilities grew, and not only did many begin to notice Mia, but she was gaining respect as well among the crews. The only break for her was when Sam's crew returned, and life was enjoyed at its peak. She looked forward to those. Everyone was so happy. Mia and Dre spent most of their time in port together. There were times when they barely left the room.

One evening, late at night, Dre told Mia that he was leaving again on a job. He was falling asleep, drifting in and out, when Mia asked where he was going.

"I don't know, after some high-value machine parts," Dre said, not knowing what he was saying, falling asleep.

"Did Selena put you up on this one?" she asked him, inching closer.

"What?" Dre asked groggily. "She always does. It's a little late for this, babe. I'm done. It's night night time." Dre rolled over and was asleep in seconds.

Mia thought of her options and did something she had never done before. She grabbed one of Dre's displays that was around and got it out of Sleep mode. She reached over very gracefully and used Dre's features to unlock his data. Her face lit up as she searched for what she needed. Scrolling, she found what she was looking for.

Mia got out of bed silently and entered the bathroom. Opening her link to the UNE outpost, she stood there in the bathroom and looked at Dre lying on the bed. She had a moment of hesitation.

What is this? I've never hesitated like this. Get your shit together, Mia. You have a mission to complete. But he means something to me now. This will hurt him.

She stood pondering and shook the idea out of her head. Her determination returned, and she switched on the comms.

"Contact made. Stand by for intel."

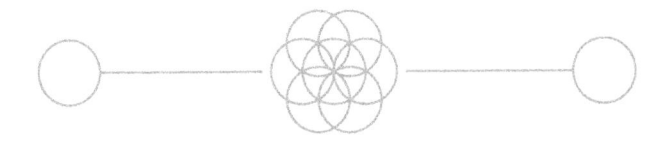

Chapter 7

Our Beginning

Sam and Vivianna walked slowly back to his place. She was right. He needed to lay low for a little bit. That aligned with his thinking because he had been away from Selena for many months, and spending time with her was always reenergizing. It was always terrible leaving after a long stay home because it was that much harder to leave.

That sounded good though. Relaxing for a couple of weeks and doing nothing, to see what happened.

What will I do with the marine? Sam thought. *We could try talking and just be honest.* If she wouldn't talk, she'd get put in a cage, and they wouldn't worry about her again. That would be Sam's worst nightmare. Sitting in a cage, rotting.

"Terrible fate," he said out loud. He told himself, as he walked with Vivianna following as she spoke to her husband, that he would never be taken alive. Never.

That would get the marine to talk—the fear of being caged. But he had another major concern that needed attention first. Where was the leak? It was a setup. He was sure of it.

Who? It could be anyone, he thought to himself. He had no idea where to look.

He walked into his dwelling, leaving Vivianna outside, still on her comms.

"Dre! What are you doing up and over here?"

"Well, looking for you, or anyone. I woke up and headed here."

"Your wounds," Sam said as he hurried over to help Dre down into Selena's chair out on the veranda. Sam took his own chair and settled in.

"It's not bad at all, honestly. The armor took most of it, just sore as shit. Couple shrapnel pieces, but I'm good, honestly. I could suit up if needed."

"Gods, some good news. Well, still, rest up, and don't push it." Sam looked over at his friend. "I'm going to lay low for a little bit myself, and the *Val* won't be leaving anytime soon."

"Lay low, huh? Not exactly good at that, Sam." Dre scratched at his developing beard. "Well, at least we can enjoy life some. I'm not going to sit around all day."

"No sitting around. We are going to be busy here unfortunately."

"Has it happened?"

Sam exhaled. "Not yet, but soon. I know it. When it happens, everything will change. We'll have to go underground. Guerilla warfare. Hit and run, raid supplies, generally be a massive pain in the dick, and when they are close to breaking, we massively strike a main target of opportunity."

Sam was in his talking-out-loud mode. The two always bounced ideas off each other. It was just easier talking to Dre sometimes. They understood each other.

"While we are laying low," Sam continued, "would you mind looking into gathering supplies? Food, medicine, weapons, and armor, Dre. Everything you can get your hands on. The armor is our main target. One Dre in armor is a formidable warrior. I asked John to do the same. Maybe you two could link up soon?"

"Yeah, no problem. I'll gather what I can and keep it at our spot. Should I let the others know so they can start getting leads?"

"That'll work, but let me explain to them when we meet later. I want an extremely low profile on this one. I want to get what we need before every psycho on the planet is stocking up for the storm and prices double overnight."

"Nothing like the fear of unknown to drive the folks mad."

Both remained silent for a moment while deep in thought. Sam more and more relied heavily on Dre for counsel, and their "strategy" sessions became more of thinking out loud for the two. For Sam, it was everything to have someone other than Selena that he could unload on, and Sam knew that Dre would never judge him. Sam knew Dre was a friend and confidant for life. A battle buddy.

"How bad will it get, Sam? I see brother turning on brother on this one. It will get very messy and will be a long, drawn-out conflict. If we are going to defeat them, then we will have to bleed them out. Your family and friends will be targeted. It will be ugly. I'd think about getting them out now."

"They'll never leave. For better or for worse, my family is the face of Mars, and they will insist on not running. They will be arrested, and after they are in their hands, who knows what will happen? But it's their call. I can't force them to do anything any more than they can force me. My family can take care of themselves. I've spoken to my sister, and she will take care of everyone and deal with the council."

"Okay, now the big question is, knowing that conflict is going to happen, do we hit first or use their aggression as a rally cry?"

"If we can avoid a war, I think we should do everything we can to avoid it, but it doesn't mean we sit here and wait for it to happen. They will come, so let's keep to the plan. Gather supplies, and we need to be ready to act when it happens."

"I'll get on it."

"Make sure to rest, Dre. I know you say you're good, but it looks like even John could take you out right now. I need you with me if we are going to pull this off."

"You need me? Why not Serg? He's been with you since the beginning."

"Serg is my closest friend, and he is an amazing pirate, but we know what is coming, and Serg is no fighter. I need a warrior's mind if we are to win, and you are that warrior. You have always been good in a fight, and you have what so many others lack."

"What's that?"

Sam looked at him. "The ability to not let the bullshit get to you. You see the core of things, like me. That's why we get along so well. None of the bullshit matters to us."

"Thank you, Sam, that means a lot. I'll do what I can. I know it's not what we do, but I want you to know, I'll be with you till the end, no matter how it turns out. If we go down, I'll be swinging right next to you."

"Hopefully, it won't come to that, but I'll make the same promise to you. We are in this together." Sam tapped Dre on the shoulder, forgetting his wound.

Dre winched and then called Sam a few choice words, then the pair laughed together. In the seriousness of it all, Sam cherished that Dre could always make him laugh.

"How the fuck did we get here?" Dre asked, getting serious again.

"I don't know, but it's what I think about at night. All the decisions we made to get us to this point. Madness. Simply madness."

"How's marine lady doing? Did she talk yet?"

"You're calling her that too? Fucking John."

The pair smiled briefly, and Sam continued, "No, not yet, which I don't understand. She's in the other room, and I'm letting her sit by herself to contemplate her thoughts, but I'll talk to her later. I'm going to tell her straight—talk or rot in a cage. Vivianna wants to talk to her too, and only the gods know why. She should be in shortly actually." Sam swung around to look toward the door. "She was just walking around outside, talking on her comms."

"Only the gods know," Dre said, eyeing Sam. "That is the truth. One of the days I'm going to get you to come to session with me."

"The gods don't speak to me like they do to you, so it is pointless. And I'm just not into that kind of . . . worship."

"It's not a cult, Sam. It's real."

"I don't like my mind altered like that. I don't like giving up control."

"That is the point, buddy, but it's not for everyone. I'm learning more about the universe each session, and it opens my eyes and mind to the possibilities."

"What possibilities?"

"That the gods are real. That there is so much more to the human story that we haven't been told. Earth and Mars are linked by our ancient history."

"See, and that is where you lose me. Dre, I'm glad you're happy seeking out the gods, but that is not my path. I do not have a relationship with our gods. That is for my father. My only concern is the UNE and their plans."

"You'll come around," Dre said, shifting in his chair.

They sat in thought for a moment as the two looked out at the Martian sky.

"Just our crew tonight, right?" Dre asked, changing the subject.

"Yes, I asked Selena to prepare the back room. No one should bother us back there."

"I was hoping to see Mia. I know she has been helping Selena." Dre cleared his throat. "Could you ask if she could be there? I actually want to see her, which is a new development for me, but fuck it."

"Don't be sorry, buddy, I get it. If anyone does, it's me. You think she is ready though? It's just that as soon as she's in there, there's no going back."

"If you and Selena are okay with it, I'll ask her. I won't tell her anything, just offer if she wants in and explain that if she's in, she's in."

"I'll talk with her, but I'm sure it will be okay. She has taken a liking to Miss Mia. Reminds her a lot of herself when she was just getting started. Mia is smart, wise, beautiful, and will cut your balls off if you mess with her. I don't know what the fuck she sees in you."

"Yeah, me neither."

The two laughed again.

"But I'm gonna sure as shit enjoy it while I can!"

"Well, I'm off."

Dre felt the conversation was at an end, and he slowly rose, indicating to Sam that he didn't need any help as he stood up.

"I'll see you at Selena's. What time?"

"Let's say 1700. I want to get serious, then drink, smoke, and fuck our problems away for just one night, then it's business until it ends."

"See you tonight. I'll get outta here before your sister shows up. I get the feeling she's not exactly fond of me."

Sam smiled widely. "She thinks you're a bad influence on me. Little does she know, it's the other way around. Dre was a happy dock worker until Sam the pirate showed up promising him riches."

"I wouldn't have called myself happy, but whatever story you wanna make up in that head of yours, it doesn't matter. I'm here now, and I ain't going anywhere. See you later."

"See ya."

Dre started moving slowly to the door, visibly in discomfort but doing his best to hide it. Right when he got to the door of Sam's dwelling, he heard the auto locks disengage and saw Vivianna alone standing at Sam's doorway.

"Dre."

"Vivianna," was all they exchanged as the two passed each other.

Vivianna closed the door behind her and found Sam still deep in thought out on the veranda overlooking the busy streets of his beloved Mars.

"I never understood why you live down here, but hey, you like what you like."

"Not this again, Vivi. I'm not coming back, and please, not today. I just like these types of people. Up there, it's like someone is always trying to get something from you. Down here, I don't know, people seem to be just people. I don't know how to explain it, more . . . *authentic*," Sam said in a higher-pitched voice as the word came to him.

The two sat while they both were deciding what to say next. They both were so busy that they really hadn't had time to talk to each other. Then Sam got the conversation going.

"You wanted to speak to the marine, and I'm allowing it because I'd do anything for my sister, so please go speak to her. I'll be right here if you need me. Just yell, and I'll be in."

"Apparently, you are not in the best of moods."

"I don't know what I am or what I'm thinking anymore. All I can think about is how bad it will be if this goes the way I think. Lots of people will get hurt, and our own lives will never be the same."

"Maybe, maybe not, Sam. It's for the gods to decide. All we can do is do the best we can with the situation we are in. I'm going in. I'll let you know how it goes."

Vivianna walked in an elegant fashion toward the prisoner, and Sam decided he had to say something.

"Vivi . . ." Sam started and paused for a moment, letting the gravity of his words set in, and then he went speechless. He just opened his mouth, but no words came out. He wanted to say "I love you" and explain the danger that their people were in. The world was out of control, and he was powerless to stop it. He wanted to say sorry, but he couldn't.

Vivianna—the older sister, confidant, and friend—just smiled, nodded her head ever so slightly, and said, "Me too."

She entered the room where the marine was in, grabbed a chair, and gracefully took her seat befitting a person of her station. Where Sam, John, and the rest of the pirates displayed their rough and rugged ways, Vivianna was the exact opposite. Elegance, charm, and beauty. Sitting with perfect posture and keeping constant eye contact with the marine, she tried to measure the woman sitting across from her. In return, the marine was also keeping eye contact but had a puzzled look on her face, wondering why someone like Vivianna would take time to see her.

"My name is Vivianna."

"I know who you are. Why are you here?"

"I want to know my enemy," she retorted immediately. "We can take this opportunity to examine each other. I answer a question, and then you answer one. How does that sound?"

"Don't talk to me like I'm a child," the marine sneered back. "What am I doing here, and what do you people want with me? Why haven't you granted me death in battle?"

"We don't kill here unless we have to, and as far as the why you are here, you'll have to take that up with my brother, as well as what they intend on doing with you. I've never seen a marine before. Are there many of you?"

"I don't know. I am a weapon of the council."

"You are a person. Weapons are disposable."

"When a weapon is no longer useful, it should be disposed."

"Do you think you will be disposed?"

"What do you want of me?"

"I want to know my enemy."

"There is only the empire. That's all you need to know."

Vivianna rose from her seat again in an elegant manner. "Empire? Interesting." She stepped slightly closer to the marine. "Thank you for speaking with me. Sam and John said you weren't talking."

The marine only fiercely gazed in response.

"I'll come back in a couple days and see how you're doing. Do you need anything?"

The marine still only gazed.

"Okay. Until next time. Good afternoon."

Vivianna spun around and walked to the door then turned back quickly and said, "How rude of me. In my excitement, it completely left my mind to ask your name. I think if we are going to have conversations in the future, I'd be nice to know how to address you."

"You can call me Commander of Marine Squad Charlie."

"Nice to meet you, Commander. Good day," Vivianna said, quickly leaving the room and securing the door.

"How was she?" Sam asked, still on the veranda. "She give you the same silent treatment?"

"Actually, no, she spoke to me. It was interesting. She said 'the empire,' not 'the UNE.' She is most likely brainwashed, and I got her name. 'Commander of Charlie Squad' was all she said."

"Dear gods, what a piece of work. What do you think?"

"It's too much to process," she said, shaking her head. "Let her sit, and let me work with her if you don't mind. I think I can break through to her." She pointed at the door. "I imagine she has had a difficult life thus far. Maybe a soft mother figure is what it will take."

"One less thing I have to worry about, so have at it, Mama. Which reminds me," Sam said, quickly changing the topic, "we need a better place to hold her. Renting a room out is not what I had in mind."

"Sam." Vivianna looked at her younger brother. "We both know you haven't even been here unless you are on watch. Don't be a goober."

"A what?"

"Goober, Sam. Don't be a goob."

"Whatever with your made-up words."

"I love you, bro. This isn't all on your shoulders. You have friends and loved ones. Like me . . . Selena, John, Dre. You aren't alone. You must let us help."

"I do, Viv. Taking that thing in there," Sam said, pointing to the door, "is very helpful. Thank you. What I mean is, just, thank you," Sam said, fumbling with finding the words. There was too much on his mind.

"I have to get back to the others," Vivianna said, filling the pause in the conversation. "It has been a madhouse since this came out."

"Mom and Dad pissed?"

"No, just deep in work right now, as we all are. Give it time, Sam." Vivianna softened up, saying, "Dear gods, you have barely been back a week."

Vivianna gave her little brother and friend a quick hug, then the slightest smack on the cheek with her famous smile, and then departed. Her smile quickly faded away as she immediately switched to the next item on her agenda. She had time to mentally prep on the ride back. Her father had requested a meeting in private.

* * *

Vivianna had to prep on the ride back because a council member officially requested a meeting. That was not unusual. What was unusual was that it was her father that had requested the meeting, and he requested it in the Library of Jazeera of all places. She exited her transport and was surprised to see Gerard there waiting for her.

"Hello. You look beautiful as always." The elder statesman gave his daughter a healthy hug. "Thank you for coming, and this is going to be hard to hear, but what do I always tell my children?"

"You always tell the truth. Your version at least."

Gerard surveyed the surroundings and took a deep breath and exhaled dramatically. "I have been waiting for this moment since you were born. I have always known you were the one, but now that it is here, it's still hard to comprehend."

"Dad, what are you talking about?" Vivianna was puzzled and surprised, which was very rare for her. She and her dad had always been close, and the old Gerard smiled widely as it brought him back to when she was a child.

"Here. Come with me." Gerard took his daughter's arm in his, and the two walked up the grand stairs to the library.

"You have grown into a beautiful woman, and I'm proud of you." He grinned ear to ear. "I can still see you running through here when you were a little girl, and it brings me much happiness in these troubled times."

They reached the top and were greeted by massive stone columns that surrounded the entire complex. They walked into the open air courtyard and came to a familiar structure that everyone on Mars visited.

"Do you remember where this came from?" Gerard asked his daughter.

"You are kidding me, right? Every child knows this is a copy of the Great Sphinx from Earth."

"Who built it?"

"Dad . . ."

"Come on, indulge me."

"The first settlers built it."

Gerard smiled at his daughter. "Come with me."

The two walked through the public area and descended to the lower levels of the library. Every piece of art that could be transported was brought by the first settlers. Art, statues, whole buildings, brick by brick, anything that people wanted, but especially books.

"We were not running. We were leaving to preserve our history. Our true history. Let me ask you this question . . ." Gerard paused his walk and looked at his daughter. "Do you think this is the first time we have been here?"

"We traveled to Mars many times before we colonized it, but yes. It was mankind's greatest achievement. Colonizing this place and building it from nothing was our greatest achievement as a people."

"What if I told you that the Sphinx wasn't built? We found it."

Vivianna's face showed her confusion as she processed what her father had said.

"When we arrived, we did start in the caves, and I'm bringing you to the first one. It was here that we learned we were not the first to live on Mars. The human species had been here before."

Gerard paused to let his words soak in with his daughter. Vivianna's head was spinning. They continued deeper into the ground.

"We were running here to preserve the last remnants of the old ways. There is an ancient technology here that once unlocked would change the universe forever. The differences between us would vanish in an instant, and I believe we could have peace in our time."

"A weapon?" Vivianna asked.

"No, not like what you are thinking of. This technology could be a weapon in the wrong hands. Anything can be a weapon, that is why it stays hidden until the entire planet is ready for it."

"I . . . don't understand."

"We are almost there, and hopefully, you will see. I was skeptical when my father brought me down here, and I'm sure your son will be skeptical too if he is chosen."

"You're starting to frighten me, Dad. I've never heard you talk like this."

Geard put his arm around her. "In these times, we have decided to pass on our knowledge to our heirs. This is the burden that I have been talking about. You will know but must never say unless with three. There is always three."

"Dad, I don't understand anything you are saying, and this sounds like some weird cult group talk those cave drillers always rave about."

"They are like all the other old religions. Just a different perspective with rules."

They walked further down the stairs and came to one of the most elaborate doors Vivianna had ever seen. It was marked with strange markings that she had never seen before.

Two large eyes stared at her—one eye was the sun, and the other eye was the moon of earth. It was surrounded by geometric symbols in no apparent pattern. The door came to life when Gerard approached it. The symbols on the massive door began to shift and changed into one circle, and the door opened for the pair.

"This place is old, and many realize the magic it holds. This is the spot, Vivianna. This is where we, and our ancient ancestors, first touched down on this planet."

Her eyes bulged from her head, and her breath was taken away as she entered the massive cave. Many stories below, the massive cavern was lit with magnificent lighting. It was like nothing she had seen before.

The cavern was round, and as she spun and took it in, she realized that the room was a dome. The doom was sectioned off into massive segments, and each section was carved with the most elaborate figures she had ever seen.

"This is our history!" Gerard announced to the empty cavern. "This is what our dream is. We want to share this with both us and Earth. We are one people, but if this fell into the wrong hands, then it would lead to the same outcome that has plagued humanity since its creation. That is why it must stay hidden until enough of us understand the potential that is locked in each of us. There are schematics for gadgets here within these carvings. That is not what I'm talking about. The true knowledge of our mother and father is in here. Where we come from."

Gerard eyed the majesty of the room and looked at his bewildered daughter.

"This place runs on water and cleans its own air. . . Crazy, right?"

"'Crazy' is an understatement, Dad. So . . . what is my part in this?" She said with her eyes wide and mouth half open. She was still holding her dad tightly.

"Ha! That is for the gods to decide. But do not be afraid, my dear. We do not live in fear. Be yourself, and be proud of who you are. You have nothing to fear if your intensions are pure. Do you see the shape in the center of the floor?"

He walked her over to the center of the dome where Vivianna saw large circles woven together.

"The original Flower of Life on this planet. This is where Mother Mars was born. This is where you will be judged my daughter. When my time comes to walk away, your first task will be to make it through your judgment day."

Vivianna started to cry, overcome with emotion. She, too, knew this day was coming.

"I can do nothing for you when this day comes, and you must face this alone. Only then are you worthy of the knowledge we possess."

Gerard turned his daughter to him and looked into his child's eyes. The same eyes he looked into when she was born. It was in that instant when she came into the universe that he learned what love at first sight was.

"No matter what happens to us, I will always love you. Feel that in your heart when you stand before them. Your father will love you no matter the outcome."

*　*　*

Mia panicked when she saw Sam and his crew return. Her assumption was that she was almost done with this assignment, but she had been informed of the failed mission moments after it happened. Knowing that they were landing had put her in a panicked state that she had not been in since she was a girl. No one in the city knew what had happened.

"Mia? You okay?" It was Cap, the ship's mechanic, standing next to her now. She hadn't even noticed when or how she approached.

"You snuck up on me!" Mia said, startled and surprised.

"I didn't have to try too hard. You had a blank, glossy look on your face, staring off in La La Land."

Mia didn't have many encounters with Cap. She wasn't important enough and merely a drone, so Mia disregarded her for the most part.

"What brings you here?" was all she said.

"Same as you. Waitin' on the crew to land." She snorted a little as she laughed and was immediately embarrassed. "Hey!" she thought out loud. "I wonder what the score is. Have you heard yet?"

"No, and I'd keep your voice down if I were you."

"Ah, who cares? Everyone knows what we do here."

Mia turned to Cap. "No, not everyone knows. Everyone thinks they know. So keep your voice down, or I will see to it that it is down."

"Geeze, Mia, what's got into you?"

"Nothing has got to me, Cap. You're just an idiot, and I don't have time for idiots now."

Cap's mouth opened to speak, but as it did, the pair heard the *Val* on approach. It started to land, and Mia and Cap sheltered themselves from the debris getting stirred around.

When it landed, Mia stood in place, and Cap gave her an awkward glance and headed to the *Validus* with Sam coming out of it.

Mia saw Sam become frustrated in encountering Cap and smirked to herself, knowing that she was not the only one annoyed by the mechanic. Ameera and Cap spoke for a while, then the rest of the crew came out one by one until all were out. Mia didn't see Dre, and the panic set back in. She walked up to the rest of the crew, who had formed a circle. Serg noticed Mia and moved quickly to get to her.

"Mia, fancy seeing you here."

"I was looking for Dre . . . He around?"

"He is . . . unavailable at the moment." Then he quickly inserted, "He's fine, Mia, just unavailable, and I can't say more."

"Gods' sake, Sergio! Let the woman see him," Ameera yelled over her shoulder at the pair.

"All right, all right. Sorry, Mia. You know how it is. He's in the auto doc. Right up the ramp and to the left. You'll see him in there."

She had never been inside the famous *Validus*. Few had. She froze when she saw Dre in the med station. He was so drugged up he just smiled from ear to ear, waving his hand.

"Hey, girl! It's been like weeks, and Mongo needs some lovin'. You look like you're on fire! Come on over here!" He waved with his wounded shoulder and winced.

Mia rushed over to him as he chuckled under the discomfort. "Dre?" She couldn't hold back her tears, and it made her panic more. "I mean . . . I . . . You . . . We . . . I have to . . . "

"What are you saying? Ha ha. You're funny! Is that like a language or something? Ha ha."

"Huh?" Mia hadn't noticed Dre was so drugged. Her panic started to instantly fade because she wasn't feeling the threat anymore.

They weren't on to her. No one knew yet, but they would be looking. She knew Selena would not rest until she discovered the leak, but no one knew it was Mia. She just had to keep telling herself that. There was no way anyone could know.

"We got in a fight," Dre said, sounding intoxicated. "I'm not sure, but I think I lost, ha ha."

Mia got a drink for him, covered him, and sat next to him as he rambled until the drugs kicked in again. It was a unique feeling. Her mission failed, but she was glad.

Then she thought to herself, *Wait, I'm in the fucking* Val.

Dre was out again, and this was an opportunity even she couldn't pass up. Instinct kicked in, and she couldn't control it or herself. Everyone had left. She stuck her head out of the med bay, looked around, and saw no one. How could she be this lucky?

No, she thought, *I made this happen. Yes. I did.*

She walked as softly as she could but tried to look as natural as possible in case she was caught. The "I got lost" always worked. She reached the end of the corridor, and while turning, she ran right into John, with someone who was unmistakable to Mia. She had seen her before on Earth. Commander of Charlie. She was the marines of marines. Her fights on Earth were legendary, and Mia was starstruck.

John saved her by saying, "Hey, Mia, what are you doing here?"

Mia used her preplanned script. "Dre wanted something to eat, so I was looking for wherever you keep that shit." Her experience kicked back in, and she was Mia again.

"I'm sorry, Mia, I forgot about you two. This one," he said, indicating to the captured marine, "has to use the facilities. Hey, would you mind helping her?"

"I got it. Come on please," she asked the commander. "And keep your distance."

"She's very dangerous, so don't let her charm her way out of anything."

Mia pulled out her sidearm and led the commander away. In the bathroom, Mia noticed a wound on the marine so small that it was, in fact, just a small cut. But this gave Mia her in.

"I know it's not much, but let me get something for that cut."

The commander frowned and gave the cut a quick glance, seeming to dismiss it immediately. Mia came with a bandage, placed it on the cut, and at the same time dropped a small tracker into a small pocket on the marine's uniform. The commander, looking away, did not notice, and Mia finished up.

By the door right outside, John knocked. "Everything good?"

Mia opened the door. "Yes, all good."

"Thanks, I appreciate it. Come on, marine lady, back to bed."

Mia thought to herself, *How the fuck did that happen? Oh yes, I remember, I made it happen. Me.*

She was glowing with excitement. She was finally invited to the inner circle. Selena had asked her to attend a get-together and talked for what seemed an eternity. Yes, yes, she agreed to everything Selena talked about. Trust and loyalty. Little did she know, her loyalty was already secured to herself and herself alone. Tonight was the night, she knew it. She took out her direct link, which had been stowed away these past months, turned it on, and keyed the Transmit button.

"Contact made. Stand by for intel."

This time the son of Mars would not escape. She had given them a perfect scenario to kidnap the prince before. Out in space, isolated, and nowhere to run. Her mission should have been over, but he wouldn't escape a second time. She was personally going to see to it.

***

It wasn't exactly the big party Sam was hoping for. Everyone was too somber to let loose. It was the same talk he had with Dre. Everyone was to gather what they could and move to their "base."

During the terraforming of Mars, the very first inhabitants lived in deep underground man-made caves. Some people of Mars still preferred the darkness and security of the caves, but most had moved into the open once terraforming had done most of its work, and that left miles and miles of uncharted cavern system throughout the entire planet.

Sam and his crew, along with almost all the pirate crews, had similar base caves around the planet to stash their ships as well as their pirated goods. Sam told them to prepare for a very long stay underground until this was all over, so it wasn't a surprise that there wouldn't be many cheerful spirits in the air. After the crew divided the duties one by one, they started leaving until only a handful remained.

"Well, this was a dud of an evening," Selena said in frustration.

"You can't blame them. Even Dre brought out 'Mongo' tonight, and even he couldn't break the mood. No trying after that, honestly. You know, I share in their discomfort of hiding. We have grown accustomed to raiding and coming back to a carefree home and living lavishly."

"No, Sam, we are not soft. I just wanted to let loose tonight, but now I'm going to help the bar. We are busy, and the girls need help. Mia, are you coming?"

"Whatever you need, Selena."

Sam rose. "If my goddess is leaving, then I shall retire for the evening as well. I have to tend to our guest anyway. I'll stay the night with her to give everyone a break from watch."

"Guest?" Mia asked.

"Yes, a guest that requires some supervision. Need to know, Miss Mia."

Mia looked over to John, who was just shaking his head wide-eyed. He was terrified, thinking he would be in trouble for Mia already knowing.

"My apologies," she said, both hoping to conceal her excitement and calming John down. She had just confirmed Sam would be with the tracker. Now, that was luck.

"No, I'm sorry," Sam said, looking at Selena. "If you are one of us now, then you have a right to know. We have a UNE prisoner that we intend to gather some intel from, and that's all that you need to know for now. Understand, Mia, that since you just entered our little circle of thieves, you are at the bottom of the barrel, and like Selena told you on your weapons run, every day is a test. Selena and Dre might know you, but I do not."

"I understand, Sam."

"Thank you. I'm going to my place now. If you need anything, I'll be there. Selena, could you walk with me for a moment."

Mia was again bursting with inner excitement. She had a time window and a place. She watched as the two got up from the table and walked away.

Dre stood, looking at Mia. "I'm gonna have another drink, you want one?"

"Absolutely! Now that the downers are gone, let's have some fun, you fucking pirate."

"Oh shit, gonna be one of those nights, huh?"

"Yes, it is. Think you can keep up?"

"We'll see who can keep up, and I ain't talking 'bout drinking anymore." He left, heading to the bar, not giving her a chance to reply.

Mia smiled and became aroused. The thought of having Dre and her target in one night was too much. And then she suddenly became somber, thinking it was more than likely her last night on Mars.

She looked around the room, as she constantly did out of habit. She was close enough to barely hear Sam and Selena next to the door, which led out to the back room. Dre slid past the two, keeping his head down. The auto doors opened and closed behind him. The two had been talking all the while, but now they had Mia's full attention while the rest of the crew spoke next to each other.

"I love you. Don't worry about rushing over. I need some time with my thoughts anyway."

"I was going to close anyway for the girls. I like your idea of taking watch tonight. I'm going to give my people a break too. It'll be very early when I get over."

"If it's too late, stay at your place. I'm a big boy. I'll be all right one night away from you."

"We don't have too many nights left here if we are going into hiding."

"I never asked. You are coming with me?"

"Sam, you pirate, where did you think I'd go?"

"I know, but if anything happened to you, I don't know if I could make it without you. It'll be dangerous on a new level."

"It's you and me. It's always been you and me, and it will always be you and me."

"You know, I had something come to me. We've been hiding for so long, hiding who we truly are to the world, hiding our love." He pulled her in closer. "No more hiding, my love."

They embraced like they never had before. Even Mia was moved by the passion she witnessed. She couldn't even comprehend what giving yourself completely to another even felt like. She had been so guarded—that constant barrier always up, always alert, never at ease. All she knew was that at that moment, she knew she wanted something like that, and she always got what she wanted. She looked over at Dre and felt a spark watching him grab some drinks. There was something about him. Just something different.

"Mia, you okay?" Selena asked, walking up to her.

Mia hadn't even realized she was in a daze. "I'm sorry, just a lot goin' on up there," Mia explained while pointing to her head. "I didn't want to ask during the meeting, but what is my role in all of this?"

"I'm happy you asked because that's what I wanted to talk about. I need someone here, Mia. Would you like to be my eyes here? They know all of us. You are new, so hopefully, they'll fall for it."

"I wouldn't know the first thing about doing that," Mia said as, internally, she felt her heart beat harder. She didn't have to fake it. "I mean, so many questions, but how do I even start?"

"Tell them you'd never go against the UNE, and when I told you to leave, we had a disagreement. Do whatever they ask. Play the loyalist, and when the time is right, I'll contact you somehow."

"So run the bar and get what info I can. Any of the girls I can trust?"

"I'll leave that to you. It's your bar after tonight. I'll close up, and then Sam and I are gone. What do you say? I have little time, so I need an answer now."

After a slight pause, Mia put on the greatest display of acting she had ever performed and stated, "I'll do it."

All the while, she was internally already scheming how to best play this out. She had no idea where they were actually running to hide, but it confirmed that tonight was night. They had to make their move, but she couldn't compromise herself.

She had a direct connection. With her help, the UNE could wipe the resistance off Mars within months. Her demands would be great. Enough that she could get out of this work and pursue her own interests, but that meant possibly many more months here. It wouldn't be half bad. Mia suddenly realized that she actually didn't mind being here on Mars.

What is wrong with me?

She quickly dismissed the idea and went into mission mode. She had a pirate to catch. She had given them information before, and they blew it. This time she would get her prize.

"I did it," she said, muffled. "Me."

"Here you go, one famous Martian brew," Dre said, bringing her a drink.

They cheered and took a healthy gulp. Mia stopped, not wanting to get too intoxicated, but Dre kept going. She was saddened at the thought of not having Dre. He was so much fun at first, but then she quickly discovered he's not just a goofball. He had wisdom. Passion. Love. Faith. He was always positive and hopeful. It was this that drew Mia to him. In the dark world of Earth with negativity and despair as a constant, this passion was what Mia was always missing.

Dre finally brought his drink down, which was almost gone.

"Mongo come out, woman. Me Mongo!" Dre finished his drink, slammed it down on the table, and swept Mia off her feet.

Mia giggled and grabbed on to him while Dre repeated, "Me Mongo!"

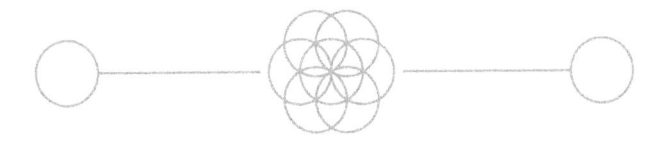

Chapter 8

Our Awakening

The initial explosion rocked Sam. When he came to, he was in a massive daze. His ears were ringing. He had trouble focusing on where he was, and even before he could gather himself, he was being violently thrown over and tied up. They—whoever they were—threw a bag over Sam's head, and two of them jerked him up while someone tied his feet up. Within seconds, he was being dragged outside and then thrown into some sort of container. He felt it move. His senses were beginning to return, and he was starting to put things together.

Oh my gods, I'm fucked. It has to be the UNE. Gods, Selena. Dear gods, please tell me she is okay. My parents. Vivianna. The crew. What have I done? Dear gods, what have I done? Let me know she is okay...

* * *

Selena was locking up. It took her a considerable amount of time to get her affairs in order. She thought she had everything in line, but as the night drew on, she kept finding things she needed to do until she realized she'd never be done. She just had to quit, lock up, and go to Sam.

As she was locking up, she had an overwhelming moment of sadness. She might never see this place again. All her work. She started when she was barely seventeen. She didn't have a thing except her will to win and her intelligence. She was proud of it. Then, as she turned away, she thought to herself, she did it once, she could do it again and even better. First, she had a war to win.

She had not taken three steps when she heard the explosion. It came from the direction of only one thing she could think of—Sam's place. She took off sprinting as fast as her legs could take her, wanting to get to him. She rounded a corner and saw from a little distance people taking someone tied up with a hood on to a transport. It was Sam—she was sure of it. The transport screamed off along with the UNE forces that had raided Sam's place.

Selena activated her link and screamed, keying the all-hands comms, "Help! Help! They have Sam! Anyone, help!"

She continued running with full speed toward the transport. They were headed toward what had to be the port.

"Gods," she said out loud. "They are taking him off world. They are taking him to the port! Help! Anyone!"

"Me and Dre are coming!" Sergio yelled out as he and Dre also felt the explosion and were racing to see what it was.

Selena was running as she came up to the port and saw a UNE vessel performing a combat drop, no doubt to gather Sam. They pulled him out and ripped off his hood. She saw Sam. They pulled out a scanner, scanned his face, and then violently injected something in him. He turned as the UNE officer checked the scanner. He looked around in a daze, not knowing where he was and what was going on, and then he saw her running.

Selena saw Sam smile. Just a little smirk, and then he saw that she was not stopping. They never broke eye contact with each other. Sam shook his head, telling her not to come closer. Selena stopped, looking like one so shocked that part of her soul was being ripped out. Sam gave a little smirk again as the UNE officer confirmed the target.

"Asset confirms target. We're done. FALL BACK! WE ARE DONE HERE!" the UNE officer barked.

The two holding Sam dragged him on board as Sam was losing consciousness.

He was okay with it all. Selena was safe. That was all that mattered, and then there was instant sadness because he couldn't go to her.

"Be strong, my love," he said, trying to reach out to Selena. "You have to."

Then Sam gave in to the drugs that had been pumped into him.

* * *

Fransico was tossing and turning in his bed next to Vivianna. The consequences of the decisions of the times were making him restless.

Would this be the great turning point in the history of Mars, or will this be just a footnote in the great histories of the UNE?

They must be extremely delicate while dealing with the UNE representatives already stationed on Mars. They no doubt would be nervous as well if they had any sense to him.

However, it would be showing a sign of respect if we formally asked for an audience.

Then again, the people of Mars who were fiercely opposed to the UNE "occupation" would see that as an act of treason. To what, Fransico had no idea. Mars wasn't a nation. Mars was just a collection of settlers just happy to be alive and fed.

The council has no authority over anyone. We would have to organize an entire planet. Who would the collective people of Mars want to lead them? Every rebellion needs a heroic leader.

Then the idea struck him.

Sam. He could rally everyone. No, it would not be possible. Rebelling against the UNE would be suicide. They have such an advantage in weapons, material, and trained professional soldiers that it would be hopeless.

Vivianna rose from the bed, also unable to sleep and rubbing her eyes as she rose. "Can't sleep either?"

"Just too much running through my mind. I think I'm going to take a walk. I can't sleep anyway."

"A walk?" Vivianna questioned in a puzzled tone, half asleep still. "Where in the gods' name are you going to walk to at this hour?"

"I don't know. I'll just start walking. I need to pace around, you know, it's just what I do."

"But at this hour?"

"Uncharted times we live in."

"Understatement of the century. Be careful, babe."

"Be careful of what, my dear?" he said as he slowly rose from bed. He gave out a yawn and stretched slightly. "Everyone is asleep anyway."

"Why is everyone in my life so darn difficult? All the flipping men in my life."

"I'm the easy one," he said, giving her a kiss on her cheek. "It's our son you will have to worry about."

"We have a new understatement of the century."

* * *

After witnessing what had happened to Sam, Selena bolted to the royal residence to get his family out. She didn't make it far when she saw massive waves of UNE forces landing all around the city of Jazeera. Drop ships came thundering down, opening their doors, allowing floods of UNE marines and regular soldiers to pour out. They came out wildly, like a swarm of insects in all directions, quickly causing chaos and killing indiscriminately the people who had come outside to see what the commotion was.

Selena had continued her sprint to the royal residence when she came upon Fransico running in the same direction.

"Hey!" Selena shouted over the sounds of ships dropping from orbit.

Francisco stopped dead in his tracks, looking with utter shock back at Selena. He recognized her but could not remember her name.

"We need to get to them!" he shouted back at her, turned, and continued toward his family.

Selena dropped her head and sprinted with all her might to catch up. They ran forever up the hill toward the city center. Her legs were heavy, and her chest felt as if it was about to explode, but she pushed on harder and harder, eager to at least get his family out. That's what Sam would want her to do. Pure adrenaline was coursing through her, and it was all that was keeping her from falling over when she suddenly came to a stop not a hundred feet from the palace. She had run into Fransico, who was bent over, breathing heavily.

"They are all over," he said, gasping for air and referring to the UNE forces that had surrounded the government center. "What do we do?"

"Let's look for a way in. Follow me, and stay low and quiet."

She moved past Francisco, this time using her adrenaline to focus her senses. They inched closer and closer, moving around the entire palace through the gardens, desperately looking for a way in. They used cover to weave in and out of sight and to inspect the building from all angles. She stopped in front of the palace, having looped completely around. They moved and hid in between two of the public buildings that surrounded the complex. The sun was coming up on the horizon.

"I didn't see anything," Fransisco whispered as he crept up to Selena.

"Too many," Selena said, both to Fransisco and to herself. "There's too many. I can't see a way in."

"I didn't see any of our people either, just UNE everywhere."

"Theres a squad of marines in armor."

"Selena, it's suicide to try now. We won't do them any good by dying now. Vivi can take care of them, I promise."

"What? We have to try!"

"We will die if we go in!"

"I can't just walk away. I fucking can't," she said as she dropped her head and started to cry. "They took Sam. Sam is gone."

"He's gone?" Fransico looked at Selena and then back at the marines getting closer.

"Vivi can more than take care of herself and the family. Sam would know that. He wouldn't want you to waste your life. You know he wouldn't. Vivi has told me," he continued, placing his hand gently on her shoulder. "I know why you are hurting."

She began sobbing.

"Come on, time to go."

Selena looked up at Sam's home, the man she loved, with heavy tears. Her world torn apart, her love gone, she could do nothing but slump over, defeated.

"Come on, let's go," he said as he picked her up. "Where are we going?"

* * *

"We have him, Counselor."

"Excellent. I want an update every fifteen minutes until he is here and in a detention cell for processing."

"Yes, sir. I will inform the escorting marines of that update."

"And the rest of the operation?"

"We have secured most of the planet. The entire first family was taken as well as a large majority of the leading figures."

"Very well. Include in your message my approval of the outcome of the operation. That is all. Dismissed."

"Aye, sir!" The aid gave a crisp salute then turned swiftly and exited the room.

Success, the counselor thought to himself.

Not only would he be showered in glory, but the First Panel would be sure to be impressed with him. If only to make the First Panel—the absolute authority over the empire. But first, he would indulge in his pleasure for the time being.

He would make an example of this one. No quick death. He needed to break him. Make him beg for his death. Beg to be released from this world. The counselor felt himself becoming aroused. The mere thought of it was enticing pleasure already. He had just the idea for him to start out. He grinned ear to ear, thinking about it.

He would indeed break him and make him an example to the rest of them. He wouldn't make him a martyr. He wanted to publicly display the son of Mars a broken man for all to see, and if he broke, then what hope did they have? He was going to overwhelmingly destroy Mars and bend it to his will.

He was put here to solve the Martian crisis. Crisis it was. Not many were privy to the information that Earth was teetering on a knife's edge. The Martian food supply was everything to Earth, and without it, Earth would starve. They were months away from running out of food, and the pirating was taking its toll even though to the public, the pirates were mere gnats. Something had to be done, and the counselor decided on a critical action: kidnap the "leader of the pirates," make him squirm with fear, and break him—at the same time breaking Mars's spirit.

He was becoming aroused again. With a coordinated massive invasion, the peasants would be helpless. The asset proved invaluable. He made a note to check the asset's status. Breaking the pirate and Mars. He needed to release the pleasure now. Just then the door opened.

"Sir, prisoner is secure and unconscious. Marines report no contacts, all clear. Proceeding at maximum speed."

"Have one of the girls sent up, and do not disturb me unless there is any change in reports whatsoever. If something changes and you do not inform me, I will have you sent to a penal colony where you will no doubt be killed within minutes of arriving for no reason other than to steal your shoes. Now, do you understand me?"

"Yes, sir!" the aid barked and again smartly left the room.

"Now, where was I?" the counselor said out loud.

* * *

When Sam came to, he felt the ship slowing down and breaking atmosphere. He had no idea how long he was out. He blinked a couple times and tried to gather some saliva because his mouth was so dry. He looked up and saw his marine prisoner herself restrained.

He tried to say something, but nothing came out. The drugs he was administered had to be extremely powerful. The ship landed, and Sam, getting pulled up, noticed that he had soiled himself. The smell of piss and shit filled his nose. The rear of the ship opened, and to Sam's utter shock, he was on the mother planet. In shock and trying to make sense of the situation he was in, he hadn't realized he'd been out for the entire trip. He wasn't in a hood anymore. There were drone cameras all over, recording Sam from all angles being dragged down the ramp of the transport.

Earth. What a paradise it used to be. The once beautiful, lush, green planet was all but gone, having been replaced with city after city until there was scarcely any vast country left. There was still the Siberian penal sector that was not developed, but the rest of the planet had been consumed by the ever-spreading people of Earth.

There used to be a balance between the people of Earth and the actual planet. Back during the days of nations, there was a very serious commitment to keeping the Earth as beautiful as possible. During this time, the people of Earth decided to commit to the terraforming of Mars as a way of population control. The United Nations gathered worldwide resources with an almost unprecedented cooperation of all the nations, and the mission to colonize Mars began. Everything started out beautifully. And then the eventual decline of man started, as it had time and time again throughout the histories.

With the massive success of colonizing Mars, the UN was seen by many over the world as a unifying body. "No more wars" was the rallying slogan. One by one, the nations of Earth fell into the collective body of the UN. It turned into "If you're not with us, then you're against us." Even old enemies gave in and in return were granted a seat at the First Council, or rather a committee of leading members. Greed, power hunger, lies, and deceit became the regular traits necessary to survive the halls of the UN, recently renamed the United Nations of Earth.

Over time, more freedoms were stripped for the good of the people, and the First Council, or First Panel, gained more and more power until their rule over the people of Earth was complete. With no more wars to fight, the new enemy of the UNE became the people of Earth. Lockdowns, scans, curfews, mandates, indoctrination. Those who saw the coming storm fled to Mars, and the wealth that was taken to Mars jumpstarted the colonization and terraforming.

The people of Mars, having fled the horrors of what a brutal authority figure could do to a population, decided no government and complete freedom. There was a Council of Peers established to guide the people of Mars, but it had absolutely zero authority to force any person to do anything. Local law officials were elected every year solely based on performance, and any politicking was strictly forbidden, and anyone so much as accused of it was run quickly from office. The main rule was, no lifetime bureaucrats. They had been destroying people for centuries. No government and minimal law, and surprisingly, it worked. People, it turned out, behaved themselves when they knew everyone was armed.

Back on Earth, the oppression continued until, generation after generation, the everyday person of Earth thought it normal to have every detail of one's life controlled. Let the UNE take care of everyday needs so you could enjoy your time off work. It all spiraled further and further.

All Sam could see was the crowd of raging, dirty people yelling and throwing garbage at him. The escorting marines even had to smash a couple of the swarming people to deter others from trying to put their hands on him. Slowly, they moved Sam through the crowd. He was dodging garbage, human feces, and whatever else people could get their hands on. He could see on the displays all over that the news of the hour was that the villainous pirate Samuel Cleber had finally been captured and that UNE forces had secured most of the planet of Mars. He was in a complete whirlwind, and all the while, endless thoughts and possibilities were running through his head.

Fuck fucking people. Where are they taking me? Am I about ready to be executed? I'm not ready yet. So many things are left undone. Selena. I'll never see her again.

Sam's fate became apparent on his face.

Fuck it. If I'm going, I'm going out like a fucking man. Sam's eyes lit up with fire. *Whatever is going to happen, I'll face it.*

There was a tug at the back of Sam's restraints, and he turned to see what it was.

The marine. What the fuck is she doing... Oh, she fucked up. They are going to make an example. Fuck her.

Sam laughed at her. "Looks like you're fucked as well."

One of the marines struck Sam so hard he saw stars and was knocked down to his feet. The marine, with no emotion, said, "No talking!" then struck Sam again.

Only this time Sam didn't see any stars; he only saw blackness.

* * *

He woke up at the same time as every day at four. He was on the day shift this quarter, and it took him every minute of the remaining two hours until work to arrive. He quickly rose from his creaky bed stained significantly from the years of neglect and walked the couple of steps to get to his toilet, which was open to the room. He performed his necessaries into the discolored commode and stepped over to the sink, splashing water on his face, and then grabbed a ration bar and went out the door in less than three minutes. His building was cleaner than most due to his security clearance and rank in the UNE, but that didn't matter to him. Hygiene and cleanliness were not his best qualities.

He got down to the street and was overjoyed to see it was a pleasant outside. He couldn't see the sky through the clouds and permanent layer of smog that had settled over the First District, but it wasn't too hot out yet, and he wouldn't be drenched in sweat when he got to his station. He weaved his way through the crowds, easily doing so due to his massive size and the fact that he hadn't bathed in many weeks. Most people weaved around him actually.

He got to the underground transport, which were used by the masses. There was, of course, aboveground transport that connected to every corner of the globe, but the underground ones were solely used by the working class. He stepped onto the crowded train and let out a massive fart that could be heard by all. Giggling to himself as a child would, he watched as many pugged their noses or left that transport for another due to the rancid smell.

Stupid people, he thought.

The standing ride took him an hour to complete, taking him to the workstation assigned to him when he was eighteen.

So many years, he thought to himself. *It had to be a couple decades at least, even possibly three or more.* He didn't know.

After eighteen, your age did not matter. You worked until you couldn't, then afterward, you are placed in a lesser manual labor district to take on the less important tasks of the UNE. If you couldn't work anymore, you were sent to a retirement community, which was another name for death camp. The upside was, you got a day to live in luxury. Hot water, real food, and a good bed, then lights out.

What a terrible fate, he thought.

"I'm gonna stay here as long as I can," he said out loud as he stepped out of the transport.

There was only a short walk to the first checkpoint, but this was always the longest line and the longest wait time. There were only two at the station today, meaning he was going to cut it extremely close getting to his station on time. The large man started to peak around the line, trying to will the two with his mind to hurry their checks.

It's just a simple scan. Why is this taking so long?

The displays came to life.

"All citizens of this great United Nations of Earth," the announcement started coming from the longtime spokesperson of the First Panel. "The First Panel proudly reports to its people that once again, we have prevailed. The First Panel has captured the leader of the pirates of Mars."

The displays switched to a ragged person being dragged by marines and followed by another. Then one of the marines struck the person, and down he went. The other prisoner was ordered at weapon point to pick up the unconscious prisoner, and the group continued its walk.

"Along with the prince of Mars, UNE forces captured the renegade marine who killed her own squad and let the pirate escape. The marine will be held accountable for their crimes against the UNE. Citizens of Earth, rejoice. A complete UNE victory over the scum of Mars. UNE forces have completely occupied and taken total control of the planet. The pirate sum have been eliminated. Once again, the UNE does what the people need.

"To celebrate this glorious occasion, the First Panel have decreed that from now on until the end of time, this shall be a global day of celebration. Pleasure centers, alcohol stations, and drug carts will flow throughout the cities. Indulge yourselves, and help the UNE celebrate . . . victory!" He paused. "Along with this grand victory, the First Panel has decided to rename the United Nations of Earth to the United Empire of Earth. Help me, people of the empire, to celebrate this great victory and the birth of our glorious empire! And with this renaming, we shall add another day of global celebration all provided by the empire. For the empire!"

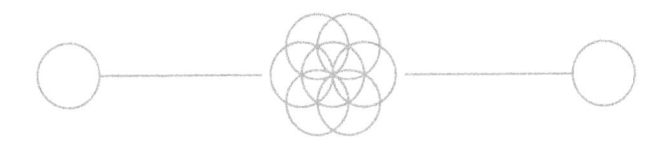

Chapter 9

Our Battle

What a day, he thought to himself as he continued to wait in line, but now his eagerness to get to his assigned work was even higher. *They have to bring him there. Where else would they bring him? Curse this line. Why is everyone stopping and smiling? Oh yeah! Pleasure houses.*

He would have to wait until his shift was over to hit the houses himself. The wait was excruciating, but eventually, he got there and was scanned in by his fellow worker and off to his next checkpoint. He entered the large opening and headed to the prison district of the military complex. It was the central hub, and his district was one of the branches. This checkpoint was less crowded. People were already searching for the nearest cart or house, but still, it had a longer line than usual.

Shit, I'm gonna be late for sure. Fuck it, nothing I can do. I'll have to earn a work credit somehow to make up for it.

He finished the wait for that checkpoint, bringing him into the medium-security section, and as quickly as he could, which wasn't at all for a man of his size, he made his way to the elevator and descended the many levels to his last checkpoint. Here they scanned his chip and his retina, and he made his way into the maximum-security district far underground. He went down the hall and saw the other lift out of the lower levels. He called it the fun elevator. He walked down this long corridor that only he and a select few could walk down. He passed another door, and it smelled of pure human filth and despair. He was home.

"Is he here yet?" he asked another overseer.

"He's on his way. They are processing him. He's getting his chip, scans, the works."

"Not many need a full process anymore."

"Peasants."

"Where are we putting him? Definitely in 8, right?"

The other guard laughed out loud. "Yeah, 8 for this one, and put the other next to him. That one is no better, far as I see it."

"I like that. What they gonna do with this one? Torture? Starvation? Execution?"

"Neither actually. This one is going to be made an example of. The other, not sure yet. They say maybe starvation. Keep her around for a rainy day. Ha ha."

"Let's move them around. We don't want Mr. Cleber to feel unwelcome when he arrives."

"Ha ha ha. Should we wash it out? Protocol says rinse it."

"Looks clean to me," he said as the pair laughed and went about their work.

Sam entered the cell block being dragged by the marine. She was laboring slightly as she finished the chore of dragging Sam.

"You're not done yet," one of the disgusting jailers said.

The smell was overpowering since she entered the lower level.

"Put him in that one. Then you go to that one," was all he said, pointing to the two cells side by side.

She did as she was directed in a quick and military fashion, placing Sam in a garbage pit of a cell, then went into hers. The solid doors slowly shut, and then she heard the heavy thud of the locking mechanism engaging. It was over. They had been captured and detained.

* * *

"Fuck!" Dre was yelling, tearing their makeshift camp apart.

"Calm down!"

"Fuck you, Serg!"

"Fuck me? I'll show you fuck me. Come on, Mr. Badass. 'Bout time me and you throw down."

Dre spun, got wild in the eyes, and charged straight at Sergio, jumping over the mess he'd made in the process. Sergio likewise charged at Dre, both wanting to let out the rage they had built up in the hours after the invasion. They clashed together, both trying to punish the other man. Both landed heavy blows but quickly were pulled apart by the others.

John stepped in. "Cut the shit!" He paused, looking at them both. "It doesn't help anyone, fighting among ourselves. What does everyone know? I was moving shit out here and was asleep when it happened. All I saw was hundreds of ships landing.

Apparently, they fucking have Sam, right?" John couldn't help getting choked up as his brother's name came out of his mouth. His eyes watered as the crew looked at John with sympathy. "I don't know what became of my family. I don't know anything, so what the fuck do we know?"

"They got us tonight," Dre spoke up, panting from the fight. "They fucking kicked the shit outta us with one move."

"We knew this was coming," Tucker exclaimed as he was sitting against the wall with Helena in his arms. "That's why we were all moving this shit. We knew it was coming."

"We didn't even get a fraction of the shit we were counting on moving," Serg said, throwing a bloody rag into the dirt in the cave.

The low light in the cave showed through the dust Dre and Serg drew up as the crew looked around in silence.

"Guys!" Ameera shouted as she continued her search into the network. "They have your family and nearly all of the council! They are alive."

"Gods!" John said as he turned away.

"I got people saying UNE is all over the city, and they are continuing the planetwide invasion throughout the day."

"Did more of us get out?" Helena asked.

"Lots of traffic on the network. I'm not sure about anything except it looks like that Jazeera is totally in control by the UNE."

"Your kids, Ameera?"

"In the *Val*, sleeping. Thank the gods, we had them out here while we set up."

"How much did we get, Serg?" Dre asked, rising and looking directly into Serg's eyes.

"Handful of weapons and whatever else was in the *Val*. Why?"

"Because it's time to fight back," John proclaimed, inserting himself into the conversation.

Dre nodded his head in agreement, "Exactly."

"Okay, so we got four of us. Against a whole invasion force. Where we going?" Serg shrugged his shoulders as he asked the question.

"I say we hit the port, grab what we can," Dre said then pointed to the port. "In"—and then behind his shoulder—"and then we get the fuck out. Smash and grab!"

"If we go anywhere, it's to get my family," John shouted.

"The palace and the surrounding district has a large number of the fucking rat UNE! It would be a very hard fight and even less of a chance to actually get them out!"

"Listen, John, and look around. We just got fucked up, but we aren't out of this fight. We are still breathing. When the time is right, we will get your family out," Dre motioned in a calmer tone.

John registered what Dre had just told him. Nodding his head, he looked at Dre and said, "Okay, we hit the port."

"All right," Dre said as he gave a slight pound on the chest to John. "Let's get suited up, boys!"

Tucker rose, releasing Helena from his arm. He gave her a look, kissed her deeply, and made his way to the *Validus*.

"Okay, crazies, we don't even know what's out there, but fuck it. Let's go down swinging." Serg chuckled.

"We got ten mikes, and we move!" Dre roared.

Serg stopped at Ameera and gave her a kiss on her forehead. "Take care of my babies."

"They'll be fine with Cap, honey. I'm going too." She reached up and put her hands on Sergio's face, cutting him off before he could speak. "After this, we'll never both be at risk, but we're all doing this one together."

* * *

The UNE forces by this time in the day had been awake for many hours, and sleep was becoming an issue. Most of the regular soldiers were scattered out around the city, concentrating their numbers at the port and the government center. All the marine squads were either scattered throughout the city to round up all council members or were well outside Jazeera performing search and destroy patrols. Jazeera was effectively being completely surrounded.

"General, by all reports, it looks like we have achieved total surprise. There was no organized resistance anywhere in the, city and marine squads are reporting zero military contacts.

They have, however, been neutralizing anyone approaching the city."

General Nikto Klaatu Barada turned from his own display and gave a quick glance at the display one of his staff was holding. He gave the staff a nod and went back to scanning the display, which previously had his attention. All around him, the makeshift command center was alive with activity. Soldiers with links installed were jacked into the system, making up the perimeter of the command station. They were completely immersed, processing all the information coming in from the linked marine squads, as well as monitoring all regular comms traffic. The general stood in the middle, monitoring everyone doing their jobs and listening to anything that might need his attention. Staff members came to him regularly, reporting the status of their assignments and in turn receiving further instruction from the general.

The door opened, and two marine guards escorted the first citizen of Mars into the command room. Gerard Cleber looked in amazement at the surrounding command room but then quickly refocused his attention on the general.

"Mr. Cleber, I am General Nikto Barada, supreme commander of the United Nations of Earth. I am hereby instructed to inform you that the First Panel of the United Nations of Earth has taken control of the planet Mars, and it is forever to be known as the First Colony of the United Empire. You are to surrender all authority immediately to the empire and inform the colony of Mars what has transpired."

"General, what gives you the right to claim our planet?"

"Why, we have the strength to take it, Mr. Cleber. Now, are you going to comply and relinquish authority, or do I have to take it?"

"What authority, General? I hold no authority over anyone but myself."

"Then I have to take it. I am going to squeeze my hand, and as my grip tightens, so will the suffering of your people that you have no authority over. If you change your mind, you know where to find me."

The marines ripped Gerard from the room, and the general spun, quickly returning to his duties.

An aid approached him. "General, Yankee Squad reports 90 percent of the council has been apprehended. They have divided to search for the remainder."

The general again nodded and returned to scanning the room.

"General, Captain Talbert reports contact, and he is need of armor support immediately!" came the shout of one of his staff.

The general spun to address the marine monitoring station, "Who is the closest?"

"Yankee is closest but scattered throughout the city," the jacked-in UNE soldier said in a monotone voice, never lifting his gaze from the display he was monitoring.

"Dispatch orders immediately to converge on the port! Send beckons to pinpoint location, and tell him to move on the double!" He then turned to the fleet station. "Air support to the port immediately, and I want eyes on the port now."

"Inbound, ETA, five mikes," came the same identical monotone voice.

The general returned to his scan but was thinking to himself where they came from.

Either the city or outside the city. If outside the city, then that means they got past the marine patrols. That's possible, but highly unlikely. The more logical explanation would be that desperate colonists were trying to escape the city and attacking from within. We haven't had time to sweep building to building. It had to come from the city, but we need information. I've reinforced and called air support. Let's be overcautious.

"Send Lima Squad to support, and inform Delta to widen their patrol."

The staff issued commands, and the general returned to his position scanning the room.

"Where's my eyes?"

"Coming up, General."

* * *

The UNE forces at the port were still alert but visibly getting tired. Their eyes were red, their shoulders started to slump, and some were even starting to drag their feet. They had secured the port hours ago and had since then been setting up their defenses and consolidating food, weapons, spare armor, medical supplies, and all the other essential gear necessary to conduct an invasion and occupation of an entire planet.

The sun was falling, having passed its zenith hours ago. The invasion was almost over, and then the occupation would commence. Rotations would begin, going from patrol, then to guard duty, then rest, then to quick reaction. Each rotation having an assigned number of battalions to execute each assignment.

One of the soldiers who knew she would be on guard duty at the first rotation pulled her antisleep pills out from a pocket of her gear. She popped the pills into her mouth and started chewing them without anything to wash them down. She had performed countless patrols on Earth, and she was actually looking forward to seeing the city on patrol, but first, she had to stay awake for her shift. The antisleep pills would definitely do its job.

She scanned her zone, looking out intensely at the surrounding buildings. They were mostly what appeared to be storehouses, but she did notice a few what appeared to be dwellings scattered in her zone. She moved her head from side to side, scanning the horizon and shifting slightly from leg to leg. Out of the corner of her eye, she spotted movement. She didn't have time to react. Someone in armor came thundering down and smashed her using its armored foot, killing her instantly.

Dre had used his heel to dispatch his first soldier and then quickly raised his head and found his next target, aided by his OB. He activated his thrusters again, this time leaping and firing his weapons as he drifted to his next soldier to smash. He came down violently again, using his knee to crush the soldier to death with his thousand-pound battle armor. He looked to his right and saw his squad mates crash into the port on the adjacent side, smashing, shooting, and tearing anything UNE that they could find. Each one fired a thruster, leaping over soldiers, firing desperately trying to at least hold the onslaught, but there was nothing they could do.

Most rounds made an impact but barely made an impression on the armor. Out of the sky came the roar of the *Validus* performing a combat landing, fiercely firing its thruster to slow its descent, all the while firing its weapons into the already-faltering UNE forces.

Helena on the weapons was destroying everything in her view. Ships, both military and civilian transports, were turned into flaming balls of destruction. While she covered them, the others started loading what they could into the *Val* as quickly as they could, not even caring what they were grabbing. John did spot some armor and grabbed two at a time, throwing both over his shoulders and bouncing to the *Validus* to unload and grab more.

Dre was still circling the parameter, seeking out every UNE soldier he could find and ripping them apart with his armor. He had run out of ammunition; all he had left were his hands. His OB notified him that it was time to leave. He turned and fired his thruster, making his way back to the others, bouncing with each thrust as he cleared building after building. John, Serg, and Tucker were hurriedly loading what they could with Helena in control of the *Val*'s weapons, covering the crew and blasting the odd UNE soldier that was left.

John heard his own OB and grabbed the last amount of supplies he could carry and fired to the ship. Midbounce, John heard Serg scream to watch out, and he was hit so suddenly that he had little time to register anything at all. A UNE marine had crashed into John and was holding John with one hand and firing with the other at the rest of the crew. Both Tucker and Serg froze, unable to fire, and scrambled to find cover. The marine turned its full attention to John and began viciously beating him, smashing his armor into John's chest.

Dre came in, landing squarely into the marine midswing, turning himself, John, and the marine into a giant ball of armor rolling on the ground. Serg and Tucker had run into the fray, each grabbing an appendage of the marine and holding it down. Dre scrambled to his feet, grabbed the armored marine by its head, and with all his might ripped the armored head off its body and, in doing so, partially ripped the marine's head off as well. The marine went limp, and the four of them rose and looked at Dre, who was covered in blood.

"Load up, we are out of here now!"

All four of the crew grabbed one last armful of supplies and bounced into the ship's open cargo bay.

"All on board! Punch it!"

The engines, which had been continuously running, powered to full, and the *Validus* started lifting into the Maritain sky. Another UNE marine came crashing down into the port and made a massive thrust, desperately trying to grab on to the *Val*. The marine came within feet of grabbing the rising ship and, after having missed the grab, turned to fire. The *Validus* was too far away by the time another marine got his weapons on the ship and held his fire. He crashed down on the ground and watched as the ship engaged its main engines and was gone in an instant. They were clear.

* * *

"How long till they find our tunnel system?" Serg asked as he was organizing the supplies they had recently acquired.

"Who says they will?" Tucker questioned.

"It's the UNE. It's only a matter of time until they find it."

"We need to move again. It's just like out there." Serg motioned to the sky. "We never stay in one place too long. We are going to need to be moving regularly."

"Well, look at you, Commander Sergio. When did you become the general?"

"General, shit, I was just worried about my skinny ass and those of my family. I don't want to be around when they come looking, and they will."

"He's right," Dre said, entering the cargo bay, still in his blood-soaked battle armor. "We need to move now and leave nothing behind. Absolutely nothing." Dre turned to leave the cargo bay.

"Hey, Dre," Sergio said.

Dre turned back toward the two.

"What was that?" Serg asked.

"What do you mean?"

"Man, you were ripping people apart! Let's just say, I wasn't ready for that."

"What did you expect to happen?"

"Shit, man, I don't know. I just never seen anything like that. I know me and you don't have the best history, but you okay, man?"

"I'm fine. I'm going to stay in armor and keep watch. You two see to John, he is pretty rattled. And help the girls load up."

"Who the fuck made you in charge, you Mongo motherfucker? Just because you went crazy, don't think for a second that gives you the right to fucking bark at me!"

Dre just smirked at the two, turned, and went to his vantage point to keep watch. He thought to himself that Serg was right, and he lost the smirk as he fired his thrusters and bounced his way to his lookout. It took him some time to approach the city at optimal observing distance. His wounds were still way too fresh, and the pain meds were starting to wear off. He reluctantly took more meds through the store in his suit and carried on.

He was careful on his approach, staying in valleys and never exposing himself for too long on the horizon. He zoomed in on his optics and surveyed the carnage he left behind. The UNE were scattered, running around the port. The smoke was dark and thick in the sky. He saw a marine squad in the port. They were taking the fallen marine that Dre had dispatched. Two of them carried while the other two kept watch. Nothing stood out to Dre that the UNE were actively tracking them. They had hit them too fast and left even faster.

They had done it. Smash and grab—and more importantly, they just punched back. The whole planet would hear about an unknown group wreaking havoc on UNE forces. The UNE would now know that they would have a fight ahead of them.

Dre got fierce in his eyes. *Good*, he thought. *If they want a fight, I'll give them a fight.*

They needed to lay low for the time being though. They needed to organize, formulate a plan, train, gather numbers, hit when they could, and find a way to gather intelligence. That would take time, and Dre was already mentally preparing himself for the long war to come. It would take years, but he didn't care.

His thoughts drifted to Mia. He wondered what had happened to her. He didn't even remember seeing her when he left his room and didn't see her after he went back looking for her. He made a mental note that when the time was right, he would try to find her, but not now. It was just too risky. He needed a place to set up operations, and a thought crossed his mind.

Ali. He needed to link up with Ali. He knew the tunnel system better than anyone. His eyes danced as he formulated his strategy right there with the UNE in eyesight. He would hit, run, and then hide.

Train multiple squads to attack simultaneously, and then disappear into the tunnels. He nodded his head, agreeing with himself. Then he saw in the distance a large marine squad bouncing, patrolling the area headed straight for him.

It was time to go, and he slipped down the hillside he was on, disappearing into the Martian landscape. He bounced back at the fastest possible speed toward the group. He hoped that they had finished loading and were ready to move. He made one last jump to the edge of the cavern that the *Validus* was hidden in, looked down, then dropped and fired his thruster just before hitting the ground to ease his descent. He crunched over holding his side as he rose and began looking around the room and spotted Selena, who was in an obvious state of shock. His eyes widened. He was generally happy and excited to see her alive.

"Selena! I lost you after Sam. I tried the comms, but I didn't hear anything. I thought they took you."

"No," she said as her voice broke, unable to get the words out. "They took him."

"I know," Dre said, inching closer to her, but then he remembered he was in bloodstained armor. "How'd you get here?"

"We used the tunnels to get out."

"Who's 'we'?"

"Me and Cap and Vivianna's husband. I forgot his name."

"Fransico?"

"Yeah, that's him."

"What the fuck is he doing here? I thought they had the residence sealed tight."

"I don't know. I just saw him while I was trying to get to his family."

"I saw them dropping all around it. I just assumed they were taken, so I started to gather the others." Dre paused a moment. "It happened so fast that." He stopped, just admitting he made a mistake. "I should've looked for you harder. I'm sorry."

"Don't be," she said, dropping her head.

Dre stood and just looked at her. It was apparent that she was destroyed and beside herself with what had happened. She started crying again, and Dre's instinct was again to comfort her, but like before, he knew he was in no condition to do so. He didn't know what to say, so he just said he was sorry again and moved on. He needed to find Fransico anyway.

"Hey, Frankie boy!"

He came around from the other side of the massive cave, peering questionably around some cargo container to see who was calling him. He stepped out and walked toward Dre with a puzzled and worried face on him as he sized up the man in armor who had just called him. He was repulsed at the sight of Dre and his dried, stained armor but walked within talking distance nonetheless.

"I'm sorry, but I don't know who you are."

"How'd you get here?"

"Selena."

"Selena, I see. Well, riddle me this, and you better answer me without the bullshit. I hate repeating myself, so again, and for the last time, how the fuck did you get here?"

Fransico very calmly and numbingly looked Dre straight in the eye. "I was outside the residence when the attack came. I couldn't sleep, so I went for a walk. They landed, and I ran into Selena. We tried to get in, but there were just too many. She told me of the tunnel, ran into some girl named Cap, and here we are. So now, may I know who you are?"

"What took you so long?"

"We had to be careful. The UNE were everywhere, and the city is on lockdown. If they saw us, it was over, and besides, she was basically an anchor. Selena is broken."

"You just left your family?"

"WHAT IN THE NAME OF THE GODS WAS I SUPPOSED TO DO!" Fransico said, unhinged. "We had nothing. We would have been killed or captured and then probably killed. How was I supposed to help my family, huh? By getting myself killed? No. We live to fight another day."

"Out for a walk, you say. Convenient."

"Just what are you getting at?"

"I know there's an informer."

"And you think I'm it? Okay, you big, dumb bastard. Why would I betray my wife, my kids, my family, and Mars to those vultures? For what, huh? For what?"

Dre just peered at the man in front of him. He looked at him as Fransico was panting heavily and locked in on Dre as well.

"Finish loading. If you are joining our crew, then you are lower than my boot. Get moving, boot."

"But what am I supposed to call you?"

"Dre. But some just call me Mongo. You'll learn from the others what I'm about. Don't fuck with me, and we'll be friends. If not, well, you don't want to find out if not."

"So you're the one I've heard about."

"Yeah," said Dre, leaning into him and looking straight into his eyes. "I'm the one." He turned and walked back to the others.

Selena, who had been listening, picked her head up. "He is good. If he was in on it, he had every opportunity to fuck us but didn't."

"I guess we'll see. Why don't you get on board. It's almost dark, and I want to relocate under darkness. Take Sam's room."

Dre instantly regretted saying it, and Selena bowed her head again and started to cry. More tears this time. Dre was frustrated that he couldn't find the words to comfort her and seemed to make it worse every time he spoke. So he just backed away, boarded the ship, and removed his armor. He went back to find her and found Selena in the same spot still crying. He picked her up, put his arm around her, and without saying a word, started to walk her back to Sam's *Validus*. She didn't make it two steps, and she turned and buried her head into Dre's chest. He held her with both arms, and he himself let a single tear roll down his face as they stood embraced. They were crying for Sam, for each other, for all the people who died, and for Mars.

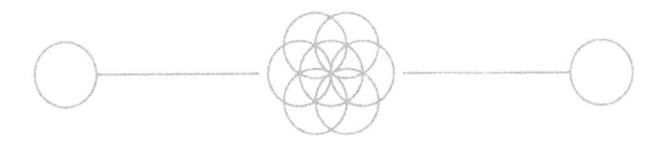

Chapter 10

Our Low

Sam started to regain his senses. His mouth was so dry that it felt like there was sandpaper in his mouth. He tried to get his saliva glands going but failed, and while still trying, he started to survey the room he was in. It was dark, so dark he couldn't make out any shapes in the room. The only thing he could see was a dim light at the top of the room hanging. He felt the surface around him, dragging his hand over the ground as he lifted his head.

Stone. Cold, damp stone was the only thing he could feel, and he realized why he couldn't see anything, because there was nothing to see. The room he was in was completely made of stone. The whole room was dark, damp, and cold. He got to his knees, still coming out of his daze. He had trouble figuring out where he was, not completely remembering how he arrived here. Then it came to him.

The UNE. Selena. It all came back. *I was captured. A cell. I'm in a cell. Gods, Selena, my parents, the crew. Where the fuck am I?*

He started to rise and groaned loudly as he stood, hunched over. He stood straight with his hands on his lower back and stretched so that he could try to walk. His legs were heavy, but he managed to take a step and put his foot down in some sort of liquid.

He smelled the air and cringed as he realized it was sewage that he stepped in, and with that realization, he couldn't get the smell out of his nose. He pulled his bare foot out of the sewage and kicked his foot so as to clear as much as he could. He felt the slime slide off. He stepped back, and his eyes were starting to focus in the dark. He could see the walls of the room. He barely had room to move around; the cell was so small. He felt the walls of the room, careful not to step in the sewage again, which was actually a trough flowing on one side of the room.

He continued to feel his way around and again stepped in liquid. This time Sam stepped out quickly, but the liquid did not feel slimy as the other did. He bent down carefully, trying to use his nose to determine what the liquid was. Not smelling anything, he pondered for a few moments, thinking of his next move. He came to his conclusion and dipped his finger into the liquid and brought it to his nose and again—no smell. So he tapped the liquid to his extremely dry tongue. It was water.

Sam immediately and with great enthusiasm cupped his hands and started to pull the water and finally wet his parched mouth. He tasted the water, and he viciously drank. He drank and drank until he was satisfied. He tasted the metallic flavor, mixed with whatever other filth was in it as well, and became overwhelmed with nausea and threw up all the water he just finished drinking.

He fell to his knees and spit directly on the floor after. He looked up and noticed another dim light. As quickly as one could, given his circumstances, he took the couple steps required to see that it was a small viewing port that was shut, but small streaks of light peered through. He felt the door and the same cold damp feeling, but it was metal. Sam knocked, and the door was no doubt very solid. He couldn't hear anything. It was dead silent. He stood around the cell surrounded by walls, metal door, vomit, and sewage. He brought his hands to his face and started to weep. He didn't make a sound, but his tears were heavy.

He paced the room, sat in silence, kicked the door and walls until he was exhausted, fell asleep, and woke up in the fetal position shivering, only to fall asleep again. He was woken this time by a sound. It was faint, but he heard something. He listened intensely, and his eyes widened as he heard the sound get louder. There was another thud, and this time he heard a creaky metal door open and then slam back to the position it came from. He heard feet shuffling and thought that the person was coming downstairs.

The person came closer, shuffling his feet, and Sam picked up the sound of heavy breathing. The port slid open, and a chunk of something was thrown in along with something else in a pan. His chunk fell into the water along with the pan, and Sam quickly snatched the chunk out as well as the upside-down pan floating in the water. He was so hungry he attacked whatever the chunk was and stopped suddenly, thinking he bit into a rock. It wasn't though. The ration bar he was given was so hard that it felt like a rock. It was so hard Sam had to gnaw at it to break any off. Still, with the pan in one hand and the bar in another, Sam yelled at the person.

"Hey!" he tried shouting, but nothing came out. He cleared his throat and tried again to get his attention because he heard the person shuffling off again.

"Hey!" a sound came out.

There was no response. Only shuffling and more ports opening and closing. He counted at least ten maybe more. A port was opened, but this time there was a pause. It lasted only a moment, and Sam heard the person say, "Pan."

It was very lazily said, and he drew the word out as he said it. Sam heard the port close and then the shuffling. Port opening, "Pan" in the exact same manner, and port closing. There was more shuffling, getting closer. "Pan." The person kept his same movement, exactly repeating what he had done previously. He finally got to Sam, slid the port open, and said the same.

"Pan."

Sam ducked his head close to the port. "Where am I? What is going on?"

Sam heard some heavy lock disengage, and the person pushed the door open, half hitting Sam as he did so. The person was massive in size. He quickly stepped into the room and bashed Sam across the head with some sort of club, and Sam fell to the ground. The person violently hit Sam three more times, catching him in the arm, his back, and finally, on his head.

Sam blacked out. The jailer, being satisfied with his work, picked up the pan, locked the door, and started to shuffle back up the stairs. This time he was grinning.

* * *

Sam came to again out of a daze, seeing the same single light flickering overhead. It was blurry, and his head felt as if someone had a vise on it. Lying on the floor, Sam reached up and felt the spot where his head hurt the most and felt a giant knot along with a lot of dried blood. It was sensitive to the touch, and he winced as he felt the wound. He felt sore on his back and arm as well, but the wound on his head had most of his attention. He could feel his heart pounding in his head because of the silence.

He smacked his mouth again, feeling the sandpaper in his lips. Driven by thirst, he belly-crawled to the trench with water and this time took small mouthfuls to quench his thirst. It was metallic and gritty again, but this time he managed to keep the water down. His stomach growled fiercely at Sam, indicating that he needed to eat, but there was nothing he could see or feel, only the light overhead barely lit. Sam rolled over, cleared his throat, and sat in the silence once more. No need to kick and scream. It would do nothing, and Sam did not feel like getting his head bashed in again, so silence it was.

"You're never going to make it at this pace."

"Who's that?" Sam's raspy voice replied.

"Your former prisoner, now your fellow condemned."

"Commander?"

"Yes."

Sam rolled back over, with his head lifted, and crawled to where he heard the voice. It was coming from the water trough but from the cell next to him. He lowered his head so low that most of his ear was submerged in the water.

"I can hear you. Can you hear me?"

"Yes, I can."

Sam uncontrollably started to tear up, and his voice cracked as he spoke, "Selena. What happened to Selena?"

"I don't know. I was taken with you."

"Gods. What about my family? What about the crew?"

"I don't know," she said, clearly frustrated at having to repeat herself.

"Where are we?"

"I don't know, but we call it the condemned. We will die here. We don't have much time. The water will rise again."

"Water rising? What are you talking about? Why are you even here?"

"I failed and was captured. I failed and brought dishonor to the corps. Now I will die an inglorious death and not meet my warriors in the afterlife."

"What the fuck is going on?" he said, thinking the jailer had hit him much harder than he thought. He felt the water rising and rising quickly. He shouted out, "Hey!"

But the water rose too fast, and Sam got nothing in response.

There was silence again. Sam sat and listened, calling out every so often to see if he could hear her. He sat and sat, calling again and again, but there was no response from the other cell. He rested his head next to the water trough and listened to his own heartbeat, and even though his head pounded, he fell asleep. He was exhausted.

He woke up again and was pissed that his head was still hurting. He drank a couple mouthfuls of water and slowly sat up. He looked up at the single light in the room and slowly rose to his feet. It took him minutes to shake off the dizziness that was overwhelming him and finally stood straight for the first time in what seemed like hours.

He looked up at the light again and reached his hand out, standing on his tiptoes, but he didn't feel the light or the ceiling at all. His eyes adjusted, and he saw that the ceiling of the cell was three times his height. He paced the room and sat in silence, becoming mad, hopeless, angry, sad, and at times content that it was him and not his loved ones in the cell. He had run his hand over every part of the cell, including the shit trench. He took a deep breath and dived his arms into the elbow-deep muck. He lost it when his hand grabbed a fat turd called a ration shit. The dehydrated ration bar made bowel movements difficult.

His train of thought was broken again by a sound. It was the jailer coming back. Sam waited by the port, eagerly waiting for the jailer to approach the same as before. The jailer shuffled closer and eventually slid open Sam's port and threw in the ration bar and the pan of mush along with it. This time Sam was ready and snatched both as they came through. He set the pan on the floor and attacked the ration bar. He gnawed and ground, taking small chunks at a time. He ate so intensely he was only broken from his food rage when he heard the jailer returning, calling for his pans back. His hair stood on his arms, and sheer panic set in. He began frantically searching for his pan with his hands, only to swipe the thing across the cell. He hurriedly rushed over, trying to find it, as his port opened.

"Pan."

"I'm getting it!" Sam said, his voice breaking at the thought of another beating.

The port closed, and the door swung open. The jailer took a couple of steps to get to Sam and beat him again with his club, picked up the pan, and left the cell, securing it behind him. Grinning while leaving the cell, he left Sam unconscious again, satisfied with his work. He loved his job. He began his shuffle back to where he came.

* * *

Sam came to again and was in such a daze and disorientation that it took him a considerable time to figure out where he was. He sat up once again, slowly, and groaned loudly as he sat up. Leaning on one elbow, he used his other hand to reach up and feel his damaged head. There were three large wounds that had formed into one, and dry blood had caked over it all. His head pounding, he dragged himself over to the water trench and carefully tried to rinse his head. He winced loudly as he cupped his hand and tried to wash his wounds with the dirty water. It stung badly, and he half wondered if it was a good idea to wash it with the disgusting water, but he thought otherwise because it would probably get infected anyway.

He cupped his hand and took a couple mouthfuls of water, not to overdo it, and slowly rose to his hands and knees. His head was still pounding, and after coming up to his knees, he became overwhelmed with dizziness and lay back down. Rolling over on his back, he felt something cold and slimy. He felt down his pants and was surprised to find that he pissed and shit himself while he was out. Sam let out a long sigh, and he once again rolled over and belly-crawled to the end of the water trench.

Once there, he removed his clothes and rinsed himself the best that he could. It took him a considerable amount of time because of his injury, and he had nothing better to do. Getting close to finishing, he saw in the dim light that the water level was beginning to drop in the trench again, and he was filled with so much excitement that he crawled to the opposite side of the trench bottomless. Anything for a chance at human contact.

"Hello, marine lady. You there?"

"Yes, I'm here."

"You do not know how good it is to hear another voice."

"I thought you were dead. You have been out a very long time. The jailer came and went. He came in your cell again, and lucky you were still out."

"How long have we been here?"

"I can't tell. There's nothing to track time. The only thing that changes is the level of water in the trench."

"So many questions," Sam pondered, leaning on his elbows next to the opening in the trench. "What happened?"

"We were captured."

"No shit. I don't remember much. Only fragments."

"You were drugged and paraded throughout the city. Then we were put here. We are deep underground."

"What are they going to do with us?"

"I don't know."

"I'm sure nothing good. Well, what now? How the fuck do we get out of here?"

"What do you mean 'we'?"

"I'm assuming you don't want to stay here. *We* need to get out of here."

"There is no escaping. We are dishonored, and the only escape is death."

Sam dropped his head in thought. No escape. Only death. No chance to see his friends and Selena ever again. He would not accept that.

"I refuse to believe that. There is always a chance. I won't give up until they kill me, and I'll fight them every chance I can get."

"You will not succeed. Better to accept your fate and try not to die a coward. 'For you will not join your comrades ever in the afterlife.'"

Sam again paused to register where the conversation was leading. It was a hopeless situation. Where was he going to go, and how could he possibly escape? His head was still pounding, and he winced again, rubbing his hand over his wound. Was death his only option?

Maybe I should just end it and not give the fucks the satisfaction. No, that is the coward's way out. Never give up. Never give in. There is always a chance.

He started running scenarios in his head. The only time the door opened was when he got beaten, and that was something he did not want to repeat. Then his eyes widened.

"Hey! It's easy, we just attack the jailer when he opens the door. A killer marine could easily overpower that fat shit."

"I don't want to. The only course for me is death. I can never regain my honor."

"Fuck your honor! Who said you can't do that? You can do whatever you want. Right now, you can decide!"

"You don't understand. In the eyes of the heavens, I am already dead. It matters not."

"But you are not dead here on this shithole of a planet. Let's get out of here, and I'll show you something great. There's nothing in the universe better than freedom. Let's get the fuck out of here, and then you can do whatever you like. Go find someone to kill, or whatever you do, or die in a battle somewhere. Come fight with us. You are sure to die then."

There was silence in both the cells. And Sam, filled with anticipation, could only hear his heart pounding with adrenaline alone with his heavy breathing.

"You dishonor me even more by thinking I would join the ranks with you."

"That's what you are concerned about? Wake up, lady! You're in a fucking prison! Snap out of it!"

Only silence was returned.

"So you're not going to talk to me now?" Sam looked up at the ceiling and the single dull light hanging. "Gods, why the fuck did you put me next to this piece-of-shit human being? Fuck!"

Sam violently kicked out and screamed at nothing. "Seriously, nothing?"

Only silence was returned.

"Fine, fuck it, I'll do it myself. A fucking coward is someone who just sits here and waits to die by the way. Fuck off."

He sat up quickly and was again reminded that his head was badly bashed in. He took his time but managed to get to his feet.

"Okay," he said to himself out loud. "If that's the way it's gonna be, then okay, fuckers."

His head became flooded with options and possibilities. He was excited. Something positive. Something to plan and execute. First, he needed to heal. He couldn't pick a fight as badly as he was hurt. He needed to rest, eat, and keep his mind and body as sharp as he could. His adrenaline was wearing off after his conversation with the marine, and he again felt his throbbing head. He decided rest was the first thing he was going to do, and he slowly lowered himself down to the cold cell floor again and fell asleep.

He continued to recuperate for what seemed an eternity. In the time between eating and sleeping, he put his mind to other tasks. He figured that it would take many weeks for his head to heal, and that was going to be his base for timekeeping. It was no exact science, but what else was he going to do? He also monitored the water trench constantly waiting for the level to dip, both to have a chance to talk and find out how often it did actually dip. To his surprise, it happened frequently, so he began to make marks on the cell floor with his nail. Time after time, he made his mark.

He called to his cellmate every time as well with no response in return. He talked anyway, because why not. It felt good to just talk and know someone was listening. He talked about everything and anything, from the decent to the not so decent. Mostly, he talked about Selena. How they met when Sam was a young and up-and-coming pirate and Selena was a struggling business owner. How they fell in love. What their dreams were. How much he missed her. What he would give to bury himself in her embrace. He talked about what he thought was happening back home. He hoped they were fighting and had not given in. He knew his friends would never, but as for the rest of the planet, he had no idea. His mind was working overtime making his plans, and his body couldn't keep up. He got nauseous, and his feet wobbled. Everything got dizzy, and he was out. Too much too fast.

He tried to squeeze himself through the water trench to get to the other cell but foolishly only got one leg through because it was so small. When the water fell, it exposed the slightest opening between the cells, and Sam was desperate to see anyone, even if the marine killed him. He even tried crawling upstream in the shit trench with the same result as before. The trench overflowed most of the time anyway. He kept marking and talking until his head, or so he thought, was completely healed.

He guessed three to four weeks to recover and counted up the marks he put in the floor and did the quick math. Twenty-five marks in total in about three to four weeks, and he concluded that the water fell once a day. That was what he was going to track anyway. At least it would give him something to do. He decided he'd give it another couple weeks to heal, and then he would make his move. He had no idea what to expect, so one battle at a time, as his sister always said. He would overpower the guard and figure it out from there.

He made a couple more marks on his wall and even tried to track when the jailer made his rounds, but it was useless. He lay in his cell, letting his mind wander, when he heard the unmistakable sound of the door opening from a distance. He sat up and waited for the shuffling but was intrigued to hear sounds of multiple footsteps this time and definitely no shuffling.

The footsteps got closer and louder, eventually stopping at Sam's door. The lock disengaged, and Sam stood quickly and braced to confront the jailer. The door swung open, and Sam was blinded by an extremely bright light directed at him. There was some sound of something electronic, which was quickly charging, and then Sam was hit with the most extreme pain that he had ever felt. His body went rigid. He tried to cry out, but even the muscles in his jaw were constricted by the shock. He fell backward, landing squarely in the shit trench, splashing the filth in all directions. The pain had died down slightly, but his body was still rigid, and he saw a figure walk in from the front of the blinding light.

"So this is the great Samuel Cleber. I'd never come down here to this level, but I think I could stomach the filth just so I get to see you wither and die." He paused for a moment. "No, no, no, Mr. Cleber. Did you think it was going to be easy? No, no, you are going to be a spectacle for the whole universe to see. We have a special place for the condemned, and you are going to fit in nicely. To tell you the truth, I like seeing people squirm. You have no idea how much pleasure you will be to me." He turned to someone next to him. "Get him ready. We have to make the show." Turning back to Sam, he said, "I'm betting they'll turn up in droves to see this one."

The stun was starting to wear off, and Sam was dragged from his cell up the stairs to the door, and for the first time in a long time, he saw something different. It was dim, but it led to a single room that had a massive set of doors on the back of the wall. The giant metal doors opened and revealed a platform. They dropped Sam on it and keyed in something, waving their hand over a control station.

The lift started to rise, slowly at first then more rapidly. It completed its ascent, finally coming to a stop and leading to a long corridor. It was made of some sort of see-through material; at least the ceiling and part of the walls were.

As Sam walked, now having regained his motor functions, he looked out at the sides of the see-through corridor and saw nothing but cells. Row and row and level after level of cells. In some he saw people rise to look at him as he walked. He had an entourage of four—what looked to be serious guards and the guy who had spoken to him earlier. He was not in the guards apparel but wore some sort of dress clothes that Sam had never seen before.

At the end of the corridor, they walked down more hallways past checkpoints and eventually came to another lift.

The man that had spoken to him turned quickly and said, "Have fun."

He continued his walk, and the guards placed him on the lift standing alone as they trained their weapons on him. The lift he was standing on began to rise slowly. The ceiling opened up, revealing a very bright light and the noise like Sam had never heard before. He shielded his eyes as he rose.

"And now, people of the Interplanetary Empire, the president and First Panel are honored to bring you the pirate, thief, and murderer, Samuel Cleber!"

Sam's look of utter shock was displayed on the largest screens he had ever seen. The noise that he hadn't heard before was the roar of a crowd, turning to rage and insults directed his way. He had never seen so many people in one place. It was extremely overwhelming, and Sam began frantically turning around, wondering where he was and what was going to happen.

The lift came to a stop and sealed the floor around him as he looked on the thousands of people gathered in an arena. His dumbfounded face was all over every screen.

"Now, before we proceed to the execution of the month, my fine people of Earth. The president thought best that this barbaric piece of human filth should first be made to suffer many punishing rounds before he is granted death."

The crowd became louder, and Sam heard many shout, "Kill him. Kill the monster."

"I hear you, but this one does not deserve a quick death. We will show him and the people of Mars how fearsome our own are. My fine people, you deserve a show and a night of celebration for your dedication to our empire. The streets will flow with liquor and all the stim you can handle, but first we need this arena to flow with the blood of our enemies. My people of the empire, I give you the Tango Squad!"

A door opened across the way from Sam in the circular arena, and he half braced himself for what was to come. The crowd roared, and the screens focused on the person walking in.

"The commander of Tango Squad drew the honor of first blood! Let the fight commence!"

Again, the crowd roared in approval.

The person walked toward Sam, and the closer he got, Sam became more and more confused. The person was a child compared to Sam. He must have been a teenager, but he was still as tall as Sam and in perfect physical shape. He looked at Sam in disgust and turned in all directions, giving the crowd a solute. He then focused on Sam with rage in his eyes.

He was so quick Sam had no time to react. The young man struck Sam square in the nose, and it exploded, spraying blood. The crowd leaped to its feet in approval. Sam was not knocked unconscious, but he was greatly dazed by the strike. When he regained his focus, he realized he was on his back, blood gushing from his nose. He was violently grabbed and pulled up from the gravel, but before he could fully stand, he was struck in the liver, and he again dropped him to the ground.

Bloody and in pain, Sam's anger finally kicked in. He grabbed a handful of the gravel covering the arena and flung it at his opponent. He followed up, trying to land a strike of his own. It was no use. It was like a child fighting, and Sam was that child. He harmlessly swung his fist, praying to land a blow. His opponent dodged everything with ease, toying with Sam.

The crowd roared in approval, and the commander of Tango Squad landed another devastating blow on Sam's leg, which dropped him to the gravel again. He was holding his leg, panting heavily, when he was brought to his feet by the commander. Sam tried to swing again but was hit by so many blows to his face that he was unconscious before he hit the gravel. The crowd voiced their approval, and the commander of Tango once again saluted the crowd. Then without any more emotion, he exited the arena toward where he had come from.

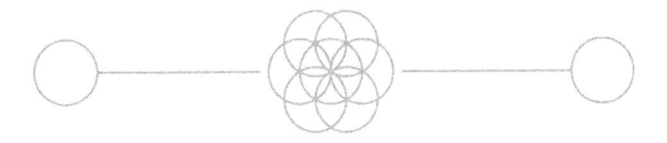

Chapter 11

Our Change

Far from Earth, the people of Mars watched the planetwide broadcast of the event. It had lasted only seconds, and most were saddened to see one of their own punished so brutally. The rest were angered to the point that they decided now was the time to fight back. If they would do that to Sam, then what would happen if they took control of Mars? The empire got a reaction, but it was not the one they had hoped for. Instead of breaking them, it only made them more resolved and unified, except for one.

One person was truly heartbroken upon watching her loved bear so much punishment. She reached out with everything she had to speak to him so far away.

I can't go on without you. Come back to me. I need you to come back to me. I can't make it without you.

* * *

Sam was unconscious for the entire return trip back to his cell and only started to regain his awareness shortly before entering. He was thrown in and rolled all the way to the rear of the cell directly into the shit trench. He rolled out as best as he could and belly-crawled once again to the dirty water to wash his wounds and grab mouthfuls of water.

He needed to stop this trend of getting beat so badly, or he would not last long. The child, if you could call him that, was so fast and hit harder than Sam had ever been hit in his lifetime. He remembered that the marines had been trained from birth and were molded heavily. He rolled over, lying on his back, and winced loudly, feeling the spot where he was kicked in his side. He was overcome with emotion, and tears started to form from his eyes. He cried in silence for a while then stopped because it did no good.

"What the fuck just happened?" he said to himself, looking at the dim light.

He reached up to feel his damaged face and winced again as he lightly touched his swollen and tender face. He figured his eye had completely swollen up, and he was still tasting blood in his mouth. He rolled over again and grabbed a few mouthfuls of water. He slurped the water cupped in one hand and afterward laid his damaged face on the cold ground. At least he had some relief doing that.

"Who did you face in the arena?"

"What?" Sam asked, lifting his head. "Is that you?"

"Yes."

"She speaks. Now you wanna talk to me."

"Who was it?"

"How the fuck should I know? Some kid named Tango or whatnot."

"Each squad is labeled this way. He was Tango One, the commander of the squad. They are young. Just finished training. They use criminals. Sometimes we beat, sometimes we kill. Eventually, you will die."

"Anything to get rid of this fucking headache?"

"You will be dishonored to die as a mere criminal. At least you get to die in battle as it should be."

"I don't need your shit right now, with your honor or whatever bullshit. Leave me alone, and sit there and die like the piece of shit you are. In case you don't understand, I'll say it different, GO FUCK YOURSELF."

* * *

In the other cell, the commander of Charlie sat up, visibly shaken by Sam's dismissal. She had been around her squad her entire life. She had never been alone for so long, and she didn't realize it herself, but she needed human contact, and Sam was it for now. She continually varied from wanting to kill Sam for the traitor he was, but then again, after hearing him talk of his life, she half wanted it. After going silent, she wanted him to continue his talks.

She was curious. She knew that Tango was a brand-new squad, replacing the Tango squad before it. She knew the old Tango. They were the top squad when she was assigned to Charlie, but like all marine squads, they eventually died until there were no more or only one survivor left standing. She was the last surviving member of Charlie. It should have been her responsibility to return and instruct the next wave of marines. Eventually, she would train the next Charlie Squad to replace her. That was the destiny she had been promised her whole life: fight and eventually be granted death to join the ranks in the afterlife.

Only the most honorable and fiercest of the marines survived to be the sole member a squad, and the highest-ranking one could achieve was instructor for the new generation. She remembered being taught it herself by the commander of Charlie she had replaced. He was fearless and supremely dedicated to the motto "semper fidelis." She wanted to be him and embody the fierceness of the corps. When she and the rest of her remaining squadmates reached adulthood, she was selected to be the new commander of Charlie.

The first task as commander of the new Charlie Squad was to send the former commander to the afterlife. There could only be one commander of Charlie. Normally, marine squads went through many commanders do to battles both external and internal. Anyone could challenge a sitting commander, and there could be only one left standing. She had retained her commander status her entire career until it was her and only three members left. They had all become hard killers over the years, exploiting weaknesses, forming intersquad alliances, doing battles because that was what they were raised to do.

Their missions, which were all but not limited to striking criminal hideouts or putting down the latest rebellion, were child's play compared to the intersquad single combats. Once per cycle, any squad member was allowed to partake in one challenge. Squad members rarely spoke to each other, but the longer the squad lasted, the more it started to overcome the internal fighting. All the hothead members had long since been dispatched, and that was why Charlie was considered the finest squad in the corps.

They had all learned to accept their status and fight external enemies. Still, they rarely spoke unless they had to, but they never left each other's side. They ate, slept, and shit all together. Now she was alone for the first time in her life. She would never admit it or show it, but internally, she was broken. She had never asked anyone for anything, but this time she needed something only someone else could provide.

"I don't know if this is the right word, but I'm sorry."

Sam's face made a frown. "What . . . ah . . . what was that again?"

"I'm sorry for you. For Selena."

Sam's frown disappeared and was replaced by tears. He didn't respond right away. He needed a few seconds to compose himself. They both needed a little compassion at the present.

"Thank you, Commander."

They both sat in their adjacent cells, joined by a sewage and now-lowered water trench, unsure of what to say next. Sam looked down in the brown liquid, which he could not see in the dim light.

"Is your water as disgusting as mine is?"

"The water rolls downhill, and we are the last cells in line. No doubt it is contaminated from the cells next to us."

"By the gods." Sam almost became nauseated at the thought of what was trickling down. "And I'm guessing it's the same for shit trench."

"Yes, that is so."

"Great conditions we have here, no?"

"I have been in worse."

"I imagine you have." Sam paused again, readjusting his broken body for comfort. "Why don't you tell me about one."

"Me tell you?"

"What else do we have to do?"

She turned the thought over in her head, still hesitant to expose herself and speak of a sensitive mission, but in the end, she was as condemned as much as anyone could be, along with Sam, so she figured there was no harm in it.

"We had to sit in a garbage collection for many days waiting in ambush positions. The waste of the commoners was all around us."

"No armor?"

"Too many days. You know this."

"That's right. I haven't been in armor for more than half a day tops. Did you get you target waiting there?"

"Until you, I have always finished a mission."

"Sorry about that, but I didn't know you back then, and I didn't want to die."

"It would have been a good death. You should have let me die."

"Ah, come on now, I thought we were past all this. How about we strike a deal? I'll talk about whatever you want, and in return, no more honor and death shit. You can still think it." Sam reached out to try to calm her. He knew he had to talk to her like she was a skittish child. "But let's not talk about that, okay?"

"Until next time, Samuel Cleber. The water rises."

* * *

The water rose and fell every day, and every day the two talked to each other every moment. The topic varied greatly, with Sam mostly interested with life on Earth and the commander of Charlie asking about Mars.

One particular day, Sam started the conversation with, "You know, I was thinking, I don't like calling you Commander. What's your, I don't know, real name?"

"I was never given one. When a squad is formed, we are all assigned numbers except for number 1. That was left for . . ."

"The commander," Sam interrupted.

"Yes, the commander. We are renumbered once in childhood, once in adolescence, and final numbers are assigned upon entering adulthood and mission readiness. As I told you, I was assigned number 1, or Charlie One."

"Is there a name you would like?"

"I have never thought on this. I do not know how to do it."

"Well, easy, just Charlie. I'll call you just plain Charlie from now on. You are the only one left of Charlie Squad, right?"

"There will be a new Charlie Squad formed, and then this will not make sense."

"Gods! Okay, just trust me. You are Charlie now, and just fucking say okay without arguing about every gods damn thing."

"I accept this name. I shall honor it."

"Okay then, Charlie, anything you want to talk about today? I feel sometimes you are just gathering intel on me for when you think they will release you."

"I am going to die here. We have been over this."

Sam exhaled, getting frustrated. She couldn't help it. It's how she had lived her whole life, but even someone as patient as Sam couldn't contain it forever.

"I know," was all Sam could say, clenching his teeth. He took another deep breath. "How about something other than Mars's military capabilities, terrain, manufacturing, blah, blah, blah? That shit is getting repetitive and boring."

The commander of Charlie—now just Charlie—was lying on her stomach with elbows up, just as Sam was.

"Tell me about love. Like you and your Selena have. I have never been instructed what it is."

"That's funny, 'instructed on love.'" Sam had to chuckle at that, refreshed by the new topic. "Well, nobody gets instructed on love. It just happens." Sam paused, breathing deeply. "There's only one way to understand. If you love something, you're willing to die for it. That's how a warrior loves. Fuck himself, fuck his possessions, everything he has. The one thing you can't live without and you're willing to die for. That's love to me, Madam Commander. And I've had about enough of this fucking shit," Sam said, getting fired up as he continued, pounding his fist together on the dank cell floor.

"I'm deciding right here and right fucking now. No more passive boo-fucking-hoo. I'm gonna fight my way out of this place to get back to the person I love or die trying. Sit in here and rot thinking about love, or fight with me to go find it out there." Sam was panting. His adrenaline had spiked, and he was now ready and his mind made up at the slightest mention of Selena.

He owed it to her and his friends to not go down like a criminal but a man. It was time to fight. There was no answer as usual, so Sam gave Charlie time to process everything.

"You are not a good enough fighter to escape."

"So fucking teach me as best as you can in a fucking cell."

Another long pause.

"I will teach you as best as I can until our cells are joined."

"Our fucking cells are joined? Are you losing it?"

"No, Sam. There is a weak point in the stone from when the trench was drilled, and it made a large crack. I started working away at it to join our cells when we first entered," Charlie paused. "I wanted to kill you myself, I must admit."

"You turd piece of shit," Sam said, grinning ear to ear.

* * *

It had been months since the invasion. The city had calmed down for the most part, settling in to the new way of things. The patrols had started almost immediately, and most of the people of the city of Jazeera came to terms with the new way of things. Life had to go on.

It wasn't that they accepted the new occupants to the city; it was all about survival. When a patrol came through the city, all the citizens dived more or less into their dwellings, giving the patrols a wide berth. The soldiers of the UNE were very harsh on the people of Jazeera. They came in, tore people's houses apart, separated families, beat the men, terrorized the women, and stole food, valuables, and whatever else they could get their hands on. But the people of Jazeera had to take it.

After securing the city, UNE soldiers did a house to house sweep, confiscated all weapons, and took anything and everything they possibly could get their hands on. They wanted to subjugate the people, and this was the uneasy understanding that had set in place inside the city.

Outside the city was a different story, the UNE patrols constantly clashed with the pirates now turning into legitimate soldiers. They did not directly attack the city, but they definitely disrupted trade and business to the point that the city was starting to struggle economically.

As bad as it was for the people of Mars, it was fantastic for Mia. The pirates were focused on UNE forces on the ground but continued their pirate raids out in space for goods, and those goods were now in high demand in Jazeera. Mia felt terrible charging what she did, but she could not give it away; she had her own expenses.

The bar was completely different. Instead of being the main hangout of the pirate crews, it was now solely frequented by UNE forces only. Mia had to stomach every day the street stories of the UNE soldiers. They hated the Martian people and yearned for home. Even the blue skies and clear air were not valued by them. They had grown so accustomed to the city lights and smog that most felt extremely uncomfortable in the new environment. What was worse for them was that they believed they were in an uncivilized world. The Martian people did not have the technology that those on Earth did; it was simpler and more personal. It's just how they chose to live.

But young Mia was different. She had started to notice that she enjoyed the Martian way of life. Among the pirates, it was refreshing to her to at least pretend what it was like to be free. Back on Earth, she was free to do as she wanted, but she had to work hard to keep it that way, always monitored, always keeping your head down. That was not freedom to her. Her UNE contacts almost immediately tried pressing her for more information. Mia advised them to bide their time and wait.

Dre and John, along with the other leading members of the pirates, were starting to exact their toll on the UNE forces, and the pressure increased even more. Mia finally decided to leak the info of where John and Dre were planning a massive strike against a forward operating base. It should have worked. UNE forces laid an ambush for the pirate rebels, and luckily for them,

John had sniffed out the ambush. Together they fought their way out of the trap and saved most of their forces. It had been a major error because now the rebels knew they had a leak, and it wouldn't take them long to figure out who it was. After all, Mia was the only person to have contact with the two sides.

But it wasn't just a random contact she was getting her information from. She had direct contact with the leadership. Not every soldier was privy to mission information, so that meant there was a very small group who could have done it. The pirates knew how to hide from the UNE. All important information was passed person to person, and no mission-critical traffic was broadcast. Everything went to low technology, except the weaponry, of course.

Now Mia had a decision to make. Her life was in jeopardy, and she could come clean. The glaring issue with this would be that the pirates more than likely would execute her. She knew Dre. He would never forgive something like this, especially after he gave his heart to her. Or so she thought. She had grown fond of Dre during their time together. He was such an interesting person to her. Back home, among his friends, he was the life of the group, always happy, just happy to be around people who cared for him.

But when it came to battle, Dre had no equal. He made a name for himself for being fearless in battle when he first signed up for one of the pirate crews with his new buddy, Sam. The *Validus* earned its reputation as being the best, and Dre always wanted to be among the best. It had happened over a long period of time, but the crew became a family, each caring and looking out for one another. In a world of thieves, loyalty and commitment did not always win, but in the crew of the *Val*, it did.

Loyalty turned to love, and love made the family. That's what Mia had betrayed. That's why Mia was sure Dre wouldn't hesitate. She had no idea if he knew for sure, but she would continue on as normal and under no circumstances give away anything to the UNE. A smart person would try to bait and give false information, but Mia was going to take the initiative and make the first move. She threw on her jacket and braced herself for the cold that was to come.

On top of everything else, one of the worst winters since the colonization of Mars had set in. Included with all the other things that had ground to a halt on the planet was the terraforming process. Many claimed that's why the weather was the way it was, but Mia didn't care about any of that. She was on a mission now, and she was hyperfocused on her present task.

She pushed open the door and was met with the extreme cold. It was nowhere near a catastrophic, total loss winter; but it froze everything—including armor, weapons, and transports. Fighting had ground to a halt, and each side was planning their next moves. When the UNE decided to continue patrols, Mia was going to leak something useful to Dre. Hopefully, that would at least buy her some time.

She made her way through the streets, trying not to slip on the random sheets of ice and additionally scanning everything she could to see if anything was out of place. The latter was not difficult because, literally, no one was outside at the moment.

She weaved from street to street, backtracking when possible, still making sure no one followed her. The wind would sweep her tracks, but she always erred on the side of caution. That's why she had survived so long in this trade after all.

She eventually came to her destination and simply closed an outside shutter to a simple view port in a dwelling. One side was white when opened, and when closed, it was a worn red. The worn red signaled a meeting as near as the tunnels as Dre could manage. The UNE had found and closed most of the tunnels next to the city, but there were always a few smaller ones that they would never find.

She did not linger and started her walk back to the bar. It wasn't unusual for her to be walking about. She always did deals around the city, and for now, the UNE didn't mind her dealings as long as they got their very large piece of the cake. She had to practice her character on the walk back. Questioning, worried, concerned. She would say that she had heard about the attack and was worried about them. Acting frantic, she would say she'd look into how they found out. Then afterward, she would say she had a piece of information, and hopefully, it would work.

* * *

All the members of the crew had settled into their respected potions. Dre, John, and Selena had taken up the leadership roles, and the three of them and the rest of the crew looked to each other for counsel and orders.

Selena was the coordinator. She ran the base camp and oversaw all forward bases and outposts. The UNE had pretty much given up on a sector of the planet, and it was there that the crews had made their main bases. Here they could rotate out of the fighting and get a few hours of worry-free rest. The crews were each captained, by way of vote, by one of their own.

Even Francisco had been voted in as a captain, and the crew called him Frankie boy. He wanted to show Vivianna that he was out there and he was coming to get her. It gave him an incredible drive and a certain fearlessness in his pursuit of his family. The palace counselor was gone at the moment, and the battle-hardened Frankie boy was shining brightly. He walked into the command center, fresh from patrol, the cold still reddening his face, which was full of whiskers. The pirate crews were living very roughly this winter. Supplies had been stocked, but it was never enough, and razors were nowhere to be found. The best people could do was take a blade to it when it got too long.

"It's way too cold for operations. We didn't get far when our armors started to act up. I had two down, and I called it. I'm very confident that they are down as well."

"We should take advantage of it. My crew is up for patrol next, so they are rested. We'll help with camp duties," John said, lending on the battle map table. He moved his crew of thirty to camp duties on the board and contacted his number 2. "Aya, patrol is canceled due to weather. I want the crew helping with camp duties. Report to Selena in the armory. I think we need to get some more armor operational."

"Copy that. I'm on it."

John turned to Dre, who had his feet up on a makeshift table they had constructed for a ragtag command center. Even with all the activity, the command center was dwarfed by the size of the cave it was in. They were deep underground where it was warmer. Dre had his eyes closed and was nodding his head in the customary fashion when someone was falling asleep. He had put some serious hours into the after-action ambush a few days ago. He was personally engaged as usual, coordinating the withdrawal, and even though he wouldn't admit it, it was a hard fight. He got back, and his armor was in such a state of disrepair that it was scraped for parts. He was worn out, but no one judged him or cared that he fell asleep. They all did it. Sleep when you could.

They had good intel on a forward operating base provided by Serg and Tucker and figured with it isolated, they could strike and destroy it. There was a four-hundred-man garrison, and Dre, John, and nine other captains linked up for a combined force. There main column of advance comprised of unarmored troops with mixed weapons and the armor element. They were on schedule, and things were looking good until the lead elements started frantically calling in contact. The sounds of battle were heard ahead of them. The captains ordered their forces into hastened defensive positions, forming a tight formation, and waited for an update. Dre was on his comms and lost contact with the forward elements. The Martians waited for the oncoming fight.

"I think we're in for one, boys! Look sharp, and pick your targets!"

Everyone found cover, and a few eager ones bounced high in their suits. They kicked in their thrusters, trying to look at the enemy coming, and they were swatted from the sky.

They heard the thuds of the bouncing armors approaching them, sounding like thunder coming from the distance. The general rule for the captains was that you needed to outnumber the marines by three to one to have a chance of victory. He saw immediately that they simply did not have the numbers as General Barada came over the ridge. He signaled the attack on the confused pirates and joined the charge. The Marines rushed the unarmored pirates and tore them to pieces before the rebel armors could concentrate to fight back. The unarmored troops stood little chance as well. By the time Dre and John gathered enough armor to fight back, almost a third of the force was gone. Dre and John, with the other armored fighters, drew a line and stood their ground.

"That's Barada," Dre said, pointing him out. "That fucker is mine!"

The fight was intense, getting hand-to-hand in some areas, and the crews suffered heavily. Barada was in his red armor, cutting a patch through the pirates. Dre came crashing down and charged at the general.

"Come to me, peasant! It's about time I get my hands on you."

Dre didn't say a word and fired his thrusters at full to meet the general. The general fired his as well, and the two met in midair. Barada had got the upper hand to fire a round at Dre, causing his armor to glow red, and his alarms started ringing.

"Come on! Let's see what you got!" Dre fired at him again, landing a glancing blow, and the general ripped a piece of Dre's armor off. He scrambled to his feet, firing at the general, who was now taking cover and picking off the random pirate in his view.

"Come on out and face me!"

"Dre! Dre, we are getting hammered. We have to pull back, or we are finished. Dre!" John was bouncing down the line, fighting where he was needed and giving support to his crew. He saw Dre go flying in front of him and saw Barada fighting off more pirates.

"Dre! I'm almost on you. Do you copy? Dre!"

Dre's armor was ringing loudly and was literally falling off him. He surveyed the battle and knew it was over.

"Pull them out, John! I'll hold them!"

"We can't lose you," John said, landing near him. "Come on, Dre! Follow me out! Dre, come on!"

Dre looked over at the general, who threw a defeated opponent to the ground. The general saw Dre falling back and stood tall. He won the engagement, and the general signaled to his marines to press the attack.

When most of the force was clear, one captain remained in place while Dre, John, and the rest pulled back. They were certain that they did not survive, but even after returning in his ragged state, he suited back up again and headed out with Serg and Tucker. They were looking for survivors. They found none, and Serg and Tucker bounced to follow the marines back to their base to observe and for a possible counterstrike. Dre got back and dived into the intel of the operation, trying to find what he had missed or how he had made such an error. He couldn't find one, and it stirred in his head, causing him to lose a lot of sleep. He fell asleep in the command center due to pure exhaustion.

"Dre," John said gently from across the room. "We are shutting down all operations for the day. Go get some rest."

"No, I'm good," Dre said, lazily wrapping his arms together to fight the cold.

John quickly dismissed him and turned to Helena, who had assumed the role of coordinating the space raiding. She had six operation crews hitting where and what they could in the mess of it all. She was keeping the crews fed and supplied for the most part, but sooner or later, that would end. Neither side had any dedicated warships, and the crews were betting that some were being built with the outbreak of the war. But so far, the crews were taking their toll. She had four crews constantly patrolling the lanes of approach and forced UNE transports to use the longer, less comfortable approaches.

All in all, it was a stalemate. Neither side had the advantage in resources or manpower to finish the war, but the pirates knew more were on the way. The UNE got stung both on the ground and on their pride. They thought they could simply walk in and assume command, and they were proven very wrong, very quickly. Mia had provided plenty of intel on numbers, equipment, and overall status of the UNE on the planet. All that proved to the pirates that they were holding their own and, in doing so, boosted their pride and moral. Both sides suffered losses, but for the pirates, each loss was much heavier.

Most people fighting had known each other for years, decades even. Some crews had multiple family and friends fighting together, and if their crew was in heavy action, sometimes whole families would cease to exist. That was the nature of the war they were fighting. Freedom to some was worth it all. There had been many people over the course of human history who had wanted their freedom, and the pirates were no different. Live your life, and I'd live mine. But it was human nature to want to take what others had. They believed incorrectly that they built it, and now the UNE wanted to take it, and they were fighting to defend it. It was a noble cause at a terrible price, and it hardened everyone involved.

"Look alive, people," Ameera barked, bursting in. "Mia signaled a meet. Must be important to risk a face-to-face."

Dre instantly woke and hopped to his feet. "I'm goin.'"

"Take Tucker and Serg with you, just in case," John said, not looking up from the map display projecting from the center of operations base.

"I'll be fine by myself. I'd prefer to be alone, and you know why."

"All right," John said, looking up from the map. "Be careful. We'd fall apart without you."

"I'm just a fucking grunt," Dre said chuckling. "Everyone is replaceable. Even me, but yes, Mommy, I'll be fine."

"You know why I'm cautious."

"Let me find out. She'd know something was up if I didn't show up alone. Let me get the proof that it wasn't her. You're wrong about her."

"Maybe, maybe not. I'm not going to do a back and forth with you. We've been over it, just watch your six. I can't lose another brother."

Dre turned instantly and walked out of the massive cave, weaving around crates, weapon racks, and people sleeping, living, and eating out of makeshift tents or just out in the open. The people were suffering, but there were still individuals smiling from time to time. When people stopped smiling altogether was when it was bad.

Dre wasn't smiling as he walked out. His eyes had swelled with water. Forcing the tears back, he prayed for Sam wherever he was. It had been a year since he had been taken. Every once in a while, they brought him out and beat him savagely. Only Dre and a few others watched. John and Selena couldn't after the first one. They couldn't stand seeing him abused in such a way.

While Dre was walking out of the command center, he ran into Selena, who had her head buried in a display. Amazingly, she still looked good in all the chaos at least physically, but emotionally, she was completely different. She raised her head, almost running into Dre as he left. She could tell he was fighting back tears. She turned off the display, didn't say a word, and hugged him. Dre let it out, and Selena didn't mind at all. Next time it would be her crying into Dre's shoulder. They needed it.

Dre looked up with red eyes. "He won't give up. That we are sure of. If there is a way, he'll find it."

"That's why I'll never quit. Not until I get him back." It was Selena's turn to water up. She knew the chance of that happening was not likely. But she would never give in. She owed Sam that. Never give in to sorrow while there was hope.

Dre continued his walk through the caves to the underground transport system they had constructed. It was being built at a slow pace, but the main tunnels had had them in place for years that most of the population had forgotten about it. Dre got in one transport and gave it its destination. The auto raced off to the city of Jazeera.

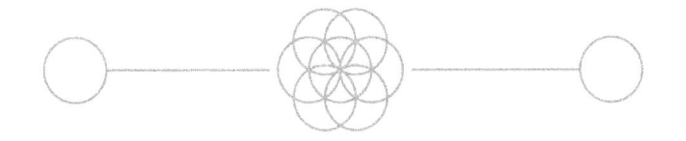

Chapter 12

Just Our Kind of Crack

The counselor had made another trip down to the dungeons to visit his prized prisoner again. He was frustrated. The peasant had put up a fight. It wasn't impressive, but he landed a blow against his opponent. It surprised everyone, including the peasant, and the marine roared in rage and beat him worse than he ever got before. Bloody and barely conscious, the guards threw him back in his cell and threw in his rations, which the counselor didn't want to guess what was in. He liked going there to see his former adversaries suffering. It drove him to collect more.

This time it was different, he thought to himself as he climbed his way out of the prison. *This time I saw life in his eyes. He never took his gaze off me. Does he think he can actually make it out of here? Stupid peasant. This time after he breaks, the empire will see for themselves that the great pirate lord is finished. Then he will be disposed of in spectacular fashion.*

The counselor's thoughts were dancing in his head as he climbed his way back to the government building. Everyone kept their distance from him and his marine guard. Each high-ranking member of the empire had their own marine squad, and it showed the counselor's status as he walked through the streets.

He liked walking among the sheep, and it showed them exactly who was governing them. He never wore outlandish clothing, opting to go for a simple look. It showed the people that he was humble like them. It was also very rare for the people of the empire to actually see someone of the panels. Most members stuck to the government districts, which were polar opposites of the commons.

The counselor got back to his inner cambers, followed by his staff.

"Status report!"

"Sir, the situation has not changed," the counselor's top military aid spoke, addressing the staff.

He pulled up his display and linked his to the room so they could see the data he had.

He continued, "The enemy has pushed us further off the lanes. By concentrating on our approach, the enemy has concentrated our defensive efforts along as well. In space, it's a stalemate. The enemy strikes where they can, and we counter. We send out recons in force, but the enemy is never sighted or hastily retreats. We follow, but like always, they dive into their caves, and we have learned not to follow. On the ground, sir, General Barada has not fared much better. He dealt the enemy a blow, but the enemy inflicted near as many casualties on us as well. With limited supplies and reinforcements, there is only so much he can do. Neither us nor the enemy has the capability to assault each other's strongholds. All action is limited to small engagements, and with the cold, nothing is happening, sir."

The high-ranking general switched off his screen.

"General Barada, with all the respect deserving of your seat, requests an updated timeline of his promised reinforcements."

"He's lucky his mother has a seat on the First Panel. Any other general would have been replaced by now. He's being outwitted by peasants!"

"Sir, they are more than peasants. Our analysis is that without the reinforcements, we simply cannot win due to supply issues."

The counselor stroked his freshly shaved chin, thinking about the possible outcomes, but quickly came to a decision.

"Have General Barada form defensive positions and hold out until our newly formed fleet and assault force arrive. Then before they know what is happening, we launch an all-out assault on their strongholds."

"Sir, I have an alternate strategy if it pleases you to hear."

"Yes, General. Share your thoughts openly. After all, your fate is surely linked to mine."

"I propose, sir, that we seal off sections of the cave system one at a time and clear them. Then we seal it after we leave. It will take time, but we will squeeze them until they are forced to meet us in the open. Then we outright defeat them, and it is over. They will have nowhere to run. Sir, I have something else to add, if I may?"

The counselor nodded his head in approval.

"This strategy will also buy you time with the First Panel who is becoming"—the general cleared his throat—"impatient. You have to convince them that this will take time, even years, to accomplish, but in the end, we will have total victory, sir. Time also gives you time to maneuver blame onto whom you desire."

"And what if I desire to serve the panel your head, General?"

"Like you said, sir, my fate is linked to yours."

The counselor sneered at the general. "A sound strategy, General, but don't be foolish enough to think I cannot depose you at a moment's notice."

The general gulped nervously but still held his chest high.

"Have the staff form a full workup, and try to run every scenario through simulation. If the panel contacts us, tell them we have a full strategy to present to them. I want this back in forty-eight hours. Get every staff member on it. Order General Barada to defensive positions, and inform him his reinforcements along with a new plan of attack is on the way. What of the asset?"

"Yes, sir. The asset gave us the latest intel on the enemy movements. I also have reports that the asset is playing both sides. She has a"—the general cleared his throat again—"love interest and is becoming attached."

"She has strayed before. She indulges herself. This is something I can understand, but very well, keep an eye on her."

* * *

Dre made his way through the cave systems wrapped in his civilian clothes that hadn't been touched much in the past year. He held his hands in his armpits and walked through the caves, watching his breath crystallize in the air. He thought of the madness in the world. At first, all he wanted was adventure, fame, excitement, but as soon as the war started, he quickly lost his appetite for it. All he wanted now was peace and happiness, and he never wanted to see war again. He met Mia as much as he could but not often enough. It had been months since they had a face-to-face meeting.

Dre picked up his pace. They made it a rule that pleasure came before business, and Dre was currently blessing the gods for that rule. He came to the entrance to the caves and approached through very clandestinely. He weaved through the junk transports, cargo containers, and whatever else was stored. Martians became conditioned to never throw anything away, so many sections of the city were public scrapyards. He was quicker than he should have been, but he was anxious to see her. He came to the meeting place that Mia had picked out and sat in silence for many moments, watching the night around him and listening.

After he was satisfied, he came to the door at the rear of the worn-out dwelling and knocked. Mia swung the door open and pulled Dre in.

She hugged him fiercely and cried out, "I heard about the attack. They were celebrating. I'm sorry, I just had to see you."

Dre hugged her back. "I'm still here, girl."

Mia hugged Dre, surprised that it was real emotion. She looked up at him, kissed him deeply, and said, "Pleasure first."

Mia had gotten Dre some first-class vape that Dre had not experienced in a long time. He eased back into their makeshift bed in the room of the dilapidated dwelling. He let the vape do its work. He inhaled deeply, taking the water-based vape into his system. It quickly put him at ease. He was fully aware of his senses and surroundings, but it took that ragged edge off. And after a year of constant fighting, he had a pronounced edge.

"Thank you so much for this. This just hits the fucking spot." He surveyed the room, still inhaling the vape to strengthen its effects. "This room, on the other hand, is shittier than where I live. Couldn't you find something better?"

"Funny you noticed after we just had at each other for almost an hour."

"You said pleasure, honey. I'm just following orders, and besides, I wasn't cold then. All we got is that shitty heater, and I'm getting cold here, all bare ass."

The room fell silent for a moment, and even still, after everything, it was still awkward in that silence. Both could feel it, but neither could say it or say why.

Mia broke it after a moment. "Can I get you anything?"

"There is one thing," Dre said, rolling onto his side to look at her. "Can you give me one hour and let me lie with you? Will you watch over me so I can let myself go? We don't have to say anything if you don't want. Can we just enjoy each other for one hour?"

"I can do that," Mia said smiling. She grabbed Dre and brought him close.

He lay down on her lap, really feeling the effects of the vape. He started to drift to sleep almost immediately and mumbled, "Gods, I love you," and closed his eyes.

* * *

He woke up startled and jumped at once, not knowing where he was. He moved into a defensive stance, kneeling on the bed, and noticed Mia lying there with a look of awe across her face.

She reached up. "It's okay, Dre. Dre, you're with me."

His widened eyes calmed down after he regained his composure. "I'm sorry, Mia. I didn't scare you, did I? I feel like a fool," he said, throwing his hands up.

"It's okay," she said, still breathing heavily. "I'm good. Here, let's sit over here. But first, you'll need to excuse me for a moment. You have been lying on me for several hours, and I've been unable to move."

Dre threw his clothes on and found the little bit of food that Mia could muster. He divided it into two and savagely dug into his meal of dehydrated bread and meat. Mia came out after a moment and joined Dre at the old, beat-up table.

"It will be hard to find these in a couple weeks. They have moved into the city center and brought in all supplies from the city. Jazeera will starve in months if nothing is done. And to add to the terrible news, they have a major strike force coming. I'm sorry, I wish I had something better."

"We'll spread the food out as best as we can. It's only a couple months of winter left. We can make it. The strike force is something else. I'll have to think on that one. Do you know the time frame?" Dre looked directly at her.

"No. When I hear something, I'll mark it. When will we see each other again?"

"I don't know, Mia. It's in the hands of the universe now, but until then, I will be anxiously waiting. If all this is true, then I expect we will be getting busier than we already are. We need something, Mia. Something to change it up. Dig for something significant."

"They just pulled back. What am I supposed to get now? I don't have any contacts in their headquarters, just the brothels and bars, honey. That's all I got. I'm not a fucking miracle worker. You were the assholes that put me there. You think I like being surrounded by those fucking people, do ya? You fucking asshole."

"Gods, Mia, fuck and then fight. Why are doing this again? There's no need for that shit."

"Okay, General Dre, savior of the planet."

"Mia, what are you doing?" Dre asked, shrugging.

Mia exhaled and finished dressing herself. "I'm done with this shit, Dre. I can't do it anymore. I'm living double lives, and I can't do it." Mia was being completely honest.

"If you want out, Mia, just say it, and you come with me now."

Mia put her hands on her hips and paced a moment. "No," she said, letting her body slump to the bed again. "We need me in there. I'll get anything I can, but I'm not a master spy. If there is someone better, show them to me."

"We need you to find out what is coming, Mia. I need you too." Dre paused, looking down at the bed. "I need you," he said and raised his head to meet hers. "I've never had anybody"—he paused again—"that I've wanted to open to more than you, but I'm terrified what you might find. I'm not saying anything other than you mean something to me now. It's hard letting people in because I've been burned before. Am I gonna get burned again?"

Mia's mouth had slightly opened while Dre spoke. Her eyes widened, and her look of bewilderment was very apparent to Dre, who started to immediately regret saying anything.

"Oh shit. Mia, I . . ."

"No, Dre, you caught me off guard, that's it. I never expected anything other than just some fun when we first met, but I've felt something too, and I'm like you," Mia said, slumping. "I have a hard time letting anyone in too. I literally don't have anyone other than you and the guys. I'm afraid of getting burned too, and I'm afraid I might do it to you because I'm a hot mess."

Dre pulled up a chair to sit across from her on the bed. "I can deal with anything, Mia. Just be honest is all I ask. We don't have to get into much tonight . . ."

"Tonight? You mean this morning." Mia pointed out the dwelling to the raising sun. She wiped her eyes.

"Listen, Mia," Dre reached out and grabbed her hands. "I'm ready if you are. No pressure."

"I can do that, but, Dre, there are things we need to talk about. Serious matters that could have serious consequences. I need time to process things."

"Process things." Did I just say that? What the fuck is going on? Go to him. No, don't. You've been here before. Don't!

"Okay, whenever you are ready." Dre laughed as he got up. "You ain't goin' anywhere anyway 'cause you hooked on Mongo now. Ha ha. Seriously, honey, come to me when you want with that, but I gotta get my head back in. The sun is coming up, and I need to move now."

"Get going then. I'm right behind you. I'll signal if I find anything. Be careful."

"You know me, honey," he said at the door. "I'm a soul of caution."

Mia just smirked at him as he threw his coat hat and gloves on.

"All right, see ya." He gave her a wink and out of the dwelling he went.

Dre shut the door, and Mia shuddered at the cold blast that had come in. She continued shaking, worried about her conversation with Dre. Alone with her thoughts, she stared at the small heating element glowing.

What will he do? What do I say? How am I going to say it? Why did I even open my mouth? Stupid girl. You can't afford to be stupid. You have to choose. You have to do it. Make a choice, Mia.

***

"I told you it would work, Samuel Cleber. A wedge will move anything."

"All right, I was wrong, Chuck."

"I wish you wouldn't call me that."

"I won't call ya that in front of anyone. It's just you and me. Am I supposed to do something over here?"

"Where is the crack forming on your side?"

"I don't know, half the length of my arm."

"Half a meter is not good. Can we fit through the hole we'll make?"

"It will be close. The more important question is, how are we going to move this thing?"

"I will not move it, Samuel. You will. You must push the stone through."

"Push it through? You want me to just push it through? This thing has to be massive. There's no way to push it."

"You have to do it. I cannot grab anything to help you. You must move it."

"Can I at least have the iron?"

Charlie grabbed the metal piece she had bent off her door when she first arrived. Her marine strength was still useful then. She initially intended to use it as a weapon to kill Sam, but now she used it to pound her wedges further. She used other pieces of stone as the wedges, and more broke than did not.

It was a long process, and Sam had four more fights in with the same result. In his last two fights, the marines were ready and did not give Sam time to breathe. They beat him savagely, but Sam had fought back and held his own.

She bent down and tied the metal to the rope system that they had made. Sam had unraveled his sleeves and used it to bring things back and forth. He had found some good stone in the shit trenches for wedges but needed the iron to get there, so the rope was made. He untied the iron and placed it against the wall.

"Well, I guess the only option is to put my back into it. There's nowhere to get the bar in."

Sam braced himself against the stone, got his feet under him, inhaled, and pushed with all his might. He exhaled and pushed more and more, but the stone did not move.

"Fucking piece of shit wall. Come on, Sam," he said, pumping himself up. "Push this fucker."

Sam pushed with all his might, and at the last second, when he was about to give up, the stone moved ever so slightly.

"Ha, fuck you, stone. I have an opening, Charlie. Hey, Charlie, I think we can do it."

"That's good, Sam."

"I'm going to pry a little. If we can get it to slide in the trench, it should be smooth from the water running and hopefully slide out."

He wiggled the metal into the opening to the desired length and put all his body weight into the metal, which bent heavily.

Sam felt it giving and wiggled the metal in a little more. This time when he put his weight on it, the large stone piece fell with a loud thud. Excitedly, Sam threw the metal down, letting it clank on the floor.

"Yeeeaa!"

"Samuel Cleber, that was too many decibels. Anyone in close proximity heard."

"As long as you call me Samuel, I'm going to call you Chuck, Chuck. And no one is down here."

Sam braced himself again and pushed again with all his might, and to his surprise, the stone moved much more easily than before. It was still taxing, but he knew he could do it. He pushed and pushed, moving his feet to a better position as he worked the stone out. The stone was in a wedge shape, and Sam had the narrow end.

As he pushed, it opened wider, until he could see light peering in. His head emerged into Charlie's cell as he ran out of room to push with his legs. It had become too narrow. He looked up, lying in the water trench with the water flowing around him, and saw for the first time in the year the marine commander he had remembered.

She was a shell of what she had been. Her hair had grown long and was matted down with yearlong dirt, slime, and blood. Sam looked closer and noticed a large wound scar at the back of her head.

"They cut it out," she said gesturing to her head.

"I can see that," he said, continuing his inspection of her. She was half of her weight, and her eyes were sunken in. She clearly needed food.

"They are trying to starve me to death. They give me enough just to survive." She could sense that she was eating away at herself, and Sam's look confirmed it.

"Shit, Charlie. We'll split our food. I can't make it out of here by myself, and you look like shit."

"I would very much like some food, Sam. I am very weak."

"Do you think you can roll that over so I can make it through?"

"Yes, I think so."

The marine commander threw what was left of her weight and strength into rolling the stone into the center of the cell. She fell onto the stone as she brought it to its final position and slid down to the floor, finishing on her stomach. She was panting heavily as Sam made his way through and crawled to her. He forgot everything and immediately reached out to Charlie and embraced her. It had been over a year since he had human contact other than the marines' fists.

Charlie, on the other hand, was used to no contact, so she stiffened as tight as she could.

Sam noticed her trembling and patted her on her back. "It's all good, Charlie. We are going to make it out of here. I vow to the gods that we are getting out of here." Sam was talking mostly to himself, but Charlie sat for a second, which was plenty for her.

"Okay, Sam. We'll get out of here, but can you let me go? I do not like this kind of contact."

"Yeah sure, no problem," Sam said, letting go. "Sorry, I, um, didn't mean to do that, just haven't . . . ya know. Okay!" he said, slapping his hands together. "I fought last week, so we have time to prepare. We split our food. Get your strength back up, and we attack the jailer and guards when they come for me. I'll sit or lie in the back of the cell, and you do your thing with them."

"We both need to work together. In our weakened state, we will be lucky to overtake the jailer and two guards."

"I'll handle the jailer, and you can take the guards with the piece of iron or whatever it is. I'll just say it, I need some fucking revenge, and it starts with him."

"I agree with your strategy. We cannot risk being found out. We have to move on the next encounter. Worst outcome is, I get a good death."

"No death seeking, please. Charlie, I have too much to show you." Sam moved closer again. "Don't give in please. For me."

Charlie stood frozen, leaning on the stone. She started to speak, and Sam cut her off.

"And speaking of that, you have something to show me. You have a couple of weeks to train me. Let's not waste time. On your feet, Commander."

* * *

Their training was nothing spectacular. Charlie had just enough time to cover basic stances, strikes, and counters, and even though he was learning quickly, he still had much to learn. Charlie had recovered slightly since they started sharing food. She was still half her weight compared to when she'd arrived here, but her starved look was disappearing slightly.

Their plan was simple. Sam would be at the back of the cell and frantically say that he wasn't going anymore. When the jailer no doubt would come in, Charlie would dart behind him and engage the guards. In the chaos, Sam would drop his act and let his rage take over. After that, Charlie would put on a guard uniform and escort Sam out of the prison. They would then find a transport, or whatever they could find, and just leave their fates to the gods.

The time was close. After more than a year, he could just start to sense it. Soon enough, the time would come, and they would give themselves to the gods and let the universe decide.

Sam's heart jumped at the sound of the door opening. He leaped to his feet, already feeling the adrenaline spike.

"Charlie, you good?"

"I am ready, Sam." She had swiftly positioned herself next to the door and held the piece of metal in her hand at the ready.

They heard the shuffling, followed by some footsteps. It did not sound like a large party to them. They gave each other a last glance and a slight head nod. They knew they had formed a strong bond that neither of them said. With that simple gesture, standing next to each other ready for battle, their bond was forever sealed. Sealed in combat. The shuffling came to the other end, and Sam heard the lock disengage. The door swung open, and Sam was temporarily blinded by the light.

"Fuck you, fat bastard! You're going to have to drag me out! Come and get me, you piece of shit!" Sam roared.

The jailer pulled his club like he always did, and Charlie made her move. With one hand she knocked the club out of the jailer's hand as he brought it up. She calculated her chance to give Sam an advantage, and she took it. Planting her foot, she lunged out of the open door behind the jailer and gave a savage strike to the neck of one of the guards with the metal. She darted off in another direction, and Sam lost sight of her. He had bigger issues.

The club that the jailer held had fallen to the ground, and Sam saw his chance. He dived next to the jailer, who was turning to see who had attacked him. Sam snatched the club, raised to his knees, and swung with all his might into the jailer's knee next to him. He heard the bones snap when he made contact. The jailer buckled, immediately falling the ground, and grabbed his knee. He fell square on his face, and Sam leaped up. He grabbed the club with two hands and brought it down on the jailer. The jailer was moving at a snail's pace, and it was almost as if time slowed down. He had been fighting lightning-fast marines.

He raised the club and with a mighty roar brought it down on the jailer's head, splitting it open, killing him instantly. Sam took a couple of deep breaths and turned his attention to Charlie.

There was no sound, and Sam rushed to see what had happened. Charlie was there, breathing slightly. She was grabbing someone by the back of his hair, holding him down and violently pulling back to expose the counselor's face grimacing with fear.

"I found this one and thought you would like him. Here." She threw him forward. "Make it quick, I move in one minute. Arm yourself, and conceal it."

She stepped over to the guard and started to strip him. Sam was surprised at first. Charlie had dispatched four marines. The ranks were thinning for the marines. He quickly turned to anger when he looked into the counselor's face. He looked around and pulled the weapon from the other guard's body. He turned and grabbed him by his hair as Charlie did. He got inches from his face and roared and then beat him multiple times with the butt of the weapon. The counselor fell to the ground, and Sam stood over him. He was barely conscious, and Sam pulled him up again off the ground.

"I should smash your head in," he said, pointing the business end right in the counselor's eye, fear all over his face. "FUCK!" he screamed. "No, you piece of shit, no easy way out for you. Just like you gave me. I swear by all the gods, I will return and burn this fucking place to the ground. Then if you're still here, you fucking worm, I will finish you myself. The next time I see your face, I will kill you!" Sam struck the counselor one more time, knocking him out. He dragged him over and threw him in Sam's old cell and locked the door behind him.

Charlie was standing watching the exchange. "Let's move, Sam!"

He ran over to her and collected the gear she found. Sam looked around at the four marines on the ground.

"Charlie, how did you just do that?"

"You have never seen me fight, Sam. Remember, marines fight each other. Where do you think we do this?"

"And you never lost," Sam was wide-eyed still with adrenaline.

She didn't say a word. She only sneered at Sam. Their blood was up.

"Let's move, Charlie!"

The two now moved with Charlie fully clothed in the guard's armor-plated uniform. She had a spare lay rifle around her shoulder, which had the other guard's clothing strapped between. She was holding one in her arms aimed at Sam as she walked him down the corridor, keeping him at a distance. Her visor was down on her helmet, and it concealed Charlie's eyes darting from point to point as she scanned the room.

They were walking down the corridor made of glass, exposing them to the outside world they had not seen in close to two years. Sam noticed Charlie shudder slightly and chose not to say anything. Best keep his head in the game. They walked as fast as they could without drawing too much attention to themselves. Each guard they passed was on their own task and gave the pair not much attention. They gave quick glances as the two walked but went back to their work, not noticing anything unusual. They then came to the only checkpoint that they knew of and walked briskly to it.

"Where's the counselor?" one guard asked as another scanned the IDs.

"He's back with the other guard and his marines . . ."—Charlie cleared her throat—"inspecting the others. He told me to get him here immediately."

"Foolish to only have one on him." The guard looked Sam over, who was playing the part of looking defeated.

"I agree," she said. "But this one is done. Anyway, orders are orders."

"Ain't that fucking right!" The guard waved his hand and let them pass.

They weaved through the mini serpentine of the checkpoint.

"Now where?" Sam said, keeping his head straight.

"I believe we go this way," she said, pulling Sam to the right. "It's been two years, but I think I remember. Look for anything that resembles a port sign, and be on the lookout for a place to change clothing."

They walked through hallways until they thought they had found a quiet spot. They ducked in a cutout from the corridor and quickly changed into their matching guard uniforms. They traded gears, each having a lay rifle sidearm. Charlie kept her helmet on, and Sam found a hat tucked in a guard's pocket. Both were dirty and matted. Charlie could pull it off, but not Sam with his long beard. He no doubt would stick out almost immediately.

"Which way?"

"Back the way we came and to the loading district. This is the main military hub of the empire. I've never been to the prison district before. We need to cross another checkpoint to the loading area, but I do not know how that is possible."

"No time to fuck around. Let's go."

They got up and went out of the prison district to the forum area. This was the crossing of all the districts in the massive military complex. This area was outside, and it so happened to be raining and gray outside. They both stepped into the rain and felt the cleansing water descend upon them. Sam looked over to Charlie and saw for the first time that she was full-out smiling. She looked at Sam, also smiling, and the two had happiness, if only for a second.

Then reality set back in.

"This is a very lucky break. Your gods are watching us," Charlie said as she directed Sam to the loading district. "This district will have plenty of transports. These ports connect the world and soon to Mars as well. We need to find a ship with the capabilities to get to Mars with enough supplies to make it there. The ship selection is your task, Sam. I will see to supplies. I say this now in case we go hot trying to make it through the checkpoint. There will be no time."

"Okay, copy."

"Let me do the talking, Sam. Stay behind me to the side, and keep your head down. I will make the first move."

They got to the checkpoint without having to wait in line too long. The rain kept most of the people's eyes down.

They were called next, and the guard immediately pointed at the pair and yelled, "Hey, you aren't supposed to have weapons. You have to check that shit! Weapon!" The guard yelled from his station. He got out and started gesturing for them to approach. "How many times do I have to remind you guards to check your weapons?"

His eyes lit up as he saw Charlie raise her lay and proceed to blow a hole through the guard's chest. She immediately swung and downed another guard and then another. She was firing so fast it was hard for Sam to keep up.

"Fire your weapon, Samuel Cleber!"

Sam realized he was just standing there still and then snapped out of it and got into the fight.

"All right, moving!" Sam raised his rifle and fired down the large corridor as he and Charlie rushed to find a ship.

They ran as fast as they could through the crowd, and Charlie had to slow to dispatch the random guard who had left his post to see what the alarm was about. It was so rare to have a major alarm sounding. Charlie downed another guard at ease, and Sam wondered how he survived their first encounter. Even with strength less than half, Charlie was making the guards look like children. Even Sam found it easy, and he grew some much-needed confidence. They stopped at a junction and quickly continued looking. They saw at the end of another large corridor another checkpoint, only this time it was a heavily defended.

"This way?" Sam asked inquisitively.

"We have to. These are military-grade vessels. Civilians are not permitted to have any vessel with interplanetary capabilities."

"I don't under—"

"You don't have to. Your home is through there, Sam."

He looked down the corridor. "There's very little cover. This is going to be difficult."

"It always is, Sam, but we do it nonetheless," the proud marine said as they walked toward the checkpoint.

He looked over at her. "Good luck, and thank you."

Charlie gave him a puzzled look.

"Just in case," he finished.

"Hold fire! They are coming this way!"

Sam and Charlie went into a run to get past the open killing zone.

"Halt! Halt, or we open fire!"

Charlie didn't wait. She already swung her rifle up and downed the closest guard. Sam followed her lead and targeted guard after guard. They darted from cover to cover that they could find. Firing and interweaving with each other, they were both hit several times. Sam took a projectile in his shoulder and another through his lower abdomen. Charlie was hit only once, but it was with a large piece of shrapnel cutting deep into her back. She fell to one knee when she was hit but kept firing. She rolled for cover and rose only to be shot again through her chest. She fell to the ground. Sam turned to his next target and finished off the remaining two still firing at Charlie. It went quiet as Sam turned to look for a target and found none.

"By the gods, Charlie . . ." He spun, searching for her.

She was on the ground coughing, and he sprinted to her.

"Okay, Charlie, I got ya," he said as he came to her.

"I think I got my death, Samuel Cleber."

"Very funny," he said, moving to pull her up.

"I'm serious, Sam. This is what I want."

"I don't give a fuck what you want. You mean something to me now, and I don't leave people I care about behind. If you stay, then I stay."

"You don't have time, Sam. Now go." She looked at him coughing. "And thank you. This is the first time in my life that I was free, and it feels just as amazing as you said it would."

"I appreciate that, Charlie, but get your ass up. Not today and not after all we endured. Get up and move. GET UP, CHARLIE!"

Sam pulled her up grabbed her by the belt and moved to area that said "Hangar" past the checkpoint. In these were the hangar workers in the massive district. Everyone was on transports. Sam threw Charlie in a vacant one and fired off from the gigantic port.

"My gods," Sam said with mouth open.

The scale was nothing like Sam had ever seen. There were dozens of military-grade massive ships neatly aligned. He saw transports and warships all with hatches open and cargo containers divided among the ships.

"They are loading them up! Charlie, how ya doing?"

"I feel like I will faint soon due to blood loss." She had grown very pale and was wheezing heavily because of her chest wound.

"Stay awake, Charlie. We'll find a ship and get you to the doc." He pressed his hand over Charlie's back to stop the blood flow. "Come on, there has to be something."

His transport was pushed to the max, moving down the long lanes of ships. He saw up ahead the auto loaders loading cargo onto a ship, and Sam realized they were in an assembly line of sorts. The ones further down had to be loaded. Sam thought he could fly one of the ships, so he picked one out, quickly stopped the transport, and ran to the other side to pull an unconscious Charlie out and up the large ramp.

He pulled her through the cargo hold to the medical station in the belly of the ship, threw her in the auto doc, and raced back to the cargo hold. He stopped midrun, noticing the fifty armored battle suits—along with ammunitions, medical supplies, food rations, and everything in between—on each transport. He climbed the stairs to the command deck and was relieved to see that he could, in fact, pilot the ship. He began the start-up sequence and was immediately pissed at the time it took to come to life. He had been spoiled by his ship's top-of-the-line gear. He thought of the *Validus*, of his Selena, and his crew. Was it really happening?

"Snap your head out of the clouds, Sam. You aren't done yet!" he barked out loud to himself. He closed the loading door and did a full system check, saying out loud, "Fuck, the OB isn't giving me access!"

He got up from the command chair, and at the same time, a countdown started on the screen.

"Holy fuck," Sam said, scrambling to find the OB to bypass or disable it. "Ha, there it is," Sam cried, pulling off the access panel of the OB. "Blow me up, you fucker! Little did you know, you're dealing with *the* fucking pirate."

He continued his work, trying to find the right component in the circuit. He found it and widely grinned. "Ha, got you, fucker!"

He pulled it out and heard the countdown stop, and his start-up continued. He ran back to the command chair, engaged the manual controls, and chuckled. "Gods, it's been a long time since I flew anything, let alone manually, but I need you now more than ever."

The green light lit up one by one as it checked seals, engine temp, anything that needed checked during preflight. It took what seemed ages, and people were starting to gather around, looking at the ship coming to life. The final green light lit, and Sam engaged thrusters. The heavy ship larboard climbed out of the sky to the atmosphere. He used the instruments normally used by the navigator to plot a course and pulled up the history of routes. This one was loading already, and Sam chose a random one and engaged the autopilot. Nothing happened.

"Fuck."

He manually turned the ship on the best course he could and fired the drive to life. The ship rocketed away. He pushed the manual controls in and turned on the comms, which barked to life with many broadcasts. The word was out that he had escaped. He swiveled in his chair to the first sounds of reports coming in that the pirate Sam Cleber was last seen boarding a ship that had just broken atmosphere.

He was headed back down to check on Charlie and thinking to himself that the race was on. Funny, he thought, it was always him chasing something down. How fates could turn. He winced in pain at his own wounds. His adrenaline had been firing, and the sharp pain he just felt reminded him that he had been shot too. He had to get patched up quickly. He had to make sure they were clear. He had too much to do.

"Almost there. I'm coming."

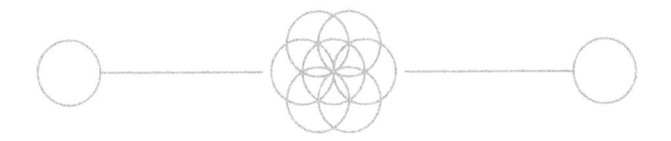

Chapter 13

Our Escape

Charlie regained consciousness and rose quickly, startled that she had no idea where she was. She grabbed at her chest, which burned as she breathed. She vaguely remembered what had happened. She took in her surroundings and turned to see Sam sleeping in a bed next to her. She found comfort that he was there and laid her head back down to drift back to sleep. The auto doc hissed as it injected Charlie with a fresh dose of sedative.

Sam woke again to see Charlie asleep like before. It had been a couple days since he had plotted his course and engaged the drives for home. He checked his route multiple times over without the help of an OB and found that it was way over his head. He was just hoping to get close and be intact. The other part of his plan meant that he needed to gain access to the comms and then try to make contact with home. He hoped they could guide him in or something like that. That part was on them. He needed every minute he could spare on the return trip home, but he was twice wounded and needed to heal. Charlie was by far the worse of the two, but Sam wasn't much better. He laid his head down again, turned over, and drifted to sleep.

Sam had woken up first, but Charlie woke up soon after. Sam wasn't even out of his bed yet when he was looking at her.

"We are in a transport that I borrowed." He smiled at her.

"What happened?"

"After the firefight, I found a transport and got us out of there, like I said I would. One day you'll figure out that I know what I'm doing."

Charlie rose from the bed, winching as she moved. Her wounds were healing but still fresh.

"Thank you, Sam," she groaned again as she swung her legs from the bed.

"Hey, easy. There's no need for you to get up so fast."

"I was ready to die," continuing without acknowledging Sam. "But I'm glad you didn't let me."

She grabbed the railings and pulled herself out of bed and stood. She wobbled slightly but gained her balance with a puzzled Sam looking at her.

"In my world, when someone saves you, you owe them the same, no matter how long it takes. So that is how it is."

"'So that is how it is'? Charlie, you don't owe me anything. Buy me a drink or something."

"No, Sam, listen!"

"No, you listen," Sam interrupted her. "That shit is from your old life, that is over. There's no life debt or any shit like that! You're family now, and family takes care of each other!" Sam turned red, immediately embarrassed that he had hurt her. "Shit, Charlie, I didn't mean it like that. We're going to stick together for a while, yes?"

She simply nodded, avoiding eye contact.

"How 'bout hang around for a while, and we'll talk about things. Something tells me you might get your wish soon enough. There's a lot of shit coming behind us, and we'll probably both die anyway."

"I will tell you I agree, Samuel, just to shut you up. Now, what do we need to do?" She snapped her head at Sam.

"You're a piece of work. How the universe brings some people together." Sam swung his legs over, groaning himself. He rose out of bed slowly, looking at Charlie's still-bloodshot eyes. "First thing, Charlie, is I'm going to find a cleansing bay and then some food. Why don't we split up, and I'm guessing you want some food first. Go take your pick, and whip up something for me. I'll get cleaned up, and then we'll switch. Once we are human again, we need to get in touch with our friends. How much do you know about these comms systems?"

He looked back at her as he started to limp to the ship's very modest living bay.

"I think it's time to start your pirate training, marine lady."

* * *

Mia continued her work from the bar. She still played both sides, but it was very noticeable to her that she was leaning heavily in favor of Dre. She blushed again at the thought of him.

Was this really going to happen? she thought to herself. *Yes, he's brave and honest, and he was so much fun before this.*

She needed the lifestyle now, and where was she going to find someone like Dre again?

Never.

She had made up her mind over the following lunars leading up to warmer weather and to the undoubtable fighting. Operations had picked up again, but ever so slightly, as each side continued their probing attacks, trying to lure the other out. The trick was not to lose so many resources to tip the scale in numbers. Mia knew that all the UNE had to do was hold out for not much longer. She had hoped that by helping Dre more, he could find a way to win before the fleet and armada showed up.

She walked back into her always deserted bar and climbed the stairs to an office that Selena had kept to have as a space to be alone. Mia quickly found out why Selena enjoyed her time in there. Sometimes she just needed to sit in silence. She opened the door and was utterly shocked to see the commander of all UNE forces on Mars, General Barada, inside.

"Mia Jackson, please join us," the general gestured, not looking up from his display.

He was sitting in Mia's chair, flanked by two armored marines. The armored marines took up much of the room, and Mia was noticeably uncomfortable. The marines were under orders to protect the general, and Mia could feel their gaze through the armor.

"Don't worry, Ms. Jackson. May I call you Ms. Jackson, or do you prefer Mia?"

"Whatever the general prefers," Mia answered, both understanding her position and telling the general she wasn't a threat. She stepped into the room and saw tucked into the corner was Cap. She just smirked at Mia when she entered the room.

"Well, Mia it is then. I believe you two know each other." The general gestured over to Cap, still not looking up from his display. "So let me ask you, *Mia*"—the general put a little extra stress on her name—"what should I do with you? You got extremely sloppy playing with your little boyfriend. Mia, I swear, we were so close to grabbing you the other day."

The general turned off his display and looked straight at Mia. He slammed his fist on the desk as he rose, startling Mia, but not the marines.

"Today is different than the other day, and well . . ." he said, continuing in his calm manner. He walked around the small desk toward her. "Playtime is over, Mia."

Mia's eyes widened as the general came close to her. She could smell his aftershave and see the tiredness in his eyes.

"Now you are going to do exactly as I ask, or your boyfriend will get this data dump I have on you, then I'll have . . . what was your name again?"

"Cap for now, General."

"Thank you, Cap. Data dump, or Cap will kill you outright. I tell you, Mia, you are a shell of what you were, and getting this was too easy for someone who had your reputation. This is what

I want, Mia. There is a ship inbound, and I want to know when and where it will arrive. I assure you," he continued, "you will know when you hear for yourself." He grabbed his general's cap and threw it on in a quick military fashion. "Marines. On me."

The general walked briskly out of the room with the marines pushing past Mia to lead the general out. The UNE had landed his transport, and his remaining marine squad stood watch in their armored suits. The general boarded his personal transport, the *Howard*, and his marine escorts took up positions around him. The transport came to life and sped away, followed by the bouncing marines protecting their general.

Cap remained behind. "I know killing you wouldn't get what we want. If he knew who you were . . ." Cap paused, circling the room. "Now, that would get us what we want now, wouldn't it, Mia? Don't think of doing anything cute now. We have so many eyes on you—well, I have my eye on you."

Mia knew it. Her experience kicked in, and she thought of her position.

"Come on, Mia," Cap continued. "Did you honestly think you were the only agent? You lost it, and now you're done, just like that." The agent snapped her fingers.

She was good as dead no matter what she did, but why betray Dre outright? She'd rather have him hate her than outright betray him.

"What do you want?"

"The same thing we always wanted, Mia. Now stop playing, or he gets your dirty secret. I can't get into the inner circle.

That's where you come in. Now stay still, this will sting a bit." Cap injected her with a tracking device. "I'm sure you're familiar with this. I don't have to remind you of the capabilities."

"How long?"

"Years, Mia. I've been here for years. Long before you. I knew who you were soon as you gave them Sam the first time. Don't you understand, Mia? You were my in." Cap paused for dramatic effect. "Give me what I want, Mia, or Dre gets your dirty secret. They'll think you are the leak while I stay here and fuck them more. Then, Mia, I will kill you and display your body for him to see."

* * *

The wires sparked as Sam twisted them together. "Did that bypass it?"

"Still nothing, Sam. I told you, you can't cut that much out. There's no return now."

They both stopped, frustrated. They had been trying for a couple of days to get the comms system off the lockdown the OB had activated before Sam could disable it.

"I hate this shit without my own OB. Shows how different it is now. We take those things as a simple tool, but they are much more, I'm afraid. How did our ancestors do it?"

"Maybe we need to go for a different approach, Samuel."

"Yeah, and what's the direction now, Commander?" Sam sat down, leaning against the bulkhead of the ship.

"There are supplies in this transport, yes?"

"Yes," Sam said, realizing where Charlie was going. "Yes, Charlie, good thinking. I knew saving you was a good idea."

Charlie snorted and smirked at Sam, which meant she was laughing inside.

The two rushed as fast as they could with their healing injuries. The auto docs did their work every night, but they were still forced to move gingerly.

"Will this armor work without an OB?" he asked, running his hand over the massive battle armor. There were dozens of suits neatly aligned. "We must be winning." Sam continued his search while he talked. "Why would they need all this shit after a year? It's because we are winning!" he said with fire in his belly.

He went through stages of extreme happiness at the thought of returning to his Selena and his life. Then he would just as quickly turn to extreme anger that he let this happen and that now was the time to make it right. He knew he was doing it, and he liked it. He was going to drive every last one from his home or die trying.

"I tell you, we are winning, Chucky. And when we get back, we are going to take it to the fuckers, but first I have to find something to call . . ." He found what he needed. "Home. Charlie!" he yelled. "I think I got it!"

He rushed to the container and opened its contents. He had been raiding for so long he knew the container very well. It was all-new, state-of-the-art comms gear. There was only one problem though.

"Charlie? Do you know how to use this?"

She came hobbling over and did a quick glance. "Of course I do, Sam. We won't know what channels they use, but we can broadcast."

"We don't need our channels, Charlie. They will be listening, ha ha! We just need to open broadcast, put it on Repeat, and wait. Who cares if the UNE listens? It's not like they don't know. Come on, Charlie, fire this thing up."

It took Charlie only moments, and she had the prepacked comms station up and running.

"It's ready, Sam. You can speak normally."

Sam inched closer to the comms station and nodded at Charlie. Charlie pushed a symbol on the touch pad, and the recorder started. Sam opened his mouth, but nothing came out. She saw his eyes dart back and forth and then begin to water. Sam tried to speak but couldn't; he was only able to drop his head. Charlie didn't quite understand Sam's reaction. She thought he would be happy at the thought of returning home. His head hung low for minutes, and Charlie stood in silence, just watching Sam.

He raised his head, his eyes red. "Sorry, Charlie. We let stuff out sometimes. It's good for the soul." He composed himself and tried again. "Any station, this is Samuel Cleber, inbound on a captured UNE vessel. We are without our onboards and are flying blind. We are being hotly pursued by a large UNE force. No more hiding, baby." He paused only for a breath and continued, "I'm coming home."

He nodded to Charlie, and she switched off the record. She navigated the touch pad and looked at Sam.

"It's ready to open broadcast, Sam, and on Repeat every five seconds."

Sam nodded again, and she switched on open broadcast. Everyone out there could now hear them.

* * *

He didn't move from the comms station anymore. They had moved it to the command deck and managed to enhance their signal by pirating some of the ship's equipment. He had made a makeshift room on the deck and only left to perform his necessaries. He sat and waited for a response.

"We are getting close," he said, leaning and looking at Charlie.

The two were used to waiting and sitting, but this was a different waiting. He was barely sleeping again and checking the comms equipment over and over.

Charlie was a different story. In a matter of days, she had inventoried the whole ship and was itching for something to do.

"Sam." The sound of Selena's voice came over the comms. "Sam, it's me."

He frantically grabbed at the comms, reaching for her. "I'm here. I'm here, honey." His eyes watered. "I can't wait to wrap my arms around you."

There was a long wait on the other end, and Sam had to make sure he still had them. "Do you copy?"

"Yeah, Sam." She had obviously been emotional. "I can't wait either. We are all here."

"Hey, buddy!" Dre said.

"How . . . how are you?" Selena asked.

"Such a long story, but we've been better. We'll make it, but I need help landing. I'm flying blind and don't have an OB."

"We have a plan, but first, you need to switch over to the channel we used for that one job where we, ya know, after."

Gods, he loved her. "I will always remember that one." He smiled from ear to ear, continuing, "Switching over immediately. This is Sam out."

* * *

The counselor heard the transmission in real time as he monitored the pursuit. He and his generals had sent a detachment to follow. The rest of the force was ready to depart. He looked up from the display toward his general and his staff.

"Send the rest."

His staff carried on to complete his orders. No one was questioning the counselor now. After Sam's escape, he had arrested or executed every last person who had a hand in his escape. Even civilians didn't escape his wrath. He claimed they stood by as the murderer ran past them. The guards that survived in the entire district were arrested or sent to labor camps. There was a clear message being sent. The counselor dug with his nails into his chair. He should have publicly executed him from the start. His memory would have faded, but after the escape, his story would be etched in stone, and the counselor would forever be known as the fool that let it happen. Sam had been captured, had fought marines in the arena, and had escaped and humiliated his captors.

* * *

"Sam, buddy, that will take too long. They are right on your six, and besides, I think Ameera has a better idea." Dre had taken over for Selena after the two made contact again.

"Sam," Ameera said, pushing herself closer, "I'll come up, and well, go manual, and I'll guide you in."

"Okay, I guess, but you all know I'm a shitty pilot. And this thing is a flying tub. It's filled with goodies that I'm sure you could use."

The group started to hear the thud of an armor approaching, and the large blast doors opened. John sprinted in to the comms station. Everyone cleared the way for John in his bright and spotless armor.

"Sam!" His voice rang from the armor.

"John!" He powered down his suit and climbed out faster than most have seen before.

"Sam! By the gods, Sam! How . . . ?"

"It's good to hear your voice. Where's everyone else?"

The room got quiet. "We don't know, Sam. We think they are alive, but they didn't make it out that night either, and we have very little to go on."

"I guess we both have a lot to talk about." Everyone could hear it in Sam's voice.

Charlie stepped forward, noticing Sam turn somber. "The entry is okay, but you need to deal with the ships in pursuit. When the UNE comes to intercept, this vessel does not have the capabilities to outrun anything."

"And who is this?" Dre asked as the room looked at each other in puzzlement.

"Former commander of Charlie Squad. You can just call me Charlie now."

John noticeably perked up. "You mean the marine lady?"

"She's good, John. Like you said, we have a lot to catch up on. You all can speak absolutely freely. She's one of us now." Sam looked at Charlie with her smirking face on and winked. "I suggest listening to her when she speaks because she doesn't do it that much."

"Well, you tell marine lady to not worry about it. We haven't been sitting here doing nothing. We'll deal with the UNE, and you work on reentry. By the way, you have twelve hours, Sam. I'm sorry, they concealed the transmission until you were practically on top of us."

"That's good for us, John, we don't have too long to wait."

* * *

Sam had strapped in, and Charlie strapped in in the nav chair next to him.

"I guess sit back and enjoy the ride." He looked over to Charlie. "Don't worry, we'll make it. We didn't just do all that shit to disintegrate at the finish line, ha ha!" He nudged Charlie with his fist. "In the hands of the gods again!"

"Sam, focus. We have inbound UNE ships. Looks like a heavy strike force. We are going to bring you in, and Serg, Tucker, and the rest of the crew will deal with the strike force."

Sam looked at Charlie with one eye raised. "Deal with the strike force?"

"Copy, Ameera, going conventional in three . . two . . .one."

The ship's drives powered down, and the ship used its conventional thrusters for maneuvering.

"Okay, Sam, I got you coming in. I'm signaling off your portside, in plane with your horizon." Sam searched to his direct left. "Okay, I see you. Coming around to port."

Sam eased the controls to the left, and the ship moaned when the thrusters engaged. Sam overturned and had to bring it back in.

"Ease off, Sam! Way too hot!"

"Copy that!" Sam quickly eased off the thrusters. "I barely touched it!"

"You're still in atmosphere! You never switched over!"

There were two different modes for ship's thrusters, and Sam didn't switch when he took off from the depot.

"Okay, hold on, I have to find it."

The moment he started to look, Charlie switched it to Space mode and snorted at Sam.

"Okay, we got it. Easing toward you."

Sam cautiously turned the ship toward Ameera, still signaling. The massive tub got close to the *Validus*.

"She looks good. I see you modified it."

"She's the *Raptor* now. Sorry, Sam, but I'm a pirate. Finders keepers."

Everyone gave a nervous chuckle.

Sam heard an explosion overhead and saw the flash of light that had to be a ship exploding. He next heard the grit and debris hit his vessel.

He saw Charlie looking out front and pointing, "Sam! Eyes front!"

Sam had taken his eyes off Ameera and didn't notice he was dangerously close to her.

"Head in the game, Sam!" Ameera roared over the comms.

"Fuck!" was all Sam said, refocusing.

The sounds of battle had picked up around him.

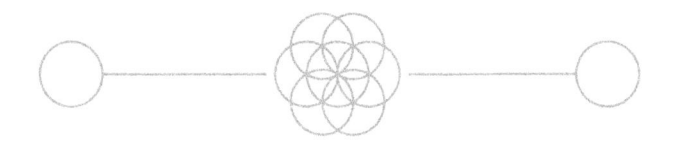

Chapter 14

Our Love

"That's one down!" Tucker screamed. "Bring her around!" he shouted orders to his crew of the corvettes. He keyed into his comms. "Taking position at his rear, Commander."

"Nicely done, Phoenix," John confirmed from the command center back home. "Okay, Serg, bring in *Big Bertha*!"

Serg came from atmosphere with his newly commissioned ship, *Big Bertha*. He made his big, lumbering ship basically all weapon and no ass. Coming in range of the developing battle, Serg and his crew started picking off targets one at a time. His large cannons, which were the first of its kind for the ragtag pirates, charged to life slowly and sent a devastating blast toward the UNE vessels. It was powerful, but it was difficult to track targets in the mess.

"John, I'm having trouble tracking."

"It's all right, only a couple more minutes until we fall back."

"That's another!" Tucker chimed in. "Time till atmosphere, Ameera?"

"Twenty seconds. Another thirty for Sam. Sam, soon as I tell you you're through, switch to manual and thrusters to atmosphere. I'm going to break off and head back up."

"Copy that, *Raptor*."

The next moments passed ever so slowly. Sam heard thuds of explosions. The occasional auto weapons firing and then another undeniable ship kill.

"Fuck, we lost Samson! Form up, people!"

Sam heard Tucker over the comms.

"Stand by . . . Fall back! Helena, you have the room. I'm getting suited up." John started walking toward his armor, steps away from the command center. "Dre, how you looking?"

"We're good here." Dre was frantic, making sure everything was where it needed to be. "I have scouts in all directions and sent backup teams. Beacon is lit for Sam. How is it up there?"

"They are falling back, and thirty seconds till he's in. I'm en route."

John flew into his suit, skipping most of the start-up procedure, and bounced quickly out of the room and onto the surface to meet his brother. Dre had no idea what the UNE would do, so he decided not to mess around. He called every available gun to be ready. His total force was on the field. If the UNE decided this was the day, then he'd be ready.

"I am on the all-comms, boys. Keep your eyes open, and if you see something, say something. Two-person confirmation on any enemy movement."

This was one of those moments again, where one minute took an eternity. Every second, the pressure continued to build.

"Confirmed contact. North by northwest directly from Jazeera!" one recon team reported.

Dre brought up his tactical map and stated his orders while bouncing to meet the threat. He made several large thrusts and had to leap over hills and down ravines until he came to the squad that had reported the movement. He landed heavily next to the squad and zoomed in his modified command armor.

"Good work, boys," he said, scanning the horizon as he heard the other units arrive and start to form a firing line. "Wait a minute. What the fuck are they doing? Are they really going to head right at us?"

"Looks like it, General," the scouts confirmed.

He saw Barada across the field as he bounced with his marines. "Why the fuck would he do that? He isn't that dumb." Dre looked down to work it out in his head.

"General! It isn't all armor!"

Dre confirmed it with his own eyes, and they lit up as he realized what was happening.

"This might be a feint attack! Jamal, move tighter around the landing zone." John came in, landing next to Dre. "John, I got this. Go help Frankie and the others."

"I'm on it." John turned instantly and bounced off again.

"We got the ground here, boys. Let them come in and pick your targets."

The oncoming marines stopped suddenly just out of range and took up positions.

"We're spotted. Hold fire, hold fire! See what they do," Dre said to himself and over the all-comms.

The UNE held their positions.

"Contact," another recon team announced. "Sizeable force moving due east. They will be on us in moments!"

"Fall back! Back to original positions. No unnecessary chatter, keep this channel open. Captains, take charge of your positions."

Each captain keyed in their acknowledgment.

"Frankie, John, gather every piece of armor you have, and meet that element. We have to meet them before they get around us. I'm sending a crew to reinforce. I got this over here." Dre switched his comms to Helena, coordinating the whole show from the command center now. "Helena, if there is any available craft available, I want them down here after Sam is back safe. Acknowledge!"

"Copy, General. Sam is pushing atmosphere. He should touch down in minutes, and I'll have Tucker and his ships engage."

"You good, Helena? The boys good upstairs?"

"There are holding their own, General."

"Copy. See if we make it out of this. Out."

Dre surveyed the terrain. He looked back quickly and saw one of his captains bouncing quickly to John and the sounds of the battle. Satisfied, he turned his full attention to his own task.

"Come on, you fuckers. I have weakened my position. Come on, come and get it." Dre was hoping for a foolish attack.

He was in a good position and had open ground between him and the still-waiting UNE forces. He heard the fight to the back of his left shoulder and dismissed it quickly. They had learned not to worry about the other. John had his mission, and he had his. He scanned constantly with his scopes and heard the sound of fighter ships overhead. Tucker and his squad were fighting low over John's position, and each ship had weapons firing wildly. Dre saw a fireball in the sky, followed by UNE fighter crafts diving to meet the crews.

An intense battle had formed. Everything hung in the balance. He was contemplating sending more to John when he heard the first bounces of the UNE charging his position. He looked back and saw them thundering as they bounced toward Dre and his fighters. They bounced at full thrust to cover the distance. Doing this made them hang in the air too long. It made them stationary targets, and Dre gave the order.

"Fire at will!"

At that moment, the whole line fired their long-range lay rifles with devastating effects. Dre watched as marine after marine dropped. A couple of ships came in to strafe the advancing unarmored forces but was blown from the sky when they fired their antiship weapons. Dre shook it off. He raised his own weapons and joined in.

"Pick your targets! We are chewing them up. Keep up the fire!"

Round after round, marine after marine, they charged; the rebels fired, and the marines fell. Eventually, only a handful of them were left when the retreat was called. They turned in unison and bounced quickly back to their original lines. Some were picked off, receiving the most shameful of wounds to the back. Dre surveyed the battlefield and looked at what had to be hundreds of armored marines lying motionless on the ground. They hadn't even reached the rebel positions, and Dre called for a head count. The captains reported minimal casualties, and they realized they had just put a serious hurting on the UNE forces.

* * *

"We are in atmosphere. Home sweet home!" Sam cheered, overcome with so many emotions.

"Sam, Serg and the boys need my help. Follow the beacon, and the rest is up to you. Welcome home, I'll see you later." Her modified *Raptor* spun and blasted off toward the ship-to-ship battle. "Serg, I'm en route. Status!"

"Here goes nothing." Sam was nervous as he eased the controls over toward the beacon.

"Sam, it's Helena, I'm going to help as best as I can. You are coming in way too hot, Sam. Hit your thruster immediately."

Sam fired his thruster, and both he and Charlie lunged forward because of the Gs.

"That's good, Sam. Bring it around more . . . That's it. All right, Sam, engage landing gear."

Charlie leaned over and flipped a switch, and the landing gear came out from underneath the ship.

"Sam, too hot still. Come on, Sam, slow that tub down."

Sam fired the thrusters, causing the ground around to kick up dust and dirt of his home planet. He saw people through the view port and picked Selena out immediately. His eyes widened, and his heart leaped from his chest. He was so close. He came down very hard, letting go of the controls that didn't matter to him anymore. He had touched down only moments before immediately unstrapping his harness and moving out of the ship as quickly as possible. He pulled the emergency hatch and leaped out of the ship into the dust. Jumping from the vessel, which landed awkwardly, he raced toward Selena. He couldn't see in the dust, but he made her out and ran toward her.

The pirates around watched as the dust settled. They saw as Sam and Selena ran toward each other, embraced, and fell to the ground. They didn't say a word at first, caught up in the moment. Sam couldn't help but place his lips directly on hers. Their love had intensified, and it was on full display for the world to see. They kissed forever, then held each other, then kissed again.

Selena reached up and placed her hand on his face. "By the gods, Sam, I never . . ." she said amid tears of joy.

"I'm home, honey. Never again. I'm never leaving you again."

They were there on their knees looking at one another, laughing, crying, embracing. Sam looked into her eyes, and for the first time in a year, he saw the universe—the possibility, true hope, love, everything good in the craziness of the world around them. They had each other, and with each other, anything was possible. Sam had fulfilled his promise. Against all odds, he came back to her.

Selena saw Charlie step toward Sam, but it didn't matter; she only had her eyes on him. The rest of the group gathered around in the clearing dust, however, did not know Charlie. They were on guard with the unknown person standing next to Sam. Sam brought Selena to her feet and embraced her again, sliding his hand down her back while feeling her hair in between. He reached the small of her back and pulled her close to him. It was the first time they ever displayed their love for each other in public.

By now, everyone knew about Sam and Selena, but this was the first time they actually saw, and then they knew why Selena was destroyed when he was taken. It was true unconditional love, displayed for all, and the two could care less. They smiled at each other in joy, and for the first time, they looked up to see everyone gathered.

Sam turned to Charlie and introduced the two, "Selena, this is Charlie. Charlie, Selena."

"I have heard much about you. I would be honored if we can speak together sometime." Charlie stepped forward crisply, nodded, and mustered a weak smile.

"She's still getting used to real people," Sam interjected. "But as far as I'm concerned, she's one of us," he said, raising his voice to announce to the crowd. "And believe me, she earned it."

Selena smiled and nodded in return, then turned back toward Sam. She frowned, inspecting Sam over, "Gods, Sam, what did they do to you?

"It's a very long story, my love. One I will tell you sometime, but for now, take me somewhere. Anywhere, I don't care."

"Come on, let's get inside."

He looked around at everyone who was smiling to see him, and the frail man smiled in return. He was a shell of his former self. Many didn't even recognize him; he was so beaten and frail. He had given himself a haircut, and shaving his head again revealed the scars that had formed. His smile faded, and he shed his fear and his sorrow and followed his love inside, followed by Charlie. He heard the sounds of fighting all around echoing in the cannons.

"What is going on?"

"We have a lot to tell you too, but never mind that. Come with me, they can handle it, trust me."

The others gathered around and watched as they headed away then turned to the UNE wreck that Sam had landed.

* * *

John had finished his fight. It was a hard slug, and they lost many. It was Frankie who turned the tide. He had led a small detachment into a weak point. The enemy had spread itself too thin, and Frankie exploited it at the cost of his own life. John had lost contact and bounced hard to get to him.

Frankie's second-in-command, Jamal, got on the comms as John bounced. "This is Captain Jamal. General Francisco is down. I am assuming command. We have a battle to win! Garcia, close it up!"

It was the next person up. Death was an everyday thing, and each death hurt. John landed next to his brother-in-law turned friend. Fransico still had his face covered by his armor, but John could still see him in his mind. He thought of his sister and his nephew. He had to get them back too.

He shook his head, saying out loud, "Head in the game."

He put his hand on Fransico's chest, which was riddled with wounds, and bowed his head. He told him he would take care of Vivianna and little Gustavo. He said, "Thank you for the time we had, the friendship that had formed." He said goodbye. Death was every day.

John stood, brought up his tactical map in his armored display, and saw that Jamal had reformed the line. He looked down at Fransico again, pausing, and then bounced off toward Jamal and the rest of his companions who were still in the fight. Death was every day.

John heard Sam had made it when he had to turn his attention to the battle. He had bounced back as quickly as possible after he was satisfied that Jamal had the situation in hand. He was bouncing when he saw Dre's contact come up on his display. He had won his battle and was bouncing hard to base as well.

"He made it!" Dre hollered over the comms.

"He made it!" John did a flip in his armor.

They ran and bounced side by side, and both had many emotions running through them.

"How'd it go?" John asked as excitedly as Dre had ever heard him. There was happiness in his voice that he hadn't heard in a long time. It brought up his spirits even more.

"Fuckin' tore them up, John. I didn't get exact numbers, but we put a hurtin' on them! How'd you guys do?"

"Not good." John paused to bounce hard over a ravine. "We pushed them back, but we suffered heavily. I don't have numbers, but it's a big loss. Francisco is gone, Dre. He was the one who turned it for us."

"Oh, Frankie," Dre exhaled. "Fuck this fucking war."

"Yeah . . . fuck it."

They both continued in silence and came to the cavern entrance they were headed. Both leaped into the deep, wide darkness of the cavern and tunnel system. Together they fired their thrusters as they landed, and both ran to get out of their armor. They were covered in sweat as they briskly walked and asked everyone where Sam was. Eventually, they found Charlie standing outside a room, and she noticed John. She turned and faced them both.

"I never expected to see you again," John was shaking his head. "How in the . . ."

"Hey, no offenses, guys, but where the fuck is Sam?" Dre interrupted.

Charlie looked at Dre, recognizing him as well. She immediately sized him up and concluded that he was a worthy threat, so she picked her words carefully and with calmness in her voice said, "Sam and Selena want to be alone for a moment. Sam needs her right now. He knows you're okay. Selena is explaining the rest."

They understood immediately.

"Yeah," Dre said, easing up. "I get it." He wanted to stay, but they all couldn't be here. Someone had to go to the command center to help Helena. "I'll head back. Let me know the minute he comes out please."

"Wait, Dre . . ." John followed.

"Nah, nah," Dre gestured with his hand. "You stay, I'll go." He turned and walked back.

John watched as he went and then looked Charlie over. "I tell you what, marine lady, you need a minute to yourself as well. When is the last time you ate?"

"Believe it or not, I have actually gained some weight back," she said straight-faced.

"I see." John didn't know what to say. What could he say? Then he said, "Come with me."

He held out his hand, and Charlie sneered and pulled back.

He frowned back and waved at her instead. "All right, crazy, come on."

Charlie just stood there.

"I'm just going to show you where to get some food and get yourself cleaned up. We don't have much, but it's okay."

Charlie turned to look at Sam's room.

"He'll be all right with her," John said. "Trust me, he is in good hands."

Charlie looked at John, then at Sam's room, then back again. "I will go with you."

"That's it . . . What should I call you? Charlie, right?"

"I am Charlie now."

"Charlie. I like Charlie."

* * *

"Barada, you fucking turd of a human being, you have lost this for us!"

"Lost it, Counselor?" he screamed into the comms. "It was your orders that led us to this."

"I ordered you to kill that fucking man, not lose half your forces."

"I told you that an attack on them was suicidal!"

"Imbecile! You will be executed along with the rest of your failures!"

"We'll see about that. You see, I'm looking at someone who lost the most important prisoner in our time then sent a suicide order to try to get him back. I am not a magician, Counselor. Perhaps it is you who needs to be branded as a failure. This whole plan was your doing. It falls on you. Don't you think I've been in contact with my mother? Don't you understand that they have been watching your every move? You are nothing to them. Nothing but disposable."

He was right. The counselor overplayed his hand.

"All is not lost. I still have my remaining forces at the center, and we are well supplied, but only for a limited time. We have the family still. They will not storm the place nor strike it from the air if they think it will hurt the family. Oh yes, Counselor, that reminds me, we also lost nearly all of our fighting crafts. The rebels are simply better than us at piloting, and their ability to adapt their aircrafts is a bewilderment," the general continued. "When do the rest of them arrive?"

"Matter of weeks. They will wait to the last before contacting you."

"Make sure and inform them of the exact situation. If you want to turn this, do not exclude anything. The commanders need to be ready for immediate action, and there's little I can do to help. Their general will not simply let us land our forces. They must be ready!"

* * *

Sam and Selena stayed in the room for many days. Selena was coming and going, and she was adamant about giving Sam some time to heal. He was in way worse shape than he had let on. His wounds needed healing even after being treated the whole way home, and he was seriously malnourished. He slept for days, waking up every so often imagining he was still in the dungeon. Selena had left and come back once to find him lying on the floor on his makeshift bed.

"Sam," she said softly, "how do you feel?"

"I'm good. I think you broke me the other night." He smirked at her. "I think I am in worse shape than I let on." He sat up quickly. "How's Charlie? Is she okay?"

"John has been watching her. I think he likes her."

"No . . . Get the fuck outta here."

"I'm serious. He goes in there all the time, I'm told."

"Where is she?"

"Down the corridor there," Selena said, pointing through the room.

"I think I've been in here long enough." He groaned as he got up. His knee popped, and he stumbled slightly. "That's a new one, honey. Some douchebag gave me a shot to the knee, and it's been screaming since."

"You need to get that looked at."

Sam laughed hard at that. "Babe, I have bigger issues at the moment."

The two laughed hard, which was the first time since Sam got back.

"I'm going to tell you every chance I get that I love you. You're the reason I'm here." Sam stretched as he looked Selena up and down. She was even more beautiful than he imagined. She walked to him, batting her eyes. "You know, on second thought," he said, watching her body move, "why don't you come here. They can wait a little longer."

"I won't break you this time, I promise." She slid her pants and shirt off, exposing her near-perfect body. Her olive skin was making Sam's heart race, and Selena came nose-to-nose with him. She smelled so good to him, and he inhaled deeply.

"Remember, my dear, I'm out of practice, and you look more beautiful than ever to me. Get ready for the best twenty-seven seconds of your life."

"You better do better than that. You have a reputation to uphold."

She started rubbing his chest and brought herself to his lips. He let go and grabbed her, ignoring his wounds. He didn't care. He had all he needed right in front of him.

The pair walked out of the room together for the first time since Sam had been back. A crowd had gathered around them, and the people began cheering. Some were clapping with wide smiles on their faces, and others flat-out cried with joy. Watching him fight in the arena time and time again had made him a hero to the people. When he actually fought back and held his own, he became a legend. After he broke out of the condemned, commandeered a transport, and made it somehow back to Mars alive, he became a son of the gods. There was not a person on the planet who didn't know of Samuel Cleber.

"They worship you now, Sam."

"I ... uh ... "

"Come this way. I'll take you to see her. Come on, Sam." She pulled him away from the gathered crowd down the corridor toward Charlie. Weaving through the people, she saw John and headed for him.

"You're out!" He jumped in the air and started running toward Sam.

Sam smiled widely as the two embraced.

"Sam . . . I didn't think I'd see you again. Everyone says you are one lucky bastard, and from now on, I'm never doubting it again."

They let go of each other and continued at a slow pace. People were still gathered around and made conversation a little difficult, but both brothers started simultaneously, "How did you—"

John nodded to his older brother, smiling.

"Charlie. It was because of Charlie, John. It wasn't luck."

"Charlie?" John frowned. How did you get her to talk? I couldn't get shit."

"Believe me, it took a while."

The two laughed and continued conversing.

"Heard you been spending time there."

"Yeah, well, she isn't so bad after all. See, I was right." John nudged his older brother.

Sam grabbed him around his neck like they used to when they were kids. "Yeah, you're right on this one, little bro." He stood up and looked at him. "If half I hear is true about you, then you should be proud of yourself, John. I'm proud of you."

"I didn't know how to bring this up, but we got it here, ya know. Me, Dre, the guys. We know what we are doing, so you can relax a bit. It hasn't been sunshine and rainbow here since you left."

"I know, Selena has been filling me in, but there is something pressing that we need to talk about. I need to tell you all, so could you have everyone meet us?"

"Will do. How worried should we be?"

Sam inhaled deeply, letting it out. "It's serious, John. No laughing matter on this one."

"We got your back," he said, clapping him on the back. "You're lucky, right?"

* * *

"Listen, Sam. I'm saying it. They are thinking it. What's up with her?" He pointed in Charlie's direction.

She sat up slightly in her chair and watched Sam turn red in the face.

"We don't have time for that!" This was the first time they heard Sam so angry. "They are coming. I saw it. We"—he pointed at Charlie—"saw it. Oh yeah, and she"—pointing at her again—"saved my life. And that's the last fucking time I hear about it."

The room got quiet, and Sam noticed. "I am sorry, guys. It's been a hard . . ."

"We know Sam, we saw," Serg spoke for everyone.

"I'm sorry, Dre."

"It's out of my mind already, so what's up? Why do you want us here?"

"I didn't want to say much over the comms, but they have a lot of firepower coming our way. Thousands of ships, armor, you name it. It's all coming."

Everyone sank with the news.

"Dre, what are our ground forces looking like?" Selena asked.

"We won, but we took a beating. I haven't seen a full head count, but with us and the others out there . . . I don't know, maybe two thousand."

"That will not be enough," Charlie pointed out. "The marines have had their ranks cut, but they are still marines. Sam can tell you that."

"How many do you think they'll have, Charlie? I saw that number easy."

"I agree, Sam. That number or more. Their fleet is the real problem. They have dedicated warships now. I have not seen your modified craft yet to assess the situation."

"We lost some ships, Sam," Ameera stepped in. "But we have the upper hand here. Don't worry," she said, winking. "We can handle that part."

"So intelligence is what we need." Selena looked over to Dre.

He stood up from the table he was half sitting on. "Let me try to find out."

"No way," Sam said a little excited. "Mia is still there?"

"Yeah, there's something we need to talk about," John interjected.

"We've been over this, John," Dre fired back. "And like Sam said, we don't have the time. I'm going, and that is that."

"What are you talking about?"

"He has to know, Dre," Sergio said.

"We have been raising some questions about her. We can skip the details for now, but Dre has a soft spot, and we are worried about him. You too, Selena. There's only one person who has all the pieces of the puzzle. Mia."

Sam looked over at Dre. "You sure?" He could read Dre instantly as he hesitated to answer. "Send people with him, John."

"No. Listen. No. We have a thing, yes, but you all knew that. I haven't said a word to her about operations. It can't be her." Dre looked around, searching for approval.

Each crew member nodded one at a time.

"Why are you doing this, Dre?" Sam asked. "Why put yourself in this position?"

He shrugged and gave up. "Because I love her."

Dre had never said that powerful word before. Some threw it around, but others, like Dre, held it tight.

He continued, "I'm bringing her back. She will run if she sees all of us coming. I don't know anymore. I thought I had things figured out, but she came, and I'm all fucked up. All this happened while fighting an interplanetary war, after losing my best friend. Now he's back, and she might be a traitor. Like you keep saying, who else?"

* * *

General Nikto Barada was on the warpath after losing the battle. All the UNE staff left kept a very wide berth from the general. A couple of eager officers spoke out of line after the defeat, and he had them executed immediately. He was not going to let chaos take over. Any talk of surrender was quickly stomped out. He knew that reinforcements were on the way, but he didn't want anyone to find out. He had a loose end, and he walked briskly to a detention cell.

"I didn't want to take a chance with you. Your pirate friends signaled another meeting, and thanks to you, we know how to signal them now. Same place as before, but he'll have new friends waiting for him. As for you, I did as I promised. I just sent the data. I'm letting it out everywhere that we brought in our top agent, Mia Jackson. Is that your real name?" The general paced the cell. "He will find out, and I will put him in here with you. I'll let him kill you, then I will kill him because of you. You were useful after all, Mia. Goodbye."

The general left the room and turned to a staff member. "How many fighting troops do we have left?"

"It doesn't look good, General. The majority of our marines were lost in the last engagement, and the remaining few are leaderless. Most of the squad commanders were lost as well."

"Tell me we have something to pull this off. There has to be."

"I can scrape a functional squad, I think," the staff confirmed.

"Full-armored assault. Quick and out. Kill him and anyone else you find."

* * *

Dre made his way back the same as before. He backtracked, weaved in and out of dark corners, and eventually, found a spot to observe the surrounding area. He breathed heavily, catching his breath, and listened. He didn't hear anything, but his sixth sense was working. He had been fighting so long that his gut told him something was wrong. It took Dre most of his life and many mistakes to finally listen to it. He became hyperaware.

He looked over at the dwelling again, and still no sign that Mia was there. She was always first to arrive. This made Dre's hair stand when he heard the unmistakable sound of thrusters and the heavy thuds of armors that followed coming at him. He turned and got up as quickly as he could. He ran for the tunnels and didn't look back as the thundering became louder. He saw the tunnel and made a turn for it. He looked up and saw a marine thrust over him and land, stopping him dead in his tracks. Another marine landed close to him, and he heard more come up from behind him. One turned to him and walked instead of bouncing toward him.

The marine kept coming, getting larger and larger, and Dre backpedaled, turning to run again. He didn't even see them or hear them as he scrambled to his feet. There were three of them who violently attacked the marines. He noticed John but didn't recognize the other two in the new UNE armor.

One of them moved very quickly. He was surprised that he didn't know how to do that in armor. The person in there knew how to handle themselves. They quickly dispatched one and fired to the next. The other threw one marine into another and fired over to them both on the ground. The person in the armor held their weapon up to the armored marine and fired multiple times into each one. It was over in seconds.

John bounced over to Dre. "I told you, idiot. One of these days, you two blockheads will listen to me. We found the data, Dre. It was her."

"He's right, man," Sam's voice rang out. "Selena found it. She's as mad as I've seen her in a while."

"We need to move." It was Charlie's voice. "They might attack again."

"Dre, get on. I'll get you back. Dre, come on."

He was on his knees, and he got up and dusted himself off.

"Yeah, fuck it. Get me out of here."

He got on Sam, and they bounced off back to the tunnels.

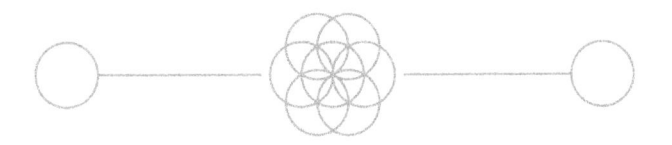

Chapter 15

Our War

"What to do? What to do? I get ordered to waste most of my forces, and now a squad can't bring one man in. What to do?"

The general paced the room. He was more irritable day by day, and some of his old vices had come back to haunt him. He spent long nights awake with his bottle as his only company.

"I can't leave, and I can't stay. So what do I do, Mr. Cleber?" He looked over to the patriarch of the family. "I mean, I'm running out of options, so it's not looking too good for you too. Your children are forcing me to consider drastic measures."

"General, the biggest mistake of your life is thinking you can outfight my boys. They will never quit. I taught them that, you know. I wish I was younger. I'd show you myself. Your threats mean nothing to me and our family. Good will win, no matter the damage you cause us. If you need to dispose of me to send a message, I would caution against that."

"You?" the general questioned. "Now, why would I use you when I have so many options? Like your daughter? Maybe your grandson?"

"What a monster you people are. Only someone who has lost their soul can threaten an innocent child." The old Gerard glared at the general.

"Mr. Cleber, do not force my hand. I extend this offer only one more time. Tell your people to lay down their weapons and surrender."

"I would never betray my family, the people, and Mars. My boys know I love them. I told them every chance I could. Do what you need to do, General."

* * *

"Guys," Helena came around the corner. "I have a message from Barada himself. He states that he and all the UNE forces will leave. He concedes the planet."

The room burst into cheers.

"Wait, people, there's more," she said, calming them down. "He will take the remaining family members as hostages. He said he's taking them to Earth."

"No fucking way," John said immediately after. "No. In no way do I accept this."

"He knew we would never accept it," Dre said from a corner. "What's he doing?"

"What do you mean?" Tucker asked.

"I don't know, just saying." He drifted to another thought about Mia, and he was gone.

The rest of the crew continued.

"He is right though. Why would he do this now?"

"He's scared," someone said.

"They are beat," another said.

"No," Dre rejoined the conversation. "He's not scared. He just buying time, people, calm down. I've been going back and forth with this guy for over a year. He isn't scared. He might be nervous, but scared, no. He personally led the ambush, and it nearly broke us. And he almost killed me for the twenty-third time."

"He's trying to get us off topic," John said, putting an end to the conversation. "What is important is the strike force coming. What are we going to do about that?"

"We meet them, John," Dre said calmly. "We are going to meet them when they are most disoriented. Right when they come in. Ha, a fucking space battle." He started laughing until he was red in the face.

"What're our options?" Ameera asked.

"There are none, unless you want to keep hiding in here for the rest of time, dodging marine patrols so you can feed your kids. I'm done with this war. One way or another, this ends."

* * *

The weeks passed slowly as they waited for the reinforcements to show. The girls had crews covering every approach they could, but they still had to watch the few remaining UNE forces. The pirates kept gathering supplies, even becoming brave enough to venture into the city more. The UNE forces had become isolated in the government building. John, Sam, and Selena spent most of their free time looking on at the center, hoping to catch a glimpse of the family.

"What will happen, Sam?" John asked, looking over the city.

They had come to a high part where most of the temple complexes were. It gave a great view of the surrounding area.

"I have no idea on this one. You guys know this Barada. What do you think?"

"He's evil enough to do it, John, if that is what you are asking." Selena was inches from Sam with her head on his shoulder.

"What do we do? We can't go in. He'll kill them all before he would let us get them back."

The crew sat and looked out across the city. They had grown accustomed to the devastation, but not Sam. He was spending a lot of time up there, looking at the city.

"I'm going to get them back," John proclaimed, slapping his brother lovingly on the arm.

"Yeah, might as well," Dre agreed.

"Hey, man," Sam said, sticking his head up around a leaning Selena. "I really haven't had the time to talk to you. Wanna sit for a minute?"

"I'll never say no to that, Sam."

"Selena, can you give us a minute?"

"Of course. I'll be right over here. I have plenty of data to look at."

Sam and Dre found a good sitting area and plopped down.

"I can't remember the last time I sat down."

They both looked completely different than the pirates they were before.

"Look at us, Dre. Who would have guessed it would end up like this? I never imagined."

"Yep. Never saw this one coming."

"Part of my Dre is missing. You haven't cracked a joke or smiled in weeks."

Dre just grunted at Sam, looking over the city.

"What do you know about her?"

"Not much. Selena found the data on her. We think it got leaked, but what does it matter. It was her all along, and we all missed it, Sam. Me, Selena, John, the crew. We all missed it."

"Was it real for you, Dre? I mean really real?"

"I think so, Sam, but now all I want is to find her. She is going to explain to me before . . . before I . . ."

"I know."

The pair sat in silence again for a while. There wasn't much strategy or planning at the moment. Everyone knew, so it was hurry up and wait. The waiting period was terrible for those in constant combat. It gave the mind time to think, and that was the worst thing that could happen in a combat setting.

"What's going to become of us, Sam? Are we going to lose?"

"Most likely, but no matter what happens, I am content. I got to see Selena again. I got to talk to you. I got to hug my brother. I thought I was going to die alone, and I can't describe it. Even though it is dire, I have my family again. Anything is possible as long as we do it together." Sam continued, "You have to let her go for the time being. We need you. I promise, after it is over, I will help you find her even if it means going to Earth. Me and you on an adventure."

"I'm done with adventures, Sam. This will be different. I'm not just going to talk to her. No one hurts my family and is allowed to get away with it. I promised the gods I would find her."

"What are we going to do, Dre?"

"We have to meet them. I don't know how to prepare for a battle like this, so we are going to wing it like back in the old days. Ameera has a sound strategy, so there is little thinking on this one. We go straight at them."

"Straight at them. I like that."

"Where do you think you're going?" Dre asked, looking at Sam out of the corner of his eye. "You can't get involved. We just got you back."

"Where the fuck do you think I'm going? Can you sit this one out, huh?" Dre was speechless. "Yeah, I didn't think so. I'm going, and I'm going to kill as many as I can."

"Did you tell Selena?"

"No, not yet. She still is fuming mad about Mia, and I'm scared she might direct it at me."

"She will, you know. No way she'll let you go up there."

"I have to. She knows it, and so do you. You might be the general, but they need me for morale. The legend of Sam Cleber has to carry on, no matter what it cost us." He breathed deeply. He didn't want the fighting anymore. He had fought long enough, but he knew they needed one more win, and then it was over. "We are close, Dre. All in. We will win."

"Dre! Sam! We got them!"

The boys jumped up and got to Selena deep in her display. "Tucker found them! Eight hours out! My gods, eight hours."

"Eight fucking hours! Shit!" Dre got on the comms. "All hands, prepare for battle! Battle stations! Only eight hours, people. I want us up there in four. Captains, get my armor up there, and get into position. Ameera, I need a ride." Dre looked at Sam and nudged his head at Selena. He got into his transport and sped off barking, "You should have had that shit ready. I can't hold your fucking hand . . ."

"I need to talk to you." Sam looked at his beautiful Selena.

She picked up her head from the display, realizing what he was going to say. "Not a fucking chance, Sam!"

"We both know I have to."

"No, you don't. How much more do you have to give, Sam? How much more has to be taken before you listen? Not again, Sam. Don't do this to me again." She fell to her knees and lost control.

Sam followed her down. "I made it back, and I will again. I don't know how to say it other than I just know I will. I have to go. I have to fight. We will win if I go. I know it. The crew is back together again. You have to know and love me enough to know I can't sit this out."

"Fuck you, Sam, and your honor. The crew? What about me, Sam? Me, Sam. I'm not a part of your crew. Stay for me, Sam. Please don't, Sam." She was growing near hysterical. "Don't go."

"I love you and will love you forever. If anything should happen, I will wait for you in the afterlife. Don't waste your life here without me. If the worst should happen, I would want you to move on. I will watch over you always."

"How would I move on without you? I can't even move now."

"Selena, come on, my love. We have to go."

"Go, Sam? What the fuck does that even mean? You mean you have to go while I stay again. I have to stay and watch you do this shit. I'm taking it with you, Sam. When you are hurting, so am I. Look at me, Samuel."

Sam looked on at the love of his life. Red-eyed and tears running down her face, she was more beautiful now than he had ever noticed before.

"It's me and you. I can't without you, Sam. I thought I lost you, and it tore me apart." Selena couldn't hold it together any longer. "No, Sam . . . no."

Sam was at a crossroad. The only passions in his life—his built-up hatred of the UNE and his devotion to his family. Selena was family, and they were together again, but then . . .

"All of it is gone if I don't. My deepest wish is to grow old and raise a family, but it's nothing and will never happen without the freedom to make it how we want. I'm doing this for you and me and our family. Selena, I'm coming back. I swear, I give my soul to the gods, and I believe I will come back. I don't know what it is. If I'm lucky or this is just the work of the universe. Is it skill? I'm just a fucking pirate, I don't know . . ." Sam stopped, unable to find the words, then he remembered his favorite quote as a boy that his father repeated to him. "We do not see but hear and feel the winds."

Selena looked up at him eyes wide and red, as Sam continued, "I'm listening, and I need you to feel with me." Sam reached his hand out and grabbed her, bringing her to him. "I need you to feel me," he said, bringing her in more. He wrapped his hand around her back, pulling her to him. "Feel with me. Feel that I will hold you again as I hold you now."

It was pure. She felt it too as they came together. Everyone around them felt it. Hope. It was bittersweet for them. Both wanted nothing more than to stay as they were, but both now knew they had to let go. Both had their own battle to win. They said goodbye. Selena had to watch Sam board the *Raptor* again and fire off the planet away from her. This time she believed as he did. But she had her own mission. Get the others to safety.

She gathered up all the families of everyone fighting and brought them to one of the most secure caravans. The young and old guarded the entrance, and Selena weaved through. She gave smiles and words of encouragement where she could. She weaved in to where Ameera and Serg had said their goodbye to the kids. They were with the elders of the community with the rest of the children. All of them played while their parents were preparing for the biggest battle of their lives. Selena couldn't even imagine what that would be like. They had asked her before leaving for battle to watch over them in case they were both killed. It gave her a chill up her spine, but she agreed in an instant. She went to where Ameera had left them.

"Where are the kids?"

"Cap has them."

"Cap?" Selena looked around, starting to panic. "Which way did they go?"

"She said that their parents told her to get them. She said she's taking the children to their parents. Is something wrong?"

"I don't know, but keep your eyes open, and let me know if you see them."

"I will, and I'll spread the word!"

She didn't want to panic. This was on her alone. She sat and let it replay in her head. She was wrong about Mia. It bothered her that she had made such an error in judgment, and she was punishing herself for it. She headed back out of the way she came, only now she started running. She didn't know why, but she had to. She got all the way back past the last guards and came to an opening in the cave. Cap was throwing the kids into a transport, and Selena sprinted to them, pulling out her weapon.

"Stop, Cap. Where are you taking them?"

Cap was behind the transport, and she pulled out her sidearm as well. "Selena, let me explain!"

"I don't give a shit! Give me the children now, or I'm coming to get them!"

"I had to, Selena, please let me explain." She came around and raised her weapon at Selena.

Selena's eyes widened as she took aim. She slowly pulled the trigger, and a blast ran out from her weapon. She watched as it hit Cap in the belly, causing her to fall over. Selena came up to her quickly as a bloody Cap looked up.

"No, Selena, you don't understand. I had to because . . ."

"I don't give a shit," Selena aimed it at her head and pulled the trigger again. "Stay where you are, kids! Hold hands, guys. I'll be right there."

Selena searched Cap quickly and found what she needed, then left her to sit there. She went around and gathered the children.

"Come on, kids. Let's get out of here."

"What happened?"

"I'll tell you one day when you're older. Come on, let's go this way."

Selena guided the kids back to safety. She looked back once at Cap as she headed away. The blood had pooled around her, and Selena was satisfied with her work. No one would do that to her or her family again.

* * *

The pirates scrambled to get what they could out of the atmosphere to meet the UNE forces on approach. Hundreds of pirate corvettes—small, modified strike crafts—and Sergio's *Big Bertha* formed up waiting for the UNE to come. The ships opened their bays and let the armor pour out, which included Dre, John, Sam, and Charlie. Ameera, Tucker, and Sergio had the fleet operations while the rest were planning on charging directly at them.

Sam switched on his channel to just his crew. "Looks like I get to go out with you buckos after all."

"One big happy family again," Ameera said while en route to her command. "Speaking of that, Sam, I've asked Selena to take the children if the worst should happen. We wanted to ask you too, but ah . . . ran out of time."

"Yes, I will. Family."

"Thank you, Sam, no one else could do it. It has to be you and Selena," Sergio confirmed.

"Guys, I don't know what to say other than I love you all. I loved almost every minute with you. Thank you all for being my friends, and if the worst should happen, I'll see you on the other side."

"See you on the other side," they all repeated.

"Love you, guys!" Dre said, organizing his forces. "I want ten-deep. Beacons set. Captains, take charge. Wait on my order."

John thrust over, gave Sam a nudge on the chest, and said, "It's all right to be nervous. On my first job, I had no idea what was going on. Just stay back, keep your eyes open, and don't fuck up."

Sam laughed loudly then placed his armored hand on his brother's. "Watch over them, John. Watch over them all. They will need you. You have to. For me. Mourn me later, but if I fall . . ."

"It won't come to that, Sam. You'll make it. Us Clebers just have luck on our side. Just like the first job we were on. There's nothing in this universe that can rattle me now because I have you with me. Let's finish this together. Then me and you have some bar nights to catch up on. I have to go, Sam. I love you." John fired off, focusing on his command. "En route. How we looking?"

Sam wobbled around in the suit a little as he watched John thrust away. He said out loud, "Steady. It's been a while, Sam. Not used to zero Gs."

"That's why we are meeting them here," Dre said, coming up to Sam. "Charlie actually suggested that one."

"No shit! That's too funny."

"Who would have thought, right?"

Charlie thrust over. "You must use every advantage, Samuel."

"Gods, Charlie. You shouldn't be here."

"And neither should you, but we do what we must. Your pirates are accustomed to fighting in zero G. The fresh marines are not. They are unskilled compared to you. I am hopeful this will make up for our lack of numbers."

"Our numbers?"

"John taught me a new saying that I'm fond of, 'Fuck them.'" Sam laughed loudly while Charlie continued, "I decided to let some of the old life go, Samuel. So fuck them."

Dre interrupted with a report over the crew channel, "Tucker reported anywhere from two thousand to five thousand based on the transport you brought back. This is going to be close. Sam, this is where we need you. You have to give them the fire. They need to hear it from you. You are the heart of this."

"Thank you, my friend. I love you, and I'm honored to call you friend and my brother."

"I know, Sam. I'll see you on the other side."

Sam thrust off so all the pirates assembled could see him. Charlie followed him.

He looked back and said, "Gods, Charlie, what are you doing? I'm serious about the life debt thing. You don't have to."

"I know that, Samuel. You told me that we are on a free planet. This is where I choose to be."

"Charlie, you're going to make me fucking cry right before a battle."

The two watched as the UNE forces entered into sight. Their thrusters were firing to slow down. They watched as hundreds of armored marines poured out of the transports.

"That is a lot of fucking devil dogs there," Sam said with his mouth half open.

"Sam," Charlie said as they turned in front of the pirates. "Use your anger now. Like you did in the arena. Fight, Samuel. Fight the people that took from you. Fight the people that took from your loved ones. I saw, Samuel. You're more of a fighter than you think you are. Don't think, Samuel. Just go! Fight!"

Sam spun and faced his pirates. His shakes started up. Adrenaline started pumping. His senses were enhanced. He didn't care about anything anymore. His attention and mind were unified on one thing. Battle. He must kill and not hesitate. Let the hate and anger out. His shaking picked up.

"Let it out," he said to himself.

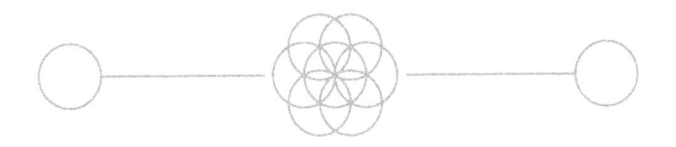

Chapter 16

Our Era

"Now. Now is the time to rid ourselves of them for good!" Sam roared over the comms.

Thousands of armored suits hovered around him as he spoke. Behind him the pirates watched as the UNE came into view and the planet glowed in the background.

"We can finish this right here, right now. Everyone and everything now hangs in balance. I need your fierceness, endurance, and faith that I have seen in your eyes over the years. I need your heart, your fire, your rage. You are more than you know. I want you to show them. Show them what we can do united. Let them know that we stand as one. That we are coming. I am coming! That Mars is coming! Are you with me?"

The once ragtag rebels roared alongside Dre, Sam, John, and Charlie. Each of them thumped their chest in the armor and roared together.

"On me!" Dre yelled and fired toward the oncoming enemy.

He was advancing quickly along with Sam. He wanted to be the first one to get at them. Sam followed closely, followed by the rest. They looked to their left and right as the ship-to-ship fighting commenced around them.

***

Sergio had brought his Bertha up along with a few escorts to keep the small fighters off him. His job was to hold a portion of the battlefield with his few crews. The UNE would see the weakened force, and the rebels hoped they would attack it. If Serg and Tucker could hold them, it would give Ameera the time to concentrate and win her sector. The UNE came into Serg's display.

"Tuck, you got 'em?"

"That's a lot of them, Serg."

"Do what we can, brother. Look after yourself."

"You too."

The rebels waited for the approaching UNE strike craft.

"Send the EMP," Serg ordered.

One hundred drones with a single purpose of locking on a target and delivering an EMP blast darted to the advancing formation. Serg followed that up with another drone salvo with armor-penetrating warheads. The UNE started to fire at the horde coming. They destroyed most, but a few of the EMP drones got through, and that was all Serg needed. Then he would destroy them one at a time while they were rebooting. They saw on the displays that the mini EMP latched on to their targets and fired. None of the crafts lost control. They kept coming right at the assembled pirates.

"Serg, all those ships have shielding. EMP is nonfactor!"

Serg got a shiver up his spine and a cold shudder that followed. The UNE antimissile fired, swatting nearly all the incoming warheads. A few went through with some hits but zero kills.

"This is going to be difficult. Tuck, keep them off me!" Serg fired his Bertha up and began picking his targets. He launched his first wave of ship-to-ship drones and gave out orders to the crew members controlling them.

"Keep them off me. I'm focusing on larger ships!"

The UNE scattered when they saw Serg's Bertha come to life. Little did they know, it was easier for Serg when they were spread out. His rate of fire was not enough though, and the UNE came in range and fired a full salvo of their own. Tucker and his crews in strike crafts evaded and joined the fray. They were simply outnumbered. Tucker downed one and then had to evade three on his tail. He dived hard and spun in the zero gravity and fired at the three pursuing him. He got two, but not in time for the third, and he evaporated in an instant.

"No! Tucker!" Serg yelled. He turned beet-red and ordered into the comms, "Fight them to the last! Hold! Hold for our brothers and sisters!"

Ameera. He had to hold for Ameera.

* * *

"Form on me." Ameera was giving her ship a last inspection. Her strike force formed on the other side of the planet. When the

UNE engaged Sergio, it was her mission to come from around the planet and strike where she could.

"Copy, *Raptor*."

The captains and their ships formed on her as she and the *Raptor* came around the planet and into view. She saw the tracers dancing in front of the stars along with a ship detonating. It brought her back.

"All right, people. Looks like they are turning to meet us. Hit them hard, and don't let up until I say stop. This is everything. See you on the other side. Going to break in three . . . two . . . one . . BREAK!"

Ameera dived with a portion of the strike force. She took a wide arc toward the underbelly of the UNE forces and downed one as she screamed directly through the formation. She circled wide and looked on to see the rest of the strike force attacking from all sides. She finished her turn and quickly thrust sideways to dodge enemy fire. She found the target firing, thrust over the charging craft, and downed it as it passed. She spun again and saw that they were winning this side of the battle. For a moment, she looked over at Serg, then darted back in, picking another target.

"*Raptor*, this is Eight. I have them turning to regroup with the other sector, should I pursue?"

"Affirmative. All captains, pursue and destroy! Serg, we're coming to you." She spun on a dime and blasted toward him.

The UNE forces she was chasing were speeding as fast as they could to reach the other sector of the battle to link up.

"Who's still here?" Ameera asked.

"Ryan is here. I'm two and a half kilometers ahead of you."

"This is Blake. I'm coming up on your keel starboard side."

"This is Paola. I have taken command. It's six of us. There's a mess, and I have major cleanup here."

"You have this sector now, I'm in pursuit."

The comms were scrambled, then Serg appeared in the ship-to-ship display breaking up.

"Serg! Can you read me? Sergio!"

Serg was barking orders to the few remaining craft he had left. "Fall back, and rejoin the others! Fall back!" Serg breathed deeply. "Fall back. I'll hold them." He turned to the display he had brought up. "It doesn't matter if you make it here, honey. We are critical." He was speaking lovingly to her. "I'm afraid this is it, darling."

"The fuck it is. I'm almost on you."

The moment she finished her statement, warnings flashed, and incoming fire followed.

"Evasive maneuvers! I'm pushing on!"

"No, honey. Not both of us. Our babies need one of us. You will not make it. I love you. Tell my children that I will be with them always."

Serg turned his display off and refocused on his disintegrating ships.

"I'm sorry, people, but this looks like this is it. Abandon ship. Suit up, you don't have much time."

His ship was critical. There were warning alarms; the OB was frantically trying to keep the ship together and keep power as well as running the battle with Sergio. He looked to see that his drones were almost gone. His antiair fire could not hold them back. He tried to fire his main weapons, but all were offline. He saw a few of the crew escape in emergency suits right before the ship detonated.

Ameera saw the bright light of what could only be Sergio's ship. She lost her breath. She was so struck. She couldn't breathe and held it long enough that she finally had to gasp for air. She let out a mournful scream in her cockpit. Strapped in and unable to move, she punched at the view port. She grabbed the controls with furious eyes and foaming at the mouth. Her veins showed through her skin. Reaching her first target, she attacked it with the rage of someone who just lost someone she loved.

* * *

For Dre, Sam, John, and Charlie, there were no tactics, no strategy, no thinking. They went straight at them. The marines facing them began their thrust as well. They got to within firing range, and thousands of projectiles littered the void of space. The two lines met with the stars and the planet in the background. Armored suits slammed into each other, and the armored center turned into a wild swarm of pure chaos.

Sam had dispatched one marine from range and blasted through the initial wave of marines, firing when he could. He slammed into one deeper in the ranks, grabbed, and fired point-blank into its armored helmet. He threw it away and saw John in his display fight a pair off.

The two were circling and firing at him. He thrust hard to disengage, but the marines were quickly on him. Sam followed and caught one of the marines in the back. He stuck his armor glove in the joint where the helmet met the chest and ripped up, pulling the helmet off, killing him instantly. John had finished the other marine off, looked toward Sam, and thrust away.

Sam found his next target and charged toward it, trying to shoot as he moved. His mini ran out of power, and he detached it from his arm. He caught another marine who was too slow to move and struck it with his extended foot. Sam was in full rage. It was pure bloodlust. Everything was let out. He grabbed the marine by both arms and, while stepping on his chest, ripped both from his body.

Sam let out a roar over the comms, "Kill them all!"

He saw Dre pass by, pumping round after round into one he had a grip on. Charlie never had left Sam's side during the fight. She picked off her former marines when she could, but she mainly watched Sam. She saw the squad coming in on him, and she thrust hard to meet them. Sam joined in, and the two fought them off together. Another squad came in clearly with orders to target Sam and Dre, and John saw the danger and acted.

"Rally to Sam! They are going after Sam!"

***

He had too many coming at him to count. All he knew was he was in a bad spot, and he thrust as hard as he could to escape his pursuers. Sam weaved in and out as he crossed the battlefield. He ran into floating bodies and debris all around him. He saw a bright light in the distance and knew a ship was destroyed. At the same instant, he didn't know what he was impacted by, but it knocked him good. He was disoriented and spun because of it. He had to right himself, and it gave the marines chasing him time to catch up.

One of them raised their rifle to fire when Charlie came from behind and blasted the marine in the back. She quickly changed direction turned and thrust to the next marine. Four came at her while the rest continued to Sam. She dispatched two using her hands, striking where she could when she felt the force and sting on her back. Her alarms rang in her suit, and she spun to see when she was struck with another round to her chest. She went limp and floated in space.

The pain. My brothers and sisters, here I come. Will they accept me? Ah, the burning. Here it comes, I'm going.

Charlie's eyes started rolling in her head, and her breathing deepened. She finally gave in and closed her eyes. She had her wish. She died in battle.

Sam couldn't worry about anyone but himself. He didn't even notice that Charlie was gone.

"I need a hand here, boys!" he called out. He righted himself and blasted away from the marines again.

"I'm right on you, Sam," Dre called.

He was almost at the edge of the battle, and he wouldn't have any cover anymore with the debris gone. The marines could target him in the open. He had faced greater odds and won. It was his destiny to bring freedom to Mars. He had no doubt in his mind, and it gave him the belief in himself that he could. He grabbed a pair of downed suits and brought them together. He made himself into the smallest target that he could and pushed toward them. He only had his auto on him, so he let them get in close. He braced himself as the marines shot at his armored shield, making it glow red. John came in smashing into them. There were many on him, and Sam couldn't sit back. He fired as hard as he could at them, bringing one down with his shotgun. Dre came firing in, joining the fray. Each were monsters going at the marines.

Sam, Dre, and John fought marine after marine. They darted among each other, catching a marine where they could, destroying it and moving to the next one. More and more poured in. Sam saw two grab John again, and he fired to help. He was too late. After everything, he had to watch as the two marines fired point-blank at John, killing him instantly. Roaring, he slammed into them, ripping at them with two hands. He didn't know what happened. He lost himself in the rage, and he tore everything with his armored hands until it was over.

Dre and Sam both heard on the comms their comrades yelling, "They are pulling back! They are pulling back!"

"All hands, hold! I say again, hold position! Rally to me and Sam." Dre wanted to gain control of the battle again. "Sam! You hear that? They are running!"

Dre turned from side to side up and down, searching for his friend. His heart picked up in his chest.

"Sam! Sam? Don't fuck around, Sam! Sam!" he called as he searched.

"Dre," Sam said in a somber voice. "Over here."

He turned to where Sam was and saw him floating next to a lifeless suit. He went over and saw that John had a gaping wound in his abdomen, and then he looked up and saw that his helmet was penetrated.

Death was something that happened every day, and every death hurt. Each knew it could happen, but everyone was still shocked when it did. The three drifted in the darkness of space, and the cheers from people quickly faded as, one by one, they came to see.

The sounds of battle were fading, and Jamal came up. "General? Request permission to . . . um."

"Go ahead, brother. Take over."

"I'm sorry," he said and turned quickly. "All right, people, I want survivors found and in the atmosphere. Captain Iwakuma, you have security see to it. The rest of you, get moving." He switched comms. "Fleet, any of you left? I have wounded . . ." And he fired off from the group.

Dre and Sam floated next to John. They couldn't believe it, nor could they take their eyes off their brother. It was not possible for him to die. He was everything to them. They just got together again, and he was now gone. Sam had never felt so alone before. He looked up and had forgotten that Dre was next to him. He was looking at Sam through his armor. Dre grabbed his shoulder and brought him in next to him. He brought his head in and lightly touched Sam's armored forehead.

"I'm sorry, Sam."

"I'm sorry too."

They drifted apart.

"I have to get them back," Sam said, looking back at the planet they had been fighting for.

Random marines drifted by, followed by pirates hunched over. Lifeless. A piece of an aircraft was drifting. Space was so vast, but it seemed small at the moment looking at all the death around them.

"I know," Dre agreed. "Let's get him home first."

"No. Not this time. No more waiting. Now."

Dre nodded through the suit. "Yeah, Sam." He keyed in to Helena. "This is Dre," he said. "How is it?"

"They are falling back! Ameera is pursuing, and they are gearing their drives up! We won!"

There was cheering all around the command center. People were giving each other hugs and high fives and jumping in joy.

Helena's smile faded, and she continued to him, "Dre?"

"I'm here."

"Sergio and Tucker are . . . gone." She had trouble getting it out.

He sighed and closed his eyes in his suit. He had told them out loud that he would take care of them.

"Say again, Dre? Dre, what is it? What happened?"

"John is gone too. Me and Sam are here. I don't know who else."

"Copy." Helena balled up both fists together and slammed them on the large display angrily. She never lost her composure, but today was a day of firsts. "Come home, guys." She slammed the table again. "Transports will be there in moments."

Dre looked around at the stars. Looked at his lifeless friend. Looked at the destruction around him. Looked at Sam. Death was every day.

* * *

The beat and battered pirates gathered what forces they could, led by both Sam and Dre. The two were in pure, uncontrollable bloodlust. They crashed into the government center and hammered every last one they could find. A bloody Sam and Dre smashed into the command center in their armor and gazed at a highly intoxicated General Nikto Klaatu Barada.

"They are not here." The general grinned as he took another drink, pulled out his service weapon, and put it to his head. "You know me," he said, looking at Dre. "Would I ever accept defeat?"

"Where are they?" Sam was bloodred in his armored suit.

"I sent them away during the battle, but don't worry," he said, grinning again. "My mother is looking after them." The general spit in the pair's direction and pulled the trigger.

* * *

They had brought the wounded back and tended to them as quickly as they could. There were not many. The fighting had turned hand-to-hand, and vacuum deaths were the main weapon. They didn't know what to do with the frozen armors and the men and women trapped inside. They brought them in as best they could and strapped them in. The casualties were horrific. More than half had departed, and including the wounded, there was a mere skeleton of the force they had started with.

Dre and Sam brought John home and would not let anyone look at him. Dre got him to a concealed room and stationed armored guards at the door. They both got out of their armors, still sweaty and grimy from the battle, and Dre went to see to the wounded. There were not many.

He came across Charlie lying on a cot with a higher-grade auto doc on her. He thought to himself that she had to be in bad shape. She lay there unconscious while the doc attempted to fix her internal wounds. He stopped only a moment and went to see Selena and Sam again. It looked like Sam was drugged. He only stared at the wall, sitting on the ground.

"Sam?" Dre approached. He gave a worried look to Selena as he came to him. "Come on, I'll get you up."

"Leave me alone, Dre."

"Sam, I . . ."

"Lucky me, right?" His head hung low, staring at the ground. "I always make it . . . Always me. I'm the lucky one, right, Dre? My whole fucking family, but I'm the lucky one!"

"Hey, buddy, come on, I under—"

"Dre. Just leave me the fuck alone."

Dre was hurt by Sam and pulled away from him quickly. He stroked his beard that had grown over the past weeks, looking down at him, and turned and left the room.

Selena followed quickly, stopping him, not wanting to stray too far from Sam. "He didn't mean it. You know that."

"He's got a lot going on." Dre put his hands on his head. "We both got a lot going on. It's always one of us, Selena. Can't you see that?" Dre, just as frantic as everyone else, now started using his arms to animate it. "Sam and I. One beating after another. We owe it to them as far as I see it. Me, you, Sam, and whoever is left." Dre's eyes watered. "We owe them that much."

"Is that what you would want if it was the other way around? Would you want one of us to owe you anything?"

"It's about making it right, Selena."

"How much will it cost us, Dre?"

"Nothing," Sam said, looking at Dre and Selena. "No more suffering for the people of Mars. We have what we wanted, right?"

"What does that even mean, Sam? Are you telling me you aren't going to go after them?"

"I never said that. All I said was that the people of Mars will no longer suffer." He stood up and walked over to them. "I'm going, but I can't without you two." He looked over to Dre. "I know why you're going." Then turned to Selena and said, "I never want to part with you again, but I . . ."

"I know, Sam. It's me and you." She placed her hand on him using her gentle touch. "Let's not worry about that now. Come with me."

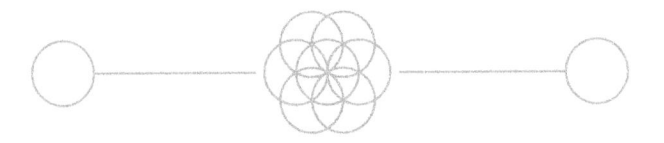

Epilogue

The people of Mars brought Johansen Cleber to the temples overlooking the city. Dre had their whole force on display in front, and Ameera flew her fleet low in the horizon. The UNE forces were gone. The free people of Mars stacked the material high and placed him on top.

Selena and all of the rebellion were there to say goodbye to their friends. The funeral pyres one by one came alight as the members of the fallen family lit them one by one. All throughout the city, they could be seen. Sam approached John, holding Selena by his side. He grabbed the lit torch from Dre and put it to the timber. The flame rose high into the night sky. He hoped his family could see it from wherever they were.

Each of them said goodbye as they watched the flames burn. One by one, they all left until only a few remained. They waited all night until the fired died and gathered a handful of ashes for each of them to keep if they wished. Selena grabbed at the ashes and filled a small vial attached to a necklace. John wished to be burned at home. He wished that everyone took a part of him so he could partake in all the adventures. He wanted it to remind them all that he would always be watching.

The fire faded, and the sun began to rise in the distance of the beautiful landscape of Mars. Dre and Sam looked over the city that had been a war zone for years. They both promised that they would get them out. They promised John. They looked on again at the sun coming up over the horizon. They had unfinished business.

They just won the most important battle in recent human history, and both could only think about how to strike back at them. How to give it back to the people that hurt them. Dre had fire in his eyes looking out. Mia was first on his list. No matter what it cost him, he was going to find her. He needed to hear it from her. They had gotten what they wanted. Their freedom was secure, but at what cost? The next generations would know of the sacrifice, but they would never feel it. Never feel the wind. The cost of freedom always faded until there were those to fight for it again. Just like the sun, freedom was on the rise.

* * *

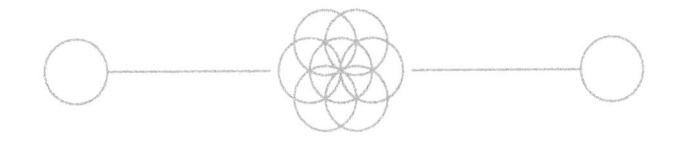

Chapter One

Our Future

"Sam, we found something in the library that you should see."

To be continued in the next book.

Join the author as he searches for answers to our future: youtube.com/@TheAmericanRoundTable